Bright Lights, Dark Nights

Also by Stephen Emond

Winter Town

Happyface

Bright Lights, Dark Nights

stephen Emond

ROARING BROOK PRESS
NEW YORK

Copyright © 2015 by Stephen Emond
Published by Roaring Brook Press
Roaring Brook Press is a division of Holtzbrinck Publishing Holdings Limited Partnership
175 Fifth Avenue, New York, New York 10010
macteenbooks.com

Library of Congress Cataloging-in-Publication Data

Emond, Stephen.
 Bright lights, dark nights / Stephen Emond. — First edition.
  pages cm
 Summary: Walter Wilcox's first love, Naomi, happens to be African American,
so when Walter's policeman father is caught in a racial profiling scandal, the teens'
bond and mutual love of the Foo Fighters may not be enough to keep them together
through the pressures they face at school, at home, and online.
 ISBN 978-1-62672-206-4 (hardback)—ISBN 978-1-62672-207-1 (e-book)
 [1. Dating (Social customs)—Fiction. 2. Race relations—Fiction. 3. Best
friends—Fiction. 4. Friendship—Fiction. 5. Single-parent families—Fiction.
6. Fathers and sons—Fiction. 7. High schools—Fiction. 8. Schools—Fiction.]
I. Title.
 PZ7.E69623Bri 2015
 [Fic]—dc23

                                                                2014047413

Roaring Brook Press books may be purchased for business or promotional use. For
information on bulk purchases please contact Macmillan Corporate and Premium Sales
Department at (800) 221-7945 x5442 or by email at specialmarkets@macmillan.com.

First edition 2015
Printed in the United States of America

1 3 5 7 9 10 8 6 4 2

Bright Lights, Dark Nights

*H*idden in the shadows of tall buildings are spots where no one looks, places where you can get away with things because nobody cares or knows any better. The court off Schrank Street, a few blocks north of our high school, was one of those places. Weeds grew out of the cracked concrete and reached about waist-high. That was how long it had been since anyone paid attention to the place.

High school kids fought there all the time. There weren't a lot of prying eyes since the buildings across the street were boarded up and condemned a year ago. When they had still been in use, worse things happened there than in the court. Two guys got into a fight last December and one guy shot the other one in the foot. It took his big toe right off. At the same building, same month, a guy was laid out in front of the door, OD'd. Cops went into his apartment and found forty bags of heroin and a pharmacy's worth of prescription meds. That had been one big crime right there, but think of how many people had bought from him, too.

The city can be seen in terms of what crimes happened and where, and there's no shortage of stories to tell. I only know the tiniest sliver, the standout stories my dad tells me, so the amount of actual no-good that happens must be staggering. Every face I pass, I can assume, has a secret locked away that they don't want anyone to find out.

Beardsley was fighting today. If no one else wanted to fight, if there was no other drama in the entirety of the school on any given day, you could count on Beardsley to show up at the court and throw some punches.

He was targeted on Bob Armstrong, a freshman kid who probably didn't know better, just over a month into the school year. Bob turned his hat backward and lowered his head, bobbing around like he was in some fighting video game, posing like an MMA fighter, throwing out kicks that went nowhere. Bob wasn't anyone at school, really. He might have been seeking attention, trying to look brave, impress some girls, but he was about to get his clock cleaned. Beardsley was a little nuts. He'd swing with all he had and didn't stop at the sight of blood like some kids did. When Beardsley fought, you knew someone was going to get hurt, and that was why we'd followed him to the court.

There were fifteen or sixteen of us there today. Lester Dooley was one. He was friends with Beardsley and was the most intimidating kid in school, if not the whole city. Built like a tree trunk, he squatted on the other side of the court with his hands clenched together, watching the fight like a gambler watching a horse race.

It was an excuse to get out of school for lunch, anyway. The wind picked up every few minutes, and the sun was feeling weaker by the day, but it still lit the sky a piercing blue, a far cry from the shadowy maze of hallways we walked the rest of the day. I reached up into the air for nothing, stretching my arm out. We stood by the chain-link fence, away from the action, me in the back. My dull jeans, dark hoodie—everything I wore screamed out *Blend in.*

"All my homework is watching movies," my friend Nate Halcomb said. He had a film history class this semester. He took a drag from his cigarette. I was Nate's nonsmoker smoking buddy when he needed to step outside. He turned to his ex-girlfriend Kate. "Walter's already devoured the entire French New Wave library."

When Nate saw a film or read a book he liked, he would casually bring it up as if it was a fact that I'd already seen or read it. The funny part was that I usually had, and he'd laugh and laugh as soon as I responded.

"You're thinking of noir movies," I said. "They came before New Wave. I have seen *Breathless*, though." I watched that one with my dad. There have been four Walter Wilcox lifetimes between the end of the noir era and now, but somehow it still clicked with me. My dad and I watch old noir movies all the time, or at least we used to. *Breathless* was French New Wave but could definitely be considered a reaction to noir. The coolness, the cynicism, the complete refusal of the Hollywood Happy Ending. And Jean-Paul Belmondo made a great replacement for Humphrey Bogart.

Nate exhaled from his cigarette, and the smoke sped away in the wind. Nate had thick-framed black glasses like mine and long blond hair and jean shorts he wore all year long. He looked anarchist-meets-Disney-show-lead with his Skrillex-lite hair and his Day-Glo green striped T-shirt on. Nate could talk to anyone about anything. When a new kid came to school, they could usually say their first friend there was Nate Halcomb. That had been the case for me. Not that I'd been a new student or anything, but the first day of fifth grade, I'd sat at a lunch table alone and Nate had picked up my stuff and said, "Come sit with us. I'm Nate." I'd been sitting with him since.

Kate put out her cigarette and pulled a sandwich out of a paper bag. They used to be Nate-and-Kate, and now they were Just Nate and Just Kate. Even rhyming names won't guarantee you *Forever*. They were still the ideal couple and the closest I'd seen to true love, whether they were together or not. Drama-free and chilled out, not at each other's throats, no jealousy, no bitterness.

No blood yet. Beardsley was on Bob's back, skinny arms wrapped around his face like tentacles. Bob was twirling and reaching at air. I'd seen enough of this kind of stuff to know better myself. I avoided standing in the center of that court like my life depended on it, since it basically did. Bob managed to throw Beardsley to the ground, looking relieved, unaware that it was the worst thing he could have done. Beardsley bounced back like a boomerang and full-on speared him to the ground.

Lester leaped to his feet. "Kick his ass!"

We had about ten minutes left before we had to go back. Nate didn't seem any different watching Beardsley hammer away at Bob than he had a few weeks ago when he was still with Kate, watching Beardsley toss around David Chamberlain. Always carefree and in the moment. Kate seemed completely at peace, eating her sandwich and squinting in the sun.

"I might get in there." Nate nodded toward the action. "What do you think?"

"Dude. Don't." Kate shook her head and dropped her eyes to the ground. "Let that kid learn his lesson."

"I'm going in," Nate said, increasingly satisfied with his decision. I've never seen Nate back off an idea when he got that look, and he's had some bad ideas. Not that he'd view this as one. The idea that people liked to do this was still an odd concept to me. This was *fun*. This was *recreational*. This was daylight activity.

"What if the cops come by?" I asked Nate. I passed out what-ifs like religious pamphlets. I could rationalize anything into inaction. "Why even bother with this stuff?"

"Why bother, Walter? Because," Nate said. "Somebody has to. That's a massacre over there. These people want a show, Walter! Without me in there, their lunch is wasted. I will bring these people change!" Nate's voice rose, becoming more theatrical, more aware of an audience. "Hold this."

Nate handed me his cigarette and made his way through the crowd, pumping his arms into the air with a roar. Everyone cheered—this lunch break would not be wasted. I squatted by Kate and pulled a weed out of the ground.

"Do you do Urban versus Suburban?" I asked Kate. She had a sweet demeanor that belied her tomboyish appearance. I mean, she looked like a girl, certainly, but she wasn't the most girly-girl person I'd ever met. I'd never seen her wear makeup. "I've heard people picking out kids and guessing where they came from before high school."

"Actually, it's called Urbs and 'Burbs, Wilcox," Kate said.

Looking at the crowd, I saw kids from both schools there. We had two middle schools, one in the suburbs and one in the city. The rich one and the poor one. In high school we were all thrust together. Kate went to school where I did, in the suburbs, before I moved to the city with my dad. "Do you remember Makiel from middle school?" Kate asked, pointing toward Makiel Romado. He was a thin kid with a baseball cap and skater clothes, but just for the fashion—there was no possible way he knew how to skate. "He used to be, like, the most suburban, computer-nerd type. Now I buy my weed from him."

Nate dove into the fight headfirst and pulled Bob back in by the sleeve of his shirt. Nate wasn't saving Bob from Beardsley. He was putting on a show, and everyone was fair game. Beardsley threw a flurry of punches into Nate's skinny ribs. I could barely watch. I didn't want to see Nate get hurt over something so dumb. I had to admit, though: it was entertaining. Bob's shirt collar had already been stretched to twice its original size. Nate caught a stray elbow and his nose started to bleed. The red on his shirt would be a badge of honor by sixth period.

"Nate's changing lives," I said. "Anything for the people."

It wouldn't have been the end of the world for me to get in there, even the score, get those two kids off Nate. That would be the code; that would be the appropriate friend move. With Nate there, we could put Beardsley down, not that there was anything we could do that wouldn't result in his picking on someone else the next day. Still. I might even get some respect from it. I didn't want to get hit, though.

"I'm gonna knock off a liquor store after school and see if I can claim a Nobel Prize," I said.

"See? Now you get it," Kate said.

Nate put Beardsley in a headlock, holding on tight like he was riding a bull. "That's my problem," I said. "I really don't get it at all."

"It's not too complicated," Kate said. Her nose ring caught a sparkle of sun. "People fight because it's what they do." They fight and they break up. Kate held a gaze on me for a second before she broke out laughing. "The way you're holding that cigarette—it just looks weird. Here, give it to me."

I gave her the cigarette.

"Don't ever smoke," she said, shaking her head. "You don't have to do what he says."

"I don't mind. It's not a big deal," I said.

"Fighting is dumb—you're absolutely right," Kate said. She looked up at me and smiled. "You're gonna make some girl really happy someday, Walter." The wind was blowing her clumpy brown hair in her face. I used to have a crush on Kate in middle school. She was my first real female friend. But once she and Nate got together, their relationship made so much sense that me and her seemed like a ridiculous thought in retrospect.

"Thanks," I said.

While Kate smoked the cigarette, Nate tossed Beardsley and Bob around like a lanky professional wrestler. Nate pumped his fists up again to more applause before Beardsley dove back into him. Lunch was almost done, and this would be a stalemate. Bob's best scenario involved Beardsley forgetting this ever happened and finding someone else to pick on. Maybe it'd be Nate, for interfering in his fight. That thought gave me some relief that I'd stayed put on the sidelines.

•   •   •

I got back around five, judging by the dimness of the hallway, and climbed two flights of stairs to home, sweet home. My dad and I had lived there since my parents divorced, so a few years now. When I opened the door, I saw a soda cup on the coffee table and an empty fast-food bag. Cheeseburger wrappers. *Judge Mathis* was on TV.

"Dad, I could have cooked," I said, dropping off my book bag and coat on a chair in the corner.

"I wasn't sure when you were getting home," Dad said, sitting up on the couch and adjusting his shirt. He looked tired. I got my expressive eyes from Dad, but lately his just seemed worn and heavy. The apartment was a mess, but that wasn't anything new, and I couldn't blame it solely on Dad.

"I can still make something," I said.

"Nah, don't." Dad leaned forward and muted the TV. He smiled so those prominent dimples came forward, warming up his face. "Look, no offense, Walter, but you're no Rachael Ray."

"Or Ronald McDonald," I said. "You're not supposed to eat that stuff." I picked up the empty bag and wrappers and took them to the garbage in the kitchen.

"It's fine. Don't worry about it," Dad said. "It's just for today." He found out he had diabetes last year, but he hated doctors and he hated hospitals, so there was no telling how long he'd actually had it. *I'm fine when I eat better*, he'd say, the problem being he never actually ate better.

When I sat down and looked at the TV, Dad pulled a heavy wrapped gift from beside the couch and placed it on my lap.

"What's this?" I asked.

"It's a Christmas present," Dad said. "What do you think it is? It's your birthday, isn't it?"

"Can I open it?" I asked.

"You've got a lot of dumb questions. Open it," Dad said with a nudge.

I tore the paper and found an oversize hardcover book on old noir movies, full of artsy black-and-white frames. All the movies we watched when we first moved here. *The Asphalt Jungle*, *The Big Sleep*. Movies where the good guys are kinda the bad guys and things usually end short of happy.

"I was at the little bookstore down the street today and thought you'd like it." Dad leaned back a bit on the couch, getting more comfortable. "Caught a punk kid running out of there. I just happened to be in the right place at the right time. Stand downtown and pay attention for an hour and you'll see a few things."

We lived in the Basement of the city; at least that's what they called it around here. It wasn't the brightest, safest section to live in, but Dad says when it gets too safe, he's out of work. It was what we could afford, these days.

"This kid comes barreling toward me like he's running from a mad dog or something," Dad said, leaning forward and using his hands to tell the story. "I'm expecting drugs or weapons to come falling out of his coat, but these Harry Potter books go flying all over the place, like the kid's some kind of book junkie. Any cop worth his salt would have picked him out even before the mad dash from the store. Big, long coat, almost seventy degrees out, middle of October. Had, like, a hundred bucks' worth of books on him. Maybe they'll give me some real work now at the station. Who knows?"

Things in general got worse after Mom left. Dad gained

weight—a lot of weight—slowed down a lot. Aged faster, if that was possible. Nothing helpful in a cop's line of work, so they stopped giving him much to do. He was always complaining about the kids they hired who got all the good jobs.

It wasn't all "*These kids today*," though. There was another side to Dad. He was kind of a legend in the city: *Officer Wilcox*. When he was working and in his uniform, out on the streets, he knew everyone, he was well-liked. He'd had people laughing while they were getting handcuffed. They could pull all the good jobs, but they couldn't take his good name.

I thumbed through the large glossy pages of the book. Humphrey Bogart as Sam Spade in *The Maltese Falcon*, about to punch out Peter Lorre. Bringing in the noir era in fine fashion.

"They didn't waste a shot back then," Dad said. "Every frame was a work of art. They could paint a whole room with light placement. You got this, too." Dad placed an envelope with Mom's handwriting on it on the book. "I don't wanna know."

I thought of saving it for later, but I went ahead and opened it. There was a card and a check for five hundred dollars. Five hundred bucks. That was something she could do now. She could give me five hundred bucks for my birthday because Mom still lives in a big house in the suburbs. But Mom moved in with her boyfriend almost immediately after the divorce and I went with Dad, and years later, he's supporting us both on one salary.

I could give the money away. I could visit Kate's weed guy. Develop a habit. *You're gonna make some girl really happy someday.*

The card said, *Happy birthday, honey! Love, Mom.* I put it in the back of the book.

"Happy birthday," Dad said, and unmuted the TV. The news was on now.

"Dad, thanks," I said, and leaned over to give him a hug. Dad got up slowly, like he was carrying another person, and turned the living room light on, then settled back onto the couch. I opened the noir book and turned the page. Orson Welles in *Touch of Evil*, bloated, drunk, and crooked. Considered the last of the film noirs.

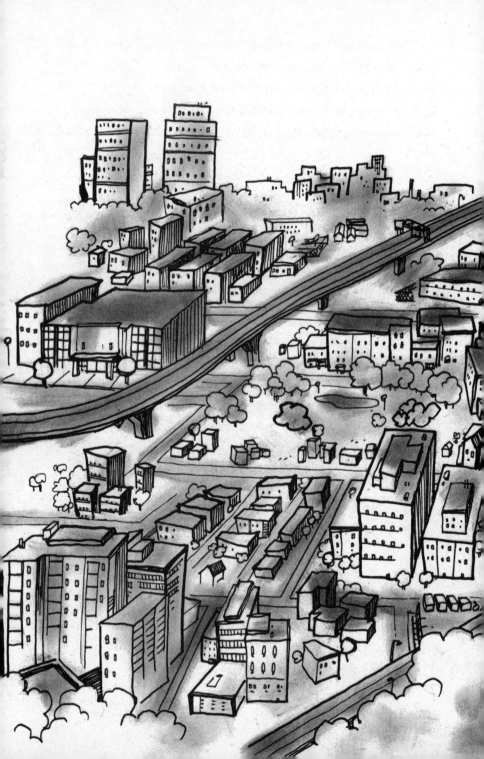

Wednesdays meant new comics and meeting up with Jason Mills at Shadows, our local comic-book store, after school.

"Okay, I got one," Jason said, playing lyrics over in his head. "Okay. This might be an easy one. *I know it's been a while, sweetheart. We hardly talk. I was doing my thang. I know it was foul, baby. Ay, babe, lately you been all on my brain.*"

"Kanye," I said. That was an easy one. "'Flashing Lights.' Come on, I used to play that on repeat. Give me a hard one, something deeper."

"All right, all right, let me think," Jason said as I browsed the new releases. This section was basically a whole wall. How did that many new comics come out every week? "My concentration is off," Jason said. "Romero's girl is here today."

Jason had a crush on the cashier's girlfriend. Romero was here pretty much every day. The only other worker was Big Dave on weekends and some nights. Romero's girlfriend hung out at the store maybe once every week or two. The only other people there at the moment were one middle-aged customer in the indie section and a couple teens I didn't recognize.

Jason actually wrote his own raps and was the only kid I knew at school who knew more rap than I did. He hadn't stumped me yet, but eventually he was going to pull out that gem.

"Show me how it's done. Your turn," Jason said.

"Me? I'm not rapping. There's people here," I said. Jason was bolder than any comic hero on the shelves. He wore bold colors, stripes, polka dots. Ridiculous outfits, but he owned them. Jason could rap in a store and pull it off; I could not. Not that I could rap anyway. That was Jason's talent. I had no sense of rhythm. I just listened to Jason and tossed out ideas when we'd talk about his forever-in-the-making demo.

"Don't be a nerd, Walter. Rap at the comic-book store with me," Jason said. "You have all the classic white lyricists to draw from. Macklemore, Eminem, Mac Miller. Vanilla Ice. What do I have, KRS-One? Fine, here's another one: *I was tryin' to get it on my own, working all night, traffic on the way home. And my uncle calling me like, 'Where ya at? I gave you the keys, told you bring it right back.'*"

"Drake. You're the biggest Drake geek there is," I said. If I did rap in the comic store, I'd go deeper than Drake. "You getting anything?"

"No, I'm broke. You?" Jason asked.

"Yeah, I think so." I had a stack of new DC comics I had to narrow down. I'd cycled through the covers a handful of times and decided to put back Teen Titans.

"Let's go now while Romero's girl is at the register," Jason said softly, suddenly excited, eyeing her at the front of the store. "Watch this. I'll show you some rapping."

Jason had the genes I lacked, the ones that made you do nutty stuff in public for attention, or say crazy stuff you don't mean to get laughs, or put yourself in actual danger to impress a girl. Anytime he said "Watch this," it was too late to turn back.

We made our way to the front of the store, where Romero was MIA and his girlfriend sat at the register reading a thick volume of Strangers in Paradise. She was cute in an odd way, with most of her head shaved, leaving a red punk Mohawk. She had a midriff on, showing off a belly-button piercing and pale white skin. Jason walked up to her, and I trailed comfortably behind. Far enough that I could pass for not being here with him.

"Excuse me. Sorry to bother you. Do you work here?" Jason asked her with a broad grin.

"I'm just watching the register, but I can—" she started to say.

"Don't mean to sound like a jerk here," Jason conversationally rapped, *"but you deserve a paycheck for attracting all these nerds in here."* Not only did I not have the genes to rap to a girl in public, but I was also flushed with embarrassment just watching. I might not be able to come to Shadows anymore.

"Um," she said, blushing as Jason leaned onto the glass counter over a lineup of highly detailed Lord of the Rings pewter figurines.

"Like my homey from the 'burbs here, he's sitting straight up like Captain Kirk's chair, full attention like a kitten with perked ears,"

Jason rapped-talked. He pointed at the graphic novel she was looking at. "Can I ask what you're reading?"

"Uh, it's—" She turned her book around to show the cover.

"Can you read between lines? Can you read what's on my mind?" Jason asked, all friendly smiles. I really felt bad for the girl.

"Bryan? Help?" she called back to the employee room. Romero came out alert but dropped the defense when he saw us. "I think this kid wants to ring out."

"You guys? Pay for your stuff and get out of here, will you?" he asked.

Outside, Jason was cracking up. I hadn't even been the one doing all that and my armpits were sweating. We started walking east from the comic shop until we reached the corner and waited for the light to turn. It was cloudy and dark out for three thirty. We were standing on the corner of Main and Laurents, famous last month for a carjacking—guy approached a stopped car after midnight and shot twice, pulled him out, and left him for dead. Police found the car a week later about two towns over, empty and clean.

"You know why that's not embarrassing?" Jason asked. He took my bag and looked through my comics picks. "I can tell you're uncomfortable, but let me teach you something. You make a fool out of yourself for a girl, and she'll shoot you down nine times out of ten. But later, when she's alone, when she's feeling lonely, guess who she thinks about? That's right, she thinks about your boy Jason, because she knows I'm with it. I planted that seed, metaphorically speaking."

"She's in her midtwenties, dude," I said. "She's not going to be thinking about you."

"Maybe not her, but other girls. Girls our age," Jason said. He dropped the comics back in the bag and handed it to me. "What are you doing now? Come over. I'll let you listen to my new demo stuff and I'll read your comics."

A door slammed open right behind us, and two guys nearly knocked me off my feet and spilled to the ground in front of Jason and me. One of the guys tried to grab a couple cartons of cigarettes that scattered. There was a struggle for a second—I half expected a knife or a gun to come out. I checked my pockets to make sure I had all my stuff.

Jason cheered them on. "Yeah! Get 'im! Knock him on his ass, son!" One of the guys kicked his feet at the other, scurried to a standing position, and took off.

"Shoplifters," the guy still with us said, and shook his head. He was big.

"I gotta get home," I said, also shaking my head.

"Why?" Jason asked blankly.

"Why do I have to get home?" I asked. Because it's safe and giants don't ram into me there. "Because I live there. I have to have dinner and stuff. My dad's expecting me."

"Have dinner at my place," Jason said. "You always gotta go home. Your dad can eat alone for a night. He doesn't care if you hang out. I'll give you some more dating tips."

I didn't do much outside of home since my sister left for college. When I used to go out, I usually tagged along with her, or we'd do something as a family. At some point I just started avoiding things, not on a conscious level. Even with Jason, I'd brush off his invites like I'd swat a mosquito. It was instinctual, if not entirely rational.

"Okay," I said. It didn't need to be a big decision. "Let me drop off my stuff at home and talk to my dad, and I'll come over." I turned to walk to my place. Noisy construction had the street closed off, so I crossed it easily.

Jason and I had been good friends for the better part of a year. I first met him when we were freshmen. I was uncharacteristically forward and approached him, knowing I wanted to be friends. It was after the talent show, in which he performed "So Fresh, So Clean" by Outkast. I told him it was "dope" and Jason cracked up, and our friendship evolved from there.

•   •   •

As I reached home, it had gotten even darker out, and the street-lights were all turned on between the buildings. Dad was outside on the stoop talking to our neighbor Rosie Maldonado. Rosie was the reason why everyone on the street knew about Mom leaving us and about Dad's diabetes and about what I had for breakfast. Dad said none of that was secret and she could talk if she wanted to.

"It could be the same kids from last summer who were taking things out of unlocked cars every night," Rosie said, nodding. "Two teenagers were doing it."

"How do you even know that?" Dad asked. "I know it—I'm a cop. How do you know that?"

"Maybe I should be a cop, too," Rosie said.

"Maybe, Rosie," Dad said. "We'll put a wire on you. I'll bet you'd bring the whole underbelly of the city down. We'll get you started in training."

Personally, I thought they liked each other. Rosie was cute and spunky. Wild hair she'd pull together with a bandanna or some barrettes. She was small, just over five feet probably, and looked really young for her age, which was maybe early forties, a good age for Dad. He could do worse.

"Kids have no respect," my dad said, and crossed his arms. I made my way up the front steps. "They want the fast dollar and they don't care who gets hurt. Right, Walter?"

"Not Walter; he's a good boy," Rosie said. Rosie liked me. She was always asking about "the love life." I knew enough to keep that to myself, or would, if such a thing existed. She was always bringing food over for us, which was nice. Chicken and rice, flan, chorizo. It was a food-gossip trade.

"My guess is the kid got spooked—he'll lie low for a couple days and pick back up," my dad continued. "This incident aside, he hasn't encountered a reason to stop yet. He doesn't know I'm waiting for him, though."

"Don't get yourself in trouble," Rosie said.

"I don't mind a reasonable amount of trouble," Dad said in classic Bogart mode. I'd seen this side of Dad before. In fact, when I was a kid, it was all I saw. But these days it came out around Rosie a lot.

"What's going on?" I asked, leaning against the railing with Dad.

"One of your friends is robbing people's homes late at night," Dad said. "All over the neighborhood, keeps happening. They got Mrs. Johnson down the street. Rosie checks in on her once a week. They got her good, emptied the place out."

"No way," I said. "What do you mean by my friends?"

"Rosie thinks it's a teenager," Dad said. "She's doing her own detective work on this one."

"Sorry, James, I know that's your job," Rosie said.

"Don't worry about it, Rosie," my dad said. "You did the right thing coming to me, and I'll personally see to it that we get this punk behind bars. Any other theories you think up, you let me know. You know where to find me."

"Thank you, James. I can't help much, but I do what I can," Rosie said. I could never tell if those two were flirting or just liked each other's company or what.

This seemed like a good thing for Dad. He stood tall when he was in cop mode, sucked in his gut. He even spoke a little sharper. There was focus and purpose there that made him look like a different person. He gave me a nod, so I dropped off my book bag and headed back out.

• • •

Just walking a few blocks was still a novelty, years after moving. It just felt different. My parents had to drive everywhere in the suburbs. I couldn't even just walk to a friend's house. Our neighbors on either side of us were kinda shut-ins when they weren't doing yard work, the big social hangout of our old neighborhood. Half the kids in our school still live out there.

We were a divided group—we'd always been divided, but when we were younger it was by town lines. The poor kids in one town, the rich kids in another. The city and the suburbs. Now, we made our own lines. We were still the poor kids and the rich kids, the white kids and the black kids, and we stuck to our own groups, for the most part. We stayed with who we grew up with, and when there was interaction between groups, it was generally a fight. That seemed to be fading with time, as we all got to know each other.

I did want to hear what Jason recorded, see if he used any of my ideas. I'd been devouring rap for years. The right beat with my eyes closed was like comfort food. When I was walking through the city and the right song was on, I felt like the most alive person there. Rap put some swag in my step, lifted my head up, had me looking people in the eye. I could get lost in drum rhythms and lyrics. Now, I don't look like the biggest rap fan. Or maybe I do—maybe everyone listens to rap these days. I could be the quintessential rap fan now. But for all my insecurities and physical shortcomings (I weigh about 120 and have densely thick glasses), when Dead Prez's "Hip Hop" comes on, I'm the toughest guy on the block. In my head, anyway.

I felt a crunch under my feet and looked down to see a pool of broken glass in the road. It belonged to the window of a car I had just walked past. Maybe Rosie was right, and these break-in kids really were expanding their business.

Jason lived in a nice row-house building. His dad greeted me at the door after buzzing me in. He was shorter and rounder than I'd pictured, not that I'd spent a lot of time picturing Jason Mills's dad. "I'm Jason's secretary," he said, looking down at an imaginary sheet of paper. "You have an appointment?"

I felt like I was in elementary

school—*Can Jason come out and play?* Jason's dad sent me upstairs, where Jason was on his phone. Five minutes later, we still hadn't actually spoken.

"Why are you picking on *me*, is what I'm saying," Jason said into his phone as he paced around his bedroom. He was always pacing and tossing out limbs like Mr. Fantastic. It was tiring to watch. "I only said the same stuff Jeff and Ty said, and they said it first anyway, and it wasn't even about you—"

I was sitting on the floor because I didn't know where else to sit. The bed was empty, but would that be weird? There was a chair Jason had sat in for all of six seconds, but I was already sitting on the floor and now this perfectly good chair was being unused.

"Just forget all that," Jason said, a sudden change in his voice. Now he was sweet Jason. "When am I gonna see you?" Jason was popular with girls. I guess he was popular with everyone, actually. He was tall, always had some kind of a cap on. The stuff girls like: tall and with hat. He had a good combination of traits. Outgoing, a goofball, good-looking, talented, and smart, although he tended to keep that to himself.

Jason hung up, and in microseconds, he was sitting beside me and showing me phone pictures of a girl's butt. Clothed, thankfully. "This is Sherry. What do you think?"

"That's who you were talking to?" I asked, looking away from the picture.

"Name a girl in school, I've got a picture of her ass," Jason said. I guessed he had no signed waivers. "Girls line up for my photography skills. I'm the Ansel Adams of butts."

Jason kept playing with his phone, and I listened to the harp music coming from downstairs. I'd seen Jason's sister Naomi lugging that thing around school before. She kept starting the same piece over again, and flubbing in the same spot.

"Check this out: remember that beat we found last week?" Jason clicked on a track in iTunes, and the beat we found online came on, soulful and bass-heavy. The speakers blasted louder than I'd expected—you could see the windows vibrating. Jason came in a few seconds after the intro.

I tried to focus on Jason's rhymes, but I really wanted to turn the volume down 50 percent. I nodded, looked around. Even in its messy state, Jason's room felt sturdy and solid somehow. Lived-in, enjoyed. All my stuff at home looked like it was going to fall over or break if it wasn't on its back or broken. Jason's room looked like it was put together with an immaculate eye to look like a messy teenager's room, straight off a TV show.

Jason sounded good—he could really do this. Lyrically, I could see where he was coming from. There was a tension to it that I felt every day. The song felt like our home, our time.

"Be honest. Is it cool?" Jason asked, back in his chair. "No? Fine, whatever. Look, be honest, all right? What do you think?"

"It's really good," I said, not lying. "It's fine as it is, but I had some thoughts, like, in general. Like, what if you looked inward more? Like, instead of just looking at the city and the people in it, talk about your own feelings."

"Feelings," Jason repeated, but not contemplatively. I'd already crossed a line. "That's your album, not mine. *By the Fireplace, with Walter Wilcox.*"

"You could be like a Drake, or a Nas," I said, knowing he would be on board with that. We could both recite "Made You Look" from start to finish. "You're essentially introducing yourself to the world with any song you write at this point. Maybe you could show more of who you are and not just where you're from, or what you can do."

"All right," Jason said, leaping from the chair over to his bed. "Or like Eminem or someone—I could just talk about my life, and my friends and family."

"Just don't kill any of them in your songs," I said. The harp started up again. Jason's sister must have stopped when he was playing his song.

"Naomi with that friggin' harp all night!" Jason blurted out, a little too loudly. He stood up and towered above me. I hadn't moved from my floor spot. "Sick of that friggin' music. What is that, anyway? Who listens to harp music?"

"Maybe we can use it," I offered. "Like, she could add on to a beat or something. It's a different sound, right?"

Jason contorted his face into a snarl. "Some kind of knights-of-the-round-table, flute-playing, castle-moat Final Fantasy chocobo rap? Nuh-uh."

Jason turned away, attention on his phone. I wondered how someone like Jason would fare without his cell phone. Maybe he would be calm, in the moment, focused and attentive, polite, get good grades in school.

"We need song ideas," Jason said, falling back in his chair and rolling across the floor. "If I'm going to talk about stuff."

"What's on your mind—what are you feeling?" I had to have some fun with it. Usually it was me feeling uncomfortable around Jason. "Does school make you sad?"

"Mr. Feelings over here," Jason said, and threw a car magazine at me. I tried to dodge it but just moved myself in the way. "You're like some straight-A, Sigmund Freud, sweater-vest-wearing bunny rabbit."

"I don't wear sweater-vests," I said. I don't really get any A's, either. And I'm not a bunny rabbit. "I'm just saying maybe you could dig even deeper."

"You're surface-level deep," Jason said. "I don't think I've ever heard you express an opinion on anything other than Superman's new costume design. What are your deep thoughts? What's your life experience? How many girls have you dated? How many places have you traveled to? What are you going to rap about?"

"But I feel stuff awesomely," I bragged.

"You sit in your bedroom all day and feel stuff," Jason said. "Feeling yourself up. I'm not picking on you. I'm trying to help. You're begging for guidance. Come out with me some weekend. What are you doing Saturday?"

I didn't think I could last a full evening out with Jason. I didn't want to try.

"The girls I could introduce you to," Jason said, taking his phone out again. *Oh god, no more pictures.* He shook the phone for emphasis. "Right in here. I could call some girls. The things they'd do to you would send shivers down your spine. And I could hook you up easy. But here's your problem, and I'm gonna be honest with you: even if I skipped all the freaks and set you up with, like, a perfect study-buddy church girl, you'd just mess it up anyway. 'Cause you're closed off."

Jason tossed his phone on his bed. He looked back at his computer and opened the Internet browser. "I mean, look at me. I'm ugly, and I get more girls than anyone, and you're actually not a bad-looking dude, for a scrawny white kid. Heck, some girls even like that. But even if they gave it up on their own, threw it at you, you wouldn't do anything. Because you don't know how to make a move. Not being mean, just trying to help. Cool?"

I played with my own phone for a bit and listened to the rain that finally broke out and came down in sheets.

"I'm not great with girls," I said. "The only one I've had any regular relationship with was my sister. And she beat me up most of the time."

"You still like girls, though, right?" Jason asked. "You still go home every night and make a mess of your bedsheets and stuff. You just need to do it to a real live human being. What kind of girls do you like? Come out with me. I'll even do the heavy lifting. You like heavy girls?"

"Maybe this is a song," I said, changing the subject. "Giving girl advice or something."

"Advice to lames," Jason said, studying me like an injured animal brought in off the street. *Do we fix it up or put it out of its misery?* "It's cool, though. It's like you're cool with being a lame, so it's kind of your thing."

"It's not my thing," I countered, although he was starting to convince me.

Jason's dad appeared in the doorway. The hall was bright and well-lit, dim in the bedroom. "Don't let this boy talk to you like that, Walter. You know he can't even pee in a toilet without messing up the seat?"

"Pop! What the hell?" Jason said, moving back to his bed.

"Hi, Mr. Mills," I said.

"Mr. Mills," his dad repeated, leaning on the doorframe and putting his hands in his pockets. "I want to say call me Kenny, but I kinda like the ring of that Mr. Mills. Are you staying over for dinner? It's raining cats and dogs and I don't know what else out there. You walked?"

I nodded.

"Okay, you're staying for dinner, then. What do you want, burger and fries? We're placing orders."

35

The first thing I noted about dinner with the Mills family was that there were no burgers or fries or fast food of any kind. The table was loaded with home-cooked food Jason's mom had made. I had smelled it cooking before, and Mr. Mills had answered the intercom at the door with "Welcome to Burger King. May I take your order?" so I had been pretty sure he was kidding. But this kind of setup was reserved for maybe Thanksgiving in my family and really not even that.

In my current situation, dinner was an afterthought. It was something my dad and I pieced together when we noticed we were hungry at some eventual point during the night. But even before, we all ate at different times, sometimes a couple of us at the table, sometimes in front of the TV.

The second noteworthy, and more important, observation was that seated at the corner of the table was Naomi Mills. She was a complete knockout. She had short dark hair, pulled back and tied together. Pronounced cheekbones that made her eyes squint a little. She always looked like she was at least partially smiling. She had the cutest smile I'd ever seen. I suddenly felt a lot more nervous.

"Walter, I'm Denise. Pleased to meet you," Jason's mom said as we got to the table. She looked nice, dressed up. I felt like a slob, but Jason was in a T-shirt and sweatpants, so I guess I had him beat, at least. I wondered how his mom stayed so thin with this kind of food around, and the ability to just make it, whenever she felt like it. What incredible power to have.

"Thanks," I said. "Denise? Is that okay?"

"Denise is fine, Walter," she said.

The small room was full. Jason's mom introduced Kenny again ("Mr. Mills," I said to a smile and a nod—I'd probably always think of him as Mr. Mills), then to Naomi, and to the latest addition to the family, baby Kelly. Naomi was too busy feeding Kelly, who sat in a high chair to the right of her, to acknowledge me. I pulled a chair out at the end of the table. A family that eats together, at the same table, at the same time.

"Sit down, man," Jason said, and I realized I'd been standing there, staring. "Grab some food if you're staying."

A pot roast was the centerpiece, so I started there. I wondered if this was a typical Wednesday when Jason left the library and came home. "Sorry, it feels weird to have so many people in the same room for dinner," I stammered, noticing how nervous I was. Everything felt more difficult when I got nervous. Talking. Breathing. Naomi was trying to spoon food into Kelly's mouth, and it dropped onto her little table.

"Mom, how do I get it in?" Naomi asked. She held a spoon

between her right thumb and index finger, and when she moved it toward Kelly, the baby closed her mouth. When she pulled the spoon back, Kelly's mouth opened. Naomi laughed and butted her head softly against Kelly's. I could admire her like nature, or art. Like a sunset you could hang up in a museum. I pulled my eyes away and looked at my plate. It was a fancy plate.

Denise got up to help Naomi. "Do you have any brothers or sisters, Walter?" she asked.

"No, it's just me and my dad," I said, before I remembered I did have a sister. So I told her that. Then I remembered I had a mom, too. My eyes darted around the room. They had paintings on the wall, chests and drawers, a chandelier. Some kind of jazz was playing in the other room. There were no windows in the dining area, so I'd even forgotten about the storm. I had to make an effort not to look awed. It was weird how weird normal could seem.

"Walter's Dad is five-o," Jason said with his mouth full. "One time, poh-lice. Right, Walter?"

"You listen to too much of that rap crap," his dad said.

"Shut up, Jason," Naomi piled on. "You think you're so funny."

"I *am* funny," Jason snapped back in a fashion that would make any stand-up proud. Even his clothes had a different effect in this context. He wasn't bold and fearless. He was the goofy character on a Nickelodeon show who absorbed every punch line thrown at him.

"If you were funny, we'd be laughing and you wouldn't be yelling at us," Naomi said. I laughed, and Denise told them both to eat their food. "I'm eating," Naomi said, taking a bite of vegetables and smiling for her mother. The first time I saw Naomi, I didn't know she was a Naomi, and especially didn't know she was a Mills.

We were passing in the hall. She had her harp and looked like she could use a hand. I was late for the bus. She was pulling the harp on a stand of some kind with wheels and lost control, and it was tipping over. I caught it. "Got it?" I'd asked, and she'd said yeah and laughed.

Kelly clapped her hands and let out a joyous squeal. I smiled because it was cute, but I'm uncomfortable around babies. I have a tendency to call them "it," and they have a tendency to scream and squirm around me. Naomi clapped her hands for Kelly, Kelly clapped her hands back, and within seconds they were having a dance party.

"How's the harp going?" I asked her, drawing on all of our history together in one power punch of an icebreaker.

"Good," she said, not quite acknowledging our connection. Naomi straightened up in her seat, almost too straight. She had a posture that matched the chair she was in. She glanced at me, and I mimicked her straightening posture, tilted my chin up. She laughed and sat up even straighter.

"Will you sit like a man?" Jason asked, only noticing my half of the conversation. "Slouch a little—damn. You're gonna be crossing your legs next."

"So your dad's a police officer, Walter?" Denise asked as she placed her fork down. "Does he work in the city?"

"He's, like, a beat cop or something, handing out parking tickets," Jason said as if the question had been addressed to him. Mouth still full of food.

"Jason, could you be any more rude? Do you need all the attention?" Denise asked.

"We're having an adult conversation," I said to Jason, and Naomi laughed. Everyone laughed, even Kelly. Naomi made a crinkled-nose face.

"I think we've got a diaper mess," she said. "I'll be right back."

"Let Mr. Funny Guy do it," Mr. Mills said, and gave a stern look to Jason.

"I'll do it. I was going to anyway," Jason said, not believably, getting up and taking the baby. "You all act like you know me, but you don't get the real me at all, okay? Let's keep that straight."

They all laughed at tough Jason. Naomi covered her mouth when she laughed or when she was eating. You could still see the laughter in her eyes, though. I stood up after Jason to refill my glass of water from the pitcher on the table. I was used to having soda with dinner, but with fancy food like this, water was fine.

"So, Walter," Denise started a few seconds later, just as Naomi said, "You're a senior, right?" I wasn't sure who to respond to before Naomi continued. "You're in Jason's grade?"

"Jason's grade? Yeah, Jason and I are seniors." She knew what grade Jason was in. "You're a what?" I said, pretending I didn't know she was a junior.

"Junior," she said, lifting her eyebrows and looking down at her plate. "Two more years until I graduate."

"Don't say it like you're getting out of prison," Denise said. "You do plenty and you know it."

"Uh-uh, I can't go to a simple concert," Naomi said, picking up on a conversation I'd guessed had been going on for a while. "Jason gets to do whatever he wants, and he did last year, too."

"There's going to be boys and alcohol there, and you're not going," Denise said. She picked up one food item at a time when she ate. I'd already mushed my food into a pile resembling Kelly's food at that point. "Besides, we have company, so this is not the time, okay?"

"Watch my eye roll, Mom. See this? This one's for you." Naomi rolled her eyes.

"That was an impressive eye roll," I said. "Just the right amount of roll."

"Mom, I've never talked to a single boy, like, ever, okay?" Naomi said, before turning her head toward me. "Do you like the Foo Fighters, Walter?"

"The Foo Fighters?" I asked. Naomi's dense sarcasm was leaching into me like a virus. "Oh, I just call them Uncle Dave's band. It's hard to even think of them as a real-life band and not just Uncle Dave and his buddies jamming in the basement."

"I need to meet your uncle Dave. You're the coolest," Naomi deadpanned with a smile. "You must be a huge rock fan with such impressive lineage."

"I listen to all kinds of stuff," I said. It was an honest answer. After my dad and I moved, I got really into music. Especially once high school started and I didn't really fit in anywhere, most of my time outside of school (and some of it in school) was spent searching for music, discovering classic albums and artists from any genre and era.

"*No way*," Naomi said with fake enthusiasm. "All kinds of stuff? That's *my* favorite, too!"

"It's the only categorizing I'll allow on my iPod, 'All Kinds Of Stuff.' Frank Sinatra is right next to the Fugees."

"And Foo Fighters," Naomi added, playing with the food on her plate.

"No, they're under 'U' for 'Uncle Dave's Band,'" I said. We had an easy banter, unlike the one I had with my sister, which generally ended in a headlock or smack. This was a girl around my age, someone I wasn't actually related to. At school I'd think of these kinds of retorts or jokes, but I never said them out loud. I never wanted the attention. But I wanted Naomi's attention.

Mr. Mills finished off his plate and excused himself. He started bringing dishes to the sink. "They won't admit it, but they get it from me, I'm the funny one in the family."

"We operate on sarcasm here. You'll fit in fine," Naomi said. I liked the sarcasm. I liked that they joked all the time and talked at dinner.

"Don't act like he's moving in," Jason said, putting Kelly in her chair before sitting back down. "My food's cold! Come on." Jason pushed his plate away in a slouchy sulk.

"Heat it up, then," Denise said, getting up and bringing more dishes to the sink, leaving me, Jason, and Naomi at the table.

"So the Foo Fighters are coming to town," Naomi said. "I assume you'll be going?"

"Not this again. Stop being random," Jason said to Naomi. "You don't even like the Foo Fighters."

"First of all, I'm not being random. I do like them, and Dave Grohl is hot, okay?" Naomi said. "He's the perfect mix of scruffy bad boy and dork."

"He's also, like, fifty," Jason said. "And stop asking about that stupid concert. You know you aren't going."

"Scruffy bad boy and dork," I said. "That definitely sounds like a can't-miss event." I wanted to add on to her every argument, like we were a team.

"Since when do you talk so much?" Jason asked me. "This kid doesn't ever talk at school."

"He's talking to me," Naomi said flatly and immediately

defusing his argument. I nodded emphatically in agreement, pointed to her and myself.

"Yeah, all right," Jason said, flustered. He brought his plate to the microwave. "Hey, can we just admit that I am funny?"

Every heated conversation around the table seemed to cool off just as fast as it had started. I guess it wasn't about having the best one-liner with the Mills family, but having the comfort to use it.

"Jason, yes, whatever," Naomi said. "You're absolutely hilarious."

"He'll be here all week folks," I said. "Be sure to tip your waitress."

Chapter Three

I didn't live too far away from school, but the bus went up and down so many blocks, stopping every couple of streets, that it felt a lot farther than it was. With the near-two-hundred pounds of Lester Dooley taking up 75 percent of our seat, the ride felt even longer than usual. He had an easygoing way about him, a nice smile, but, damn, was he a big kid. He could pass for a huge LeBron James, who's already huge. I'd only seen him on the bus a couple of times in the past.

I looked out the window and made myself as vacant and unavailable as I could. My earbuds were in and my music was loud. I wanted to zone out for the fifteen minutes it took to get home.

I was listening to the Pharcyde on my iPad, "Passin' Me By," and, before that, A Tribe Called Quest's "Bonita Applebum." It was a playlist to fit my mood. I hadn't been able to shake Naomi from my head all week, and I hadn't seen her at school anywhere since. Maybe I needed to convince Jason a weekly dinner at his place was in order. Maybe I needed to friend-request her. We did have a bonding moment. It might not be creepy.

I tried to figure out what I'd say if I did cross her path at school. Maybe *No harp!* if she didn't have her harp with her. Or if she did,

Harp! Or maybe I could bring up Uncle Dave Grohl. She seemed to think that was funny. *Uncle Dave says hi!*

Lester nudged me, and I gave a quick nod of acknowledgment. It wasn't enough, though, and Lester made the "take out your earbuds" motion. I knew it would happen eventually. I took out the earbuds like I was putting on a blindfold and stepping onto the plank.

Lester was part of a trinity of kids you generally wanted to avoid when they were together, the others being Frankie Roland and Beardsley, both also on the bus today. Frankie was a giant, too; he played football, his face was mostly forehead with brown hair parted in the middle, and he was popular but pretty quiet. Beardsley was his and Lester's overexcited pet. It really wasn't an accident that Lester ended up sitting next to me.

There were other seats he could have taken, but I'd crossed his path in gym class, stealing the ball in our basketball game just as he was taking it to the basket. I could have just let him pass, and I don't even like sports, so that would by all means have been the smarter decision, but he was right in front of me and wide open, too. Now I existed in his world. I just hoped I hadn't pissed him off.

"What's your name?" Lester asked with a nice smile. He was like Nate, one of the first people you met at the school. Good or bad, most people had had some interaction with Lester Dooley. Except me. "I must be forgetting or something."

"Walter," I said quietly.

"Wally? All right, Wally," Lester said. He pointed at my new iPad. I'd found a use for my birthday money from Mom. "You listen to rap? What do you have on there?" he asked. I didn't have a lot on my iPad, since it was still pretty new.

"Uh, the Pharcyde," I said, trying to keep my answers as brief as I could. I closed my iPad and put it in my bag. I didn't want to be on Lester's radar, and I didn't want to say anything that was going to rub him the wrong way.

I didn't actually grow up with Lester, but we were in the same grade and I'd heard all the stories by the time high school started. How he'd missed an entire winter from school to go to some mental hospital. Broke some kid's arm for calling him a racist name. How he dated a college professor, how he talked his way out of an overnight jail stay. Some rumors outlandish, others entirely believable, especially once you'd gotten a look at him. There were enough rumors to not believe any of them and still have your guard up when you passed him in the hall.

"You listen to Pusha T?" Lester asked. "I've been into trap music, that real hard stuff, myself."

I nodded. I actually liked Pusha and Clipse, but I wasn't up for that conversation. Jason, I could make an ass of myself in front of, but I didn't want to come across as some poser to Lester. Not today, anyway.

"Hey," Lester said, turning to face me. "How come I don't know you? I know everyone in this school. They don't even let you in here without going through me first. So how come I don't know you?"

I shrugged. I guess I wasn't the star I thought I was in gym class. "Not sure."

"That's what I thought." Lester laughed. "You live this far down and you got an iPad? You must have noticed we're on the poor side of town. I can't even sit next to you with that thing out. You'll get us mugged, man. They'll take your iPad and your socks and shoes. They don't even sell those here."

I laughed.

"I hope you don't expect me to stick up for you," Lester said.

"I'm running." He laughed. "My car got busted into a couple weeks ago. I had my iPod in there overnight; someone smashed a window and took it. My mom won't help me fix it. She says the window's gonna cost more than the iPod did. I gotta get it fixed before it's cold out."

We passed a liquor store that had been robbed enough times I'd cross the street to walk past it. Dad had a story for every spot in the city. One of the package-store tales had a fifty-year-old woman robbing a clerk at gunpoint. Dad said they found the gun, and it'd belonged to an actual police officer. No one knew how she'd gotten it.

I zipped my bag up and stuffed it between my feet. I looked back out the window. We were almost at my stop.

"You're quiet, Wally," Lester said. "That must be why no one knows you. You need to make a name for yourself—be somebody."

•   •   •

My bus stop was on Lincoln Street, a few blocks from home. The bus would take me right to my doorstep if I wanted to sit twenty more minutes when I could walk home in ten. Lester followed me off, along with Frankie and Beardsley, who trailed behind obediently. Beardsley walked with a slouch, his arms swinging. The fact that they were following me at all was troubling. We could turn down a path, lose the traffic, and next thing you know my book bag and iPad are gone and I'm trying to remember how standing up works.

Not that they'd done anything to warrant the fear. Lester talked to me like there was nothing he'd rather be doing on a Tuesday afternoon. "Tell me about yourself, man," Lester said. We walked

at a slow pace. He was a two-strap-backpack guy. I was a one-strapper myself. "You play b-ball, right? Into sports?"

"Not really," I said. "Just got lucky today."

"I'm not that good, either," Lester said humbly. "I watch, but I don't play. Who are you friends with? Anyone I know?"

"Probably not," I said. I couldn't help but mumble and give short answers.

"Everyone's got some friends," Lester said. "They put so many of us together in high school that by the time we all know each other, we'll be going off to college. That's why I try to talk to everyone when I get the chance."

People on the sidewalk cleared a path for us. Big Bad Lester wasn't so bad. But those rumors had been going on forever. Maybe he liked the mystique. I might, too. Maybe I'd be friends with Lester Dooley, have a crew of guys who'd take down anyone who crossed me, not that anyone would when I walked around with Lester and Frankie.

"That's my crib," Lester said, pointing out a duplex that looked remarkably like the other buildings on this street.

Everything in the city has a name, it seems. The section between Lincoln Street and Laurents Avenue is called the Jungle, partly because of the abundance of trees lining the streets and partly for some wild parties that get thrown here.

"You live that close?" I said.

"I know, right? You must have moved here," Lester said. He stuffed his hands in his coat pockets. "If we grew up blocks from each other and I just noticed you now, I must be too wrapped up in my own drama or something. And if you didn't grow up over here, that'd put you in the suburbs."

"Yeah," I said. "Moved the summer before sophomore year."

"So you were living in some big house with a lawn you didn't have to share, and you ended up here? That's a long fall, man. So what happened? Parents split up? Divorce?"

I nodded. "Divorced."

"Mine, too. Money problems? Cheating?" Lester asked. "They say half of marriages end in divorce, but I swear it's more than that. Everyone I know, their parents are split. Happens to everyone. You got any brothers or sisters?"

"Sister," I said.

"I can picture your whole family," Lester said. Frankie and Beardsley still trailed behind us, shuffling along and talking to each other. "Your dad must be an accountant or a lawyer or something, wears one of those jackets with the elbow patches, smokes a pipe."

"It wasn't like that," I said, and shook my head. "Not at all."

"Guess I misread. You like it in East Bridge?" Lester asked. "It's not for everyone or anything, but it's nice once you're out of the Basement. They've got a restaurant on every corner on Main Street. The people are good here."

"It's cool," I said. I mostly knew the people in my classes and a few of my immediate neighbors.

"I was, like, nine, ten, something like that, when my mom and pop split up," Lester said. "So you were a teenager already. And then you end up here. I'd probably be quiet, too, if I was used to birds and hanging laundry by the fence and all that."

"It's really not like that," I said. A loud chirp disrupted the proceedings, and a cop car rolled up alongside us. It was my dad. No pipe or elbow patches. Lester gave me a look, like, *Here we go.*

"This stuff always happens right near my home," Lester said. "I'll bet my mom drives by and thinks I'm up to something."

Dad and his partner, Ricky, stepped out of the car. "What's up, homeys?" Dad asked. I cringed. That was the end of my friendship with Lester.

"Hi, Officer Wilcox," they all deadpanned. "Hi, Officer Ortiz."

"Everything all right, Walter?" Dad asked. I nodded. Dad was checking out the scene, absorbing the details, but there was no story here. "Isn't that your house back there, Lester? You walking off lunch or something?"

"Just talking to my new friend, that's all," Lester said, calm and relaxed. He even threw a giant arm around me. It was like wearing a heavy neck brace.

"You know who your new friend is?" Dad asked him, pointing at me. "That's my son, Walter. So you lay a finger on him, Lester, you deal directly with me. Understand?"

"Wally *Wilcox*?" Lester said, eyebrows raised, and turned me around to get a better look at me. I apologized as best I could with just my eyes. "We didn't even know he was a celebrity. We were just talking, honest. I like this kid."

"That doesn't make me feel much better," Dad said.

"Hey, I wanted to ask you a question, actually," Lester said to my dad. "We got this homeless dude camping out in our front yard dude. What do I do about that? My mom wants me to go yell at him, but I don't know what this guy's up to."

"You can file a report," Dad said.

"At the station?" Lester asked, and twisted his mouth. "Pass. I thought maybe you could just come take a look or something."

Dad nodded. "I'll see what I can do."

"So we're all friends here. That's great," Ricky said. "Let's keep it that way, yeah?"

Dad pointed his thumb at the cruiser. "Walter, let's get in the car." I did a walk of shame to the car with my head down and ducked into the backseat.

• • •

In the car, Dad and Ricky were talking about bullies while we sat in traffic. The fact that I could have been home already if I'd finished walking popped into my mind.

"Did you know Uncle Ricky used to be a bully?" Dad asked. Ricky's not my actual uncle, but my parents had called him that since I was little. He turned to face Ricky, who was in the passenger seat. "You used to hang out with Adrian Ford—I hated that kid! He used to torture me in school."

"That doesn't make me a bully," Ricky said. "Adrian was a nice guy, if you weren't on his list."

"But I was on his list!" Dad said. I'd seen high school photos of Dad, and heard some stories. It's not like he was a nerd or anything. "And you were a bully by association."

"That's so not a thing," Ricky said. "That's like me being rich because I know a guy who owns a boat."

I took my cell out of my pocket after it buzzed. It was the cheapest phone on the family plan, but it did have a crappy version of the Internet.

Ricky turned around in his seat to face me. "This guy Adrian used to pick on your dad, Walter. He ever tell you about Adrian?"

"It's my story—let me tell it," Dad interrupted.

"Well, tell it, then!" Ricky said, settling back in his seat.

"Adrian Ford, tall, tall guy with a head like a solid boulder," Dad started. His story is a little fuzzy in my mind because I saw I had a Facebook message from Naomi Mills, and the world spun for a split second and up was down and down was up. What I remembered of the story while I was waiting for a signal to load Facebook involved my dad getting picked on at school by this guy Adrian, who'd been the king of the school, and my dad took it and took it, until one day he stood up to Adrian and told the bully to meet him after school. The bully never showed and left Dad alone after that, presumably because Dad had earned his respect or something. None of it applied to me, because Dad was a cop and had been kind of big deal. I wasn't about to call out Lester or Beardsley or anyone else at school, and as long as I was friendly, I didn't have any need to. Besides, I was pretty sure I'd seen that same story line on some sitcom repeat.

I accepted Naomi's friend request, probably just minutes after she sent it. I could risk the dorkiness.

Dad was still in lecture mode. "You gotta be careful with guys like these," he was saying. We were taking a detour, apparently, as we left the smaller streets to pass the markets. "These guys are animals. I see some pretty wild stuff. I was joking around back there, but these guys carry knives—these guys have guns.

"You can tell me if you're in trouble, you know, right?" He kept looking at me to verify I was listening. It was a little troubling with people walking on the sidewalk and crossing the street.

"Dad, I'm fine," I said.

Naomi was asking me if I wanted to go to the Foo Fighters concert. *U were a huge hit with the fam*, her message read. *My mom would totally let me go w/ u. I can work this.*

Was that a good message or bad? Was she saying I was a big nerd, but she could use me to get to the concert? Who was I kidding? I didn't care. *Operation Uncle Dave is a go*, I replied. *Count me in.*

"It's good that you stood up to them," Dad said. He just kept talking. "And those are some ugly dudes to face, too. But you can't run from problems. You tackle them head-on, right? You did good. I'm proud."

"Dad, we were walking. That's it," I said. My phone buzzed.

I was afraid to look at the screen. What if she'd changed her mind, or she'd been just joking and I'd misinterpreted it and hadn't caught the tone? What if she hadn't asked at all and I'd just responded to an imaginary message? Reception was poor, and her message took, like, ten seconds to show up, which was a very long time when you were in midconversation with Naomi Mills.

LOL that was fast! Naomi replied. Not exactly a confirmation of plans.

I'm in my dad's cop car. I think I'm under arrest. :P, I wrote back. I tried to send it, but the Internet dropped out again. Technology fail. The phone buzzed again as Dad pulled up to our building, and my eyes darted to the screen.

NOOOOO, Naomi wrote back. *Post bail! We need you free til after the concert!*

Bake me a cake with a nail file in it, I wrote.

At that exact moment, I'd have escaped Alcatraz if I needed to.

Chapter Four

10/23 10:35 WalterW1014: Hey, are you going to the Foo Fighters concert Saturday?

10/23 10:35 NateTheGreat01: Have I said or done anything to indicate I'd be going to a Foo Fighters concert? Or do I have a clone running around I need to be concerned with?

10/23 10:35 WalterW1014: I'm just wondering if I should go.

10/23 10:35 NateTheGreat01: If you have to wonder, maybe just don't go?

10/23 10:36 WalterW1014: Well, a girl I was talking to wanted to go, and I might have said I'd go too.

10/23 10:36 NateTheGreat01: Really? Who?

10/23 10:36 WalterW1014: Don't tell Kate though . . .

10/23 10:36 NateTheGreat01: Kate would demand you go, you know that right?

10/23 10:37 NateTheGreat01: So what's the dilemma? Sounds like a sweet deal.

10/23 10:37 WalterW1014: I'm not sure if it's a good idea. Believe it or not I might make a poor impression.

10/23 10:38 NateTheGreat01: If you don't go, I'll go. I'm single now. She sounds hot.

10/23 10:38 WalterW1014: I haven't said a thing about her.

10/23 10:39 WalterW1014: Here's the thing. I'm in a pretty good space now.

10/23 10:39 NateTheGreat01: Perfect, go

10/23 10:40 WalterW1014: and if I go, like her, things don't work out, bam. Distraught for the rest of high school.

10/23 10:40 NateTheGreat01: You're not in a good space, you're distraught now. This IM wouldn't be happening in a good space.

10/23 10:40 NateTheGreat01: Who is this mystery girl?

10/23 10:40 WalterW1014: She's a junior, Naomi Mills. Don't tell anyone, though.

10/23 10:41 NateTheGreat01: Really? Wow, okay

10/23 10:41 NateTheGreat01: I dig it. You should definitely go.

10/23 10:42 WalterW1014: Yeah, I guess so. I already said yes, so I guess I have to.

10/23 10:42 NateTheGreat01: Walter. Go. This is an order. I'm happy for you.

10/23 10:42 NateTheGreat01: This is going to be amazing, you'll see. Best night of your life.

It's a strange feeling when you're on the bus with a pretty girl and somehow you'd rather be in front of it. Maybe some of us are just conditioned to the bad things, and even though we hate them, it's what we know and what we're comfortable with. We've adapted to crappiness and anything more or less is unsettling.

I was already blowing it. I had to be boring her. Did she just want to go to this concert and I happened to be a decent-enough excuse to escape the family watchdogs? Was she expecting some-one else there? What if it was a guy, a secret boyfriend? Was the whole night going to be weird? Those were the questions running through my head as I sat next to the prettiest girl I'd ever seen and couldn't think of anything to say for going on three minutes. That was a lot of time for awkward silence on what could, conceivably, be a first date.

I was people-watching, trying to keep my brain distracted from all the negative thoughts, before it got me in trouble. I found more than a few people on their way to a rock concert, based on the median college age and abundance of Foo Fighters T-shirts. Naomi, on the other hand, had actual fashion sense. She wore a jean jacket better than most. And the bracelets—she accessorized. I never hung out with anyone who accessorized.

We were on our way to the High Hill section of the city, and the buildings were getting taller the closer we got; the lights were getting brighter.

"Have you seen Uncle Dave lately?" Naomi asked, breaking our epic bout of silence. "Do you see him often? Does he know you're coming?" She'd been trying to pin me down on the Uncle

Dave fib ever since that dinner. This running joke was turning into a marathon.

"Yeah, I see him when he's in town," I said, rolling with the story. "We have a secret language. If he plays 'Everlong,' it's a message to me because he knows that's my favorite." I never talked to anyone the way I talked to Naomi. It was like a game of volleyball in which neither of us ever missed, we were that in tune with each other's playing style.

"Oh wow," Naomi said. "I hope they play it. That'll be so cool for you. And I'll know the real reason they're playing it. So do you listen to *anything* but rap Rap and 'Everlong'?"

"I like everything, remember?" I said. "I like the Beatles."

"The Beatles?" Naomi asked. "Who's that? I never heard of them."

We passed a long chain-link fence, and the bus pulled into a semiempty parking lot a couple of blocks away from the uptown High Hill area. Hotels, restaurants, and venues crammed the grid. This was the section that went on the tourist brochures and state website. A five-by-five grid of lit-up, fun-for-the-family city entertainment that cast a long, dark shadow where the rest of us lived.

"I'm excited. I don't go to a lot of concerts," Naomi said. "Last one was with my sister a few years ago."

"Kelly?" I asked, remembering her baby sister.

"Kelly's, like, one year old," Naomi said, shaking her head and laughing. "How would I go to a concert with her a few years ago? No, my older sister, Alicia."

"Oh, okay," I said, unaware that she and Jason had an older sister. "What concert did you see with her?"

"Erykah Badu," Naomi said. "Look, I love Erykah Badu and I love the Foo Fighters. I'm like you, I love everything. I love Kenny Rogers."

"Everything's the best," I said. "Kenny Rogers, though? Really?"

"I've never heard his music but yes," Naomi said. "He's awesome. He's my favorite."

We walked between tall buildings, lights all around and stars in the sky if you looked straight up. I looked up too much when I walked in the city, like a kid when the whole world's taller than you. It felt like that in High Hill—like if you looked down, you'd miss half the picture. The buildings got impossibly tall and the lights impossibly bright and I felt like we were in a maze, like mice in a maze. People walked in packs and we followed the herd, down one street and up another.

We passed through people like sand through a sifter, outside the building, in the doorway, the merch area. I tried to look like I belonged and like I wasn't freaked out by the mobs even though this was my first concert. And maybe my last, since it'd taken all the money I had left from Mom's birthday present to get my ticket.

There was seating around the sides of the venue, but Naomi and I were in a busy general admission area. Naomi sprang to life once the show started, dancing up a storm while I shouldered the brunt of bodies being slammed around us. It turned out that Foo Fighters fans were much bigger than me, and more nimble and more drunk. There was no great way to know if this was a date, or just a friendly hang-out, or if she just really wanted to go to this concert. At least there wasn't a secret boyfriend. I didn't know how to nudge things in one direction or another, or if there was something expected of me at some point to cement things as romantic or friendly. I had no idea what to expect, and that was why I'd broken out in a sweat once again. I looked at the happy seated people off to the side. I could have done some gentle chair-dancing there, I was good at chair-dancing. As it was, I swayed and head-bobbed and pushed back against the wave of shoulders and elbows. I could guarantee a constant movement of my body, but I could not guarantee it was dancing.

Naomi, on the other hand, was good. I think. She looked good to me, anyway. She seemed to talk to everyone in our radius. When she wasn't doing that, she was yelling song names to me each time a new riff played. She was a legit fan. She spent more time asking people around us what their favorite albums were and what other shows they've been to than she did talking to me. A good three or four guys seemed to be interested in her. Two of them might as well have come here with her.

"This is so fun!" she shouted toward me about halfway through the set. "It's like a big family here. I love it!" It did feel like family, which is why I wanted to go to my room and shut the door. That word had different connotations for us.

There were bodies everywhere, dark bodies with splashes of red highlights on us. I watched the band and I watched Naomi as the lights on the audience went off and on in flashes to rile up energy. One of the guys kept leaning in and I couldn't hear him. Sounded

like he wanted to get her something, a drink maybe. She shook her head, and they laughed. I couldn't tell if she knew these guys or not. At the rate I was going, they were more likely to make a move than I was. I glanced at my phone and saw we had probably an hour or so left, and I debated sneaking away or going outside for air, but instead I smiled firmly and kept with the waves of crowd movement, a reluctant semimosh. If I brought Naomi home crushed or bruised or folded in half, I could count a second date out.

Naomi tried to talk to me, but I was off my game—my brain was shut down. I was holding back the moshers, the music was loud, I was deeply analyzing what this was. So I smiled and nodded a lot.

Eventually, in between sets, I was introduced to Ted, one of the guys who'd been hitting on Naomi all night. "Hey, man, I'm Ted," Ted said.

"Hey, how's it going?" I asked, as noncommittal as possible, my hands in my pocket, looking around at the dark venue. These guys seemed like they were built into the installation here, like regulars. They looked and dressed the part, cool concert-going hipsters.

"Good show, huh?" he asked. Someday I'd look back and think, *Yes, that was a damn fine show.* But right that second was not the time. "You go to a lot of shows here?" he asked. I didn't. I didn't ask for a personal tour guide or concert buddy, but the questions continued. "Do you live in the city? Ever go to New York? What kind of music do you listen to?"

I tried to pull myself away from Ted and get back to Naomi. Maybe if I hovered obviously enough, we could bail from these guys, find another place to stand. She was talking to the other dude. He wore fingerless gloves. Who wears fingerless gloves? As I got closer I caught wind of the conversation; this guy had a lot of questions, too.

"You don't have Facebook?" he asked her, leaning in. "Okay, Twitter? E-mail? Phone?"

"No, sorry, I'm completely disconnected," Naomi said, and she seemed relieved to see me. I had been wingmanned—I couldn't believe I'd missed it. The wingman and I joined Naomi and her would-be suitor. I wondered if I could take them, but decided I could not.

The band came back out and Naomi pulled me away, closer to the stage. "Let's dance" was all she said, and as much as I didn't want to dance, didn't know how to dance, it by far beat hanging out with the concert hipsters. Naomi bounced and twirled and laughed, and I tried to follow suit. I tried to bounce and laugh, and on every level I feared I looked ridiculous. But I also suddenly stopped caring if I did.

Naomi turned to face me, a big smile on her face, and I wanted to be the best dancer in the world and I didn't want to let her down. "I can't really dance," I shouted over the music. "All I know is some bad sixties dancing my mom showed me!"

"Show me the sixties dance!" Naomi shouted back.

I threw inhibition to the wind and did my mod-era hand-dancing. I did the scuba dance. My mom would have been proud. Naomi cracked up and danced badly with me. She looked down, watched my body, and copied. She had a big smile when she looked back up at me. I could move—I surprised myself and probably Naomi, too. I felt less like I was on some job interview, or even like I was on a date. I was just there, and it was fun.

She turned to face the band and backed into me, and I felt the weight of her. I didn't know if I could touch her, move my arms, or what. She turned again and touched the hair over my forehead.

"I like this curl," she shouted over the music. "I can tell you're a little bit wild because of that curl in your hair. It can't be tamed."

I needed to feel more like my hair.

•　　•　　•

After the concert, we waited for the floor to empty. Half the room cleared out immediately, but a lot of people hung around, talking and taking their time.

"I think the show's pretty much over," I said when it was us, some roadies cleaning off the stage, and maybe a few other people scattered around. The lights were on and some pop music was playing over the speakers. The place was a mess in the light.

"Finally, it's all ours," Naomi said, laughing and dancing by herself. "I don't want to go home yet. My parents won't know exactly what time they stopped playing."

"If they're signing any autographs, it'll be out by the tour bus," one of the guys cleaning said.

•   •   •

We waited outside at the end of a line by the bus, with about twenty other people. These were the hard-core fans. They probably did this often. Standing along the dark side of the building, watching for a rock star every time a door opened, chatting with one another about all the other times they stood in line and watched the doors.

"The clock is ticking, Mr. Wilcox. Uncle Dave is just feet away," Naomi said.

"He's going to be so thrilled to meet you," I said.

Those two guys from the concert were nearby, because of course they were. They walked over like they were old friends and reintroduced themselves. I introduced myself again, and Naomi immediately said, "Dave Grohl is his uncle." She really had no off button. It was one thing to joke around with her and another with these two guys I didn't know.

"Oh yeah?" one of them said. "Really? And you're in line?"

"Yeah," I said, desperate to run in any direction from there, into traffic if possible. "He doesn't actually know I'm here, so it's cool."

They laughed, unbelieving. I would have, too.

"It's real," Naomi said, somehow making it all worse. But then, "Walter's my boyfriend, so I've seen him before."

"Wow," the one with the fingerless gloves said, kind of actually genuinely impressed, and he even took a step back. Thank god she finally acknowledged the joke, indirect as it was. I wasn't sure how much further I could take it. "That's really cool. Hey, sorry, I didn't know you two were—"

"Yeah, well, we are, and you two are rude, and way too old to be dressed like that. Plus I'm sixteen, so bye," Naomi said. She smiled and leaned her head on my chest, and the two guys stepped away with their eyebrows raised. I'd have been horrifically embarrassed if I didn't like her head there so much. She could push every button I had and know exactly how to undo it all. She was a master manipulator and I didn't think she had a clue.

"No autographs tonight, everyone. Sorry," one of the roadies called out as he left the building. The stragglers dispersed with some grumbling.

"*Bye, Uncle Dave,*" I yelled at the tour buses, and Naomi yelled bye as well.

She turned to me with a look of shock as we made our way back to the parking lot our own bus was in. "Can you *believe* those guys? At least one of them was trying to ask me out! So awkward!

That doesn't happen, like, ever. And those guys must have been, like, twenty at least! Ew!"

"That's, like, forty combined," I said.

She took a deep breath of air that didn't smell like beer or sweat. "So how's it feel being Mr. Naomi Mills?" She laughed before I could answer, not that I had an answer. "I can't believe I said that. I say stupid things, Walter."

I never really liked my name until I heard it out of her mouth. And then it was all I wanted to hear. The light at the intersection turned red and the little walking guy turned white. A bunch of people crossed the street together under a smattering of traffic lights and streetlamps.

I took Naomi's hand and felt a shiver through my whole body. I was positive my hands were clammy and sweaty and my heart was ready to explode, but I didn't hesitate. I was sure that this was okay. That this was supposed to happen. I gave her hand a squeeze and she squeezed mine back. Some kind of secret communication and I didn't know what it said. Maybe *I've got you,* or *Is this more than friendship?* or maybe just *Hello.*

"I promise you I'm not a compulsive liar," I said as we walked toward the less glamorous transit bus in the parking lot.

"You promise? That's exactly what a compulsive liar would say," Naomi said. "I think you're witty. Most people would have bailed on the Uncle Dave story about three seconds after the joke, but you hung in like a trouper. I'm proud of you, man."

"Do you want to walk back?" I asked. The two guys from the concert weren't far behind us, and a line of people in the parking lot were piling onto the bus already. We could be alone, stretch this out. Have some space. "We can get a bus at the next stop unless you have to get home right away. I can protect us if we get in trouble. I'm a black belt in karate."

"Are you really or is this more compulsive lying?" Naomi asked. She let go of my hand as we passed the bus stop. My hand felt empty now.

"This is lying," I said. "I'm completely beltless. But it is pretty safe here."

"All right, let's walk. But if any ninjas pop up, you better protect me."

"Have you angered ninjas?" I asked. "No, you know what? It's a deal." We made our way through the tall uptown buildings and bright lights to the nighttime oranges of the business district. Orange lights, brown trees, yellow walk signals, and cars lined up on every curb. Everywhere we looked, there was life, even at ten, eleven, whatever time it was. The night owls were out. Nate might have been right about tonight: it just could be the best night of my life.

"Let's play a game," Naomi said as we waited to cross the street. "We each get to ask the other five questions, and by the end we'll know everything there is to know about each other. I've got, like, a thousand questions I can ask already, so it should be easy. You in?"

"I'm in," I said. The silence of the bus ride to the concert felt like ages ago. "You go first, since it's your game. I need to know if this is, like, 'your favorite letter' kind of questions or 'who would your murder if you had the chance' kind of questions."

"Those are both good," Naomi said. "But okay. First question. Walter Wilcox, what is your favorite memory?" She gave the side of my head a playful poke, and it gave me a rush.

"My favorite? Wow, that's tough," I said. She hit hard right off the bat. "I could still be thinking by the time we get to the bus stop."

"What's the first thing that popped into your head?" Naomi asked. I couldn't say the head poke or the hand-holding. Could I? No, I couldn't say that. I did have an image, though.

"I don't know if it's legitimately my favorite memory, but Disney World," I said. We crossed another street, darting through

headlight beams. "I was eight years old. My family drove all the way down there. My family never really did anything, so that was a huge deal. I was obsessed with it all year. Nobody fought. We all had a blast, so, yeah, maybe that's my favorite memory."

"How about something specific?" Naomi asked. "So I can picture it. What's the one image that captures the whole trip?" She was looking at me when she asked it, not looking at her feet like I had been doing. She was good at this. And she was really interested. I had an answer.

"Fireworks," I said. "They had this parade and these crazy fireworks that went on forever, and the sky was so bright it seemed

like daytime. They do it every night there, too. But, yeah, just sitting on this sidewalk with my family watching the fireworks, that was the image that popped into my head. My sister had her arm around me, which was rare, but it was nice."

"Good answer," Naomi said. "I feel like I know you more already. Now you ask me something." She had her hands in her jacket pockets now. I wished I could hold them again.

We were walking under a line of trees downhill toward the park bus stop while I thought up my next question. What I really wanted to know I wasn't sure how to bring up, but she did say something earlier I could use to get there. "Why was it so weird to you that those guys were trying to ask you out?" I asked. "Was it just because they were older? Or was that just really strange for you in general?"

We sat down at a bench across from a guy eating a slice of pizza. It was Saturday night but it could have been Saturday morning with the amount of foot traffic in the park.

"They were old, but it wasn't just that," Naomi said. "You go right for the personal questions. Why was that so weird? I don't know. I guess because it's never happened before? It's gotta be weird the first time someone hits on you, right?"

"I would not know," I said. That was a feet-watching answer, not a face-watching answer.

"Me, neither," Naomi said. "I'm kind of a dork. I don't really come across as super approachable or anything. Which is fine because I'm really not, my parents wouldn't let me date anyone anyway. Never mind. I'm gonna change the subject. My question. Here's an easy one: favorite color, and why."

She didn't look like a dork, that was for sure, and she didn't have a dork vibe until she was calling herself one. After a few hours with Naomi, I was starting to see it a bit, in a good way. Our differences were attractive, but the similarities were what I really enjoyed. Our mutual dorkiness.

The bus showed up, a perfect diversion from Naomi's hard-hitting question. The bus was packed and we had to stand and hold on to the rails. Naomi and I faced each other on the bus, no room for anything but face-watching and eye contact for the ride. The game was a little embarrassing with so many ears in the vicinity now.

"So my favorite color. Maybe purple?" I said. I focused on her shoulder. The dark purplish black of her jean jacket. "Like a night-sky purple. Shadows. In my head it's the color of the city, even though I can look around and not see a ton of purple. That's a bad answer, I know. I'm going to use my question to ask you the same thing. Favorite color."

"All right, but you only get to copy me this once, and only because I have an answer," Naomi said, confident smile. "I like combinations. Like blue and black, or blue and brown."

"So anything with blue, but not blue by itself," I said. I looked up, tried to match her eye contact. I didn't want to seem intense or creepy but not too soft or insecure, either. Life is difficult.

"Hey, blue goes with a lot," Naomi said. "My question. We'll get a little deeper. Who was your first crush?"

I looked around. No one was paying any attention to us. The people in seats were asleep or listening to their iPods, or talking to each other.

"I guess it was this girl Ellen, from third grade," I said. "I just picked her at random because everyone else at our lunch table were picking out their crushes. She was the first girl I saw when I looked around. Lo and behold, she became the most popular girl in elementary school, and pretty much everyone was into her by the end of the year. I think she moved out of state in fifth grade."

"Nice, so you have good taste and set trends," Naomi said, nodding. The bus stopped and we swayed toward the back for a second. "You also send girls running across the country. Hmmm."

"That's one way of looking at it," I said. We grabbed a couple of empty seats. When the bus started moving again, her body pressed into mine. She was still waiting for my next question. "What do you see in your future?" I asked.

Ideally she'd see me there, but there was pretty much no chance of her actually saying that. It would probably be troublesome if she did.

"Boring future, but not too boring," she said. We sat side by side now. I watched her knee. There was a slight rip in her jeans on the left knee. "Like, I want a husband and family, but I don't want a boring day job or to be home all the time or anything. I have too many hobbies I love, so I want to do something with one of them to make money and be fulfilled."

"Wow, there's, like, twelve follow-up questions to that," I said. This game could go all night, but our stop was next.

"That's why it's a good game," Naomi said, cutting off the subject. "Are you a good student?"

"No," I said. "Not really. I get C's in school, I strive for average. I'm a better student of life."

"Fair enough. What grades do you get in life?" Naomi asked.

We hopped off the bus at our stop, and I gave it some thought. "Life grades," I said, mulling it over. "Like, D's, if I'm honest. I'm a bad student of life. I'm a bad kid, Naomi Mills."

"Tsk. Disappointing," Naomi said. We crossed the street to her building. Her arm swung free, and I wanted to hold her hand or take her arm, or something. Anything that didn't end the night on *Tsk, disappointing*. Her stupid building was getting closer. "Ask me something," she said. And she looked at me when she said it. And maybe it was the look, or the fact that she looked at all when she asked . . .

"Can I kiss you?" I asked. I hadn't even thought of it before the words came out of my mouth, probably the only way I'd get them out. But there we were, standing outside her home and enjoying each other's company, and Jason had said you had to throw yourself out there even if they said no nine times out of ten—

"Walter, no!" Naomi said.

I'd have to remember not to listen to Jason anymore.

"I'm sorry. I wasn't expecting that," Naomi said, touching her lips and looking away from me. "Uh, let me just get to my next question. I'm sorry. Um, I was going to ask you what you found attractive, but don't say me or anything cheesy."

This took a sudden turn for the worse. At least she didn't run for the door. Instead, we walked around the block. There

were benches and trees, people walking around. The concrete was the color of the moon under the pale lights. I had to salvage this. I was running on fumes here. "Sense of humor?" I said. "Intelligence, maybe?"

"Hm. BS alarm," Naomi said. She was still acting the same with me, aside from a lot more feet-watching. Maybe I hadn't fully blown it. I should have played it cool, kept it casual. Now I'd sounded the BS alarm and it was only minutes before the BS police took me away and put me in BS jail for eternity.

"I do have an answer," I said. We were walking a slow pace, neither of us setting it. All was not lost. "Here's something. I like: oddness. Like, your typical popular high school girl—yeah, they're cute, but I like someone who's a little quirky, who maybe I can click with in a way that not everyone else in the world does. Does that make sense?"

"I'll give you that one," Naomi said as we circled back to the front of the building. "Hey, listen, I should get inside. But about that kissing question—"

"No, don't," I said. "Forget it. I didn't mean to make things weird. I don't even know what I was—"

"No, I made it weird. It was a knee-jerk reaction," Naomi said, fiddling with her pocketbook strings. "I like to be up front and real, and I don't want to leave it like that. I didn't mean to sound rude or anything, and I hope I didn't hurt your feelings. But between you and those guys at the concert, I guess it's just my night or something."

"Those guys were lame," I said. "You can't group me in with them. Where are they? I'm gonna kick their—"

"I'm just embarrassed—that's all," Naomi said. "I've never really kissed a boy or anything like that, and I don't think you're supposed to really ask—"

I scooped her toward me, my heart beating like it took up my entire chest. I leaned in and kissed her on the lips, closed mouth, but held it for a second. I didn't know if that was the right move or what, but I wanted to hold her closer and longer.

"I have one question left," I said as I let her go.

"Okay . . ." Naomi said, laughing at the discomfort of it all. She looked back at the door, probably hoping no one in her family was around. I was looking at my feet but made a point to look up.

Her eyes were reflecting the streetlights behind me.

"Did you have fun?" I asked.

She nodded. "That's an easy one. Good night, Walter," Naomi said, walking backward as if she were drunk, still in a silly mood. "Thanks for taking me."

I stood in place and watched Naomi go inside. I watched the door close, jealous I wasn't on the other side of it. I felt light on my feet but glued to that one spot. The moon was close to full and the streetlights were bright, and it felt like the middle of the day, like the fireworks at Disney World. I spun away from Naomi's and started to walk home, almost as if I were drunk, too. I smiled and waved to a passing couple. I smiled at everyone I passed on the walk back home.

I got home to find Dad consoling Rosie on the couch, a box of tissues on the coffee table. She blew her nose into one of the tissues.

"What's going on?" I asked, closing the door behind me.

"Hey, Walter, leave us alone for a minute, would you?" Dad said.

Rosie shook her head. "No, maybe he can help. It was a teenager, I think," Rosie said. Her makeup was running from the crying.

"Good, that's good. It was a kid," Dad said. He had his hand on her back, sitting right beside her on the couch, hunched in. "Was he black?" he asked. "I've heard things, some black kids doing this."

"I think so," Rosie said, nodding. I took off my coat and sat down in the chair beside the couch. On the other side of Rosie, I could see her face was bruised—she'd been hit or something.

"You think so?" Dad asked. "You didn't see what color he was? Sorry, that was rude. Take your time."

"He was black," Rosie said. "He had a hat, too, red hat." She took another tissue from the box and blew her nose again.

"Walter, get something for Rosie's eye," Dad said. "Get an ice pack and a cloth." Then to Rosie, "So go over this one more time for me."

"I went to bed early, a little after nine," I heard Rosie say as I went into the kitchen. "Long day. So I'm just falling asleep and I hear someone in my home. I should have stayed put, but I didn't. I turn on the light, go into my living room, and there's this kid, just standing there. I ask him what he's doing here; I tell him to get out before he answers. He throws me into the wall."

Rosie stopped talking there. I heard her blow her nose again. I brought the ice pack out for Rosie.

"He tells you to get him something valuable and he'll leave," Dad says. Rosie nodded. "You freeze up; he hits you and runs." Rosie nodded again, her face was all wet from crying. Rosie lived next door—this creep was on our street. We could be next.

I'd just taken Naomi through the city. I'd just walked through the Basement in the dark. There were crazy people out there, right here, right near us. It felt like something that happened to other people. Getting mugged, being attacked—that was stuff you saw on TV or read about online. My dad was a cop—how much safer could it get? But here we were.

"Rosie, I'm gonna find this kid, all right?" Dad said. "I'm gonna personally find him, and when I do, I'm gonna give him a lot worse than a black eye."

Chapter Five

ate was in love with Naomi already. It was Wednesday, lunch break, and I was with Just Nate and Just Kate on the outside staircase behind the school. We were looking over the woods and city on the third floor while Nate and Kate smoked. It was another nice day, and the leaves were red and falling. I'd explained the dinner, the date, and even the hallway passings and the harp from before I'd even officially met her, and Kate hung on to every dorky word like it was the world's worst romance novel.

"So you kissed her?" Kate asked.

"I think so," I said.

"Well, dude, you either kissed her or you didn't," Nate said. "It's that thing, with the lips touching . . ."

"Okay, yeah, I kissed her," I relented, pacing around. "But, like, right after she basically told me no, no kissing. But then she was apologizing for saying no, and she was hinting I should maybe be more assertive, but assertive feels douchey to me, so I had no way to tell if I was being an aggressive douche or romantic. I don't know if the kiss was any good. I mean I'd never really made a move like that before, and I didn't know if I should open my mouth or not. It was probably a terrible kiss, honestly. I probably was just smooshing my closed mouth into her face. I should have gone on the Internet and looked up how to kiss or something first."

"No, don't go to the Internet for love advice," Kate said. "Bad move. I'm sure your kiss was perfect. She didn't squirm or hit you or anything?"

"No, she didn't hit me," I said.

"Awww," Kate said with a big grin. "She didn't hit you! Walter!"

Nate and Kate brought it all back down to earth. It didn't feel so monumental when I said this stuff out loud, and heard their reactions. It felt like this was a normal thing that people go through. A good thing.

Nate and Kate were in some ways the most ideal couple; they fit like Legos. Somehow they could still talk, they could still be inseparable, and they could still be Nate and Kate, even though the relationship hadn't worked out. You look at the statistical probabilities of failure and heartbreak, which are astronomical, but you realize sometimes it can still end like this: decent. They were a failed romance but a spectacular failure, as these things go. You looked at Nate and Kate and you were almost not afraid to try.

"Now the issue is, what do I do next?" I said, and I'd been pacing back and forth and leaning over the railing. I'd felt nervous for a couple of days and really needed to know how to stop feeling nervous.

"You ask her out!" Kate said. "You ask her to be Walter's hot little mama."

"I'm not ready," I said. I had the jitters right then, and the jitters were bad enough. The thought of asking her out made me want to toss up everything inside me. "I'll ruin everything if I try to force it."

"Walter, you give yourself the worst advice," Nate said from his spot in the shade. "You'll ruin everything by sitting around waiting while someone else asks her out. This girl has a taste for kisses now, and if she doesn't get more Walter loving, she's gonna look for it somewhere else. It's on to the next one, son."

I'd gone to Nate and Kate because they were normal and thought normal and had normal relationships, except for right now, I guess. But they still had a better track record than I did for this stuff. Nate was right: my own advice was terrible. And what did I know? My family was a mess. I wouldn't know a normal relationship if it asked me to a Foo Fighters concert.

I was in the stage of a budding romance that I've named "The Awkwardness of What's Next." There were too many lingering questions, too many unknown variables, too many unspoken words still. I needed to find Naomi so we could figure it all out.

• • •

I skipped the bus ride home and stayed late at school to see if I could find Naomi. If I was going to ask her out or admit to feeling a certain way, I'd rather do it in person than wait for a response online. I also had the comfort that she brought me when we were face-to-face. She had a way of making me feel like I could say or do anything. This would put it to the test, if I could actually find her.

I sat at a table in the hall with my books out, halfheartedly starting some homework. But mostly I was people-watching, hoping to spot Naomi. As I waited, I overheard a conversation.

"Those sneakers were expensive," this one kid was saying. "Since when do I have to worry about my stuff being stolen in gym class? I'm gonna pound someone."

"Did you hear about Jeremy?" the other kid said. "His house got hit by the burglar. His mom's jewelry, small stuff—they didn't even realize it was missing until Sunday morning."

I couldn't actually focus on work, so I wandered. I didn't really stay at school late often, but walking home wasn't a big issue when I did have to. There were football players making their way to the gym area. People doing homework in the hall. Seven hours was generally enough for me.

I made a turn toward the lockers and bumped into Jason.

"Hey, man," he said. "I'm running late today."

"Hey, I can't make it to Shadows," I said, not expecting the conversation. I had forgotten completely that it was Wednesday, and that meant comic books. I had more important things on my mind, and not things I could talk to Jason about.

"Don't have to run it by me," Jason said, and walked past me. He didn't ask what I was doing there late, and I didn't have a reason primed if he had asked. "Catch you later."

I hadn't talked to Jason since the concert, but the way he walked past me and kept it short made me wonder if he knew about the kiss. I couldn't imagine Naomi would tell him. I didn't even know if he knew I was at the concert.

I wandered aimlessly down the hall, through the science lab wing, and turned back. I'd pretty much given up when I saw her ready to leave, walking to the exit doors. I couldn't catch her in time.

"Hey!" I shouted out, embarrassing myself. She turned around. I couldn't think of a word to follow up with. She was wearing short pink shorts and a light jacket. She had a track uniform on. Her legs were a mile long. She wore glasses on her head, like she sometimes did. I'd seen her with the glasses on her head before but rarely actually wearing them, so her eyes had to have been a lot better than mine.

"Hi, Walter," she said as I made my way over. I felt like a stalled car in a heist getaway. I couldn't get the engine in my mind to turn.

"Um, I wanted to ask you something," I sputtered out.

"I'm late for cross-country," she said, still walking. "Can we walk and talk?" She jogged in place for a second.

"You do track *and* harp?" I asked. "I'm an underachiever, aren't I?"

She smiled, and we went out the doors to the open air. I was comfortable in my layers and jeans, but Naomi was going to have to work her way up to comfort in her shorts. There were a few people waiting for rides in the parking lot, but not a lot. Nobody I knew. I was walking with the cutest girl in the school, and no one was there to witness it and prove it was real. "You wanted to ask me something?"

"Yeah. Do you like movies?" I asked with all the charm of a sociopath. Naomi laughed. "Or TV, or anything?"

It wasn't the best opening question. I might have been better off blurting out *DO YOU WANNA BE MY GIRLFRIEND?* But it could work—it could lead to a movie date, at a theater or the home version. I could work with it still. Maybe.

"That's what you had to ask me?" she asked. "I do watch TV, like, really bad TV. Singing competitions, reality shows. I'm a *Biggest Loser* junkie. Let's bump it up to a jog," she said, and started a light run. I couldn't handle my half of the conversation. Her smile was too much. I had a rush like I was skydiving. I ran after her, lugging my stuffed backpack around so it knocked me on the back with every step. I was winded within a minute.

"I had another question," I said. "That was just the appetizer."

"You want to know my favorite sports team? Book?" Naomi asked. "It's the Red Sox, and the Chronicles of Narnia. But I don't watch baseball."

Those were good answers. She looked like a posed picture you'd find in a newly purchased picture frame, and our light hobbling had already left me sweating a bit more than what was acceptable for a seventeen-year-old.

We got off the pavement and onto crunchy grass and dead leaves, cut through a line of trees, and made our way to the field, where all her teammates were warming up. We'd exhausted reality TV as a conversation subject by then. I was out of time.

"Anyway," she said as she stopped and laughed. She grabbed her foot behind her and gave it a good stretch. She was just showing off now. "I have to take off. They're waiting for me."

"Cool, yeah," I said. I couldn't find the words I needed. My mind was a black hole, a vortex that thoughts were sucked into and crushed to particles. "Hang on. Uh . . ."

Naomi laughed. "Hey, there's this Halloween party my friend was trying to get me to go to. I wasn't planning on going, but if you wanted to go, I could be convinced still . . ."

"Yeah," I said, not being completely honest. I didn't really go to parties, and the idea of going to one with Naomi was like a double shot of nerves, like I got socked in the stomach. "Yeah, that sounds good, definitely. I'm in."

Her coach was staring at us and at her stopwatch at this point, and Naomi backed away toward her team. I caught my breath. "Halloween?" I asked. "So like . . . costumes?"

"Yeah, we'll need costumes," Naomi said. "I'll talk to you later. We'll figure it out!"

•   •   •

My dad was standing in the living room and putting on a tie in the mirror when I got home. "I'm working nights this week," he said without looking over as I closed the door. "So you'll be on your own for dinners if you can handle it."

"Yeah," I said, and put my bag on the chair in the corner.

"This shirt used to fit just right," he said, tugging at the sleeves with a critical eye. "I must have shrunk it in the laundry."

"Hey, Dad?" I asked. "I'm going to a Halloween party on Friday, and I need a costume. I was thinking of going as Bogart or something, or a generic detective. I need the parts for it, though."

"Party?" he asked. I didn't go to many parties. He sat down on the couch to put his work shoes on. "There gonna be girls there?"

"I would wager it's a strong possibility," I said.

"Who are you going with?" he asked, looking up at me while hunched over tying his shoes.

"No one," I lied. "I know some people who'll be there, though."

Dad stood back up. "And you came to your old man because

your friends wanted a chaperone, right? A man of the law on the scene, to keep everything on the up and up? No, huh? I've got just the thing. Come here." I followed Dad into his room, surprised it wasn't messier. He opened his closet door and pulled a box out and opened the top.

"Authentic classic fedora." He took out the hat and put it on my head. "Belonged to your grandfather, and he got it from his father. Just need a suit and a trench coat, and you're good to go."

"Wow, thanks," I said, and adjusted the hat. I walked out to the living room to see how it looked in the mirror. It fit me just right. I had one suit that would go pretty well with it; it was my only suit. Multipurpose for school functions, weddings, and funerals.

"So do we need to have a talk?" Dad asked as he stepped out of his room and put his jacket on. "You know, with the party, and the girls."

"No," I said, instantly and definitively, and shook my head. Dad nodded.

"Fair enough," he said. "Use a condom."

"Dad, what kind of party do you think this is?" I asked. Although truthfully, I had no idea myself what kind of party it was. Parties and I don't mix—that's an accepted fact. If there were unknowns and unspokens in my budding awkwardness with Naomi, a party, well . . . I don't have to go any further.

• • •

We made our way to the fifth floor in a building in High Hill, out in the city, not too far from where we went to the concert. The idea was for Naomi and me to go to the party as a detective and a femme fatale, but Naomi had interpreted "femme fatale" as "gangsta bitch." She had baggy jeans, a loose belt, and a backward cap on. It looked like I was taking her into custody.

"We had less than a week, and I don't exactly have any nineteen forties evening wear lying around," she said. I had a cute gangsta bitch on my arm, and I couldn't pull my gaze away.

The party was essentially a room where people could talk and hang out for longer than the seconds between bell rings we got at school. Aside from a group of kids freestyle-rapping near the TV, everyone was pretty much grouped off and talking to each other. The apartment was really cool, with big windows and a nice view of the city. The lighting was dim, and the living room was fairly crowded and noisy. The music fought the TV, which fought the YouTube videos on the computer, which fought the conversation and laughter. Plastic cups all over. There was a table with food.

"Well, hellooooo," one of Naomi's friends said, two syllables that explained more than I'd ever need to know about the one named Maelynne. She gave me a once-over and Naomi an accusatory glare for springing this surprise. Apparently, I was a surprise.

"So many slutty costumes," Maelynne said, looking around. "Did you see Bethany yet?"

Naomi shook her head.

Maelynne was a tall Asian girl with sharp eyebrows and a smile that only enhanced her mischievous look. She had long hair down her back. Maelynne and Naomi's friend Kaylee were on costume-review duty. "I don't even know what the hell she is," Maelynne said. "She's wrapped in plastic or something. You can practically see everything! It's like . . . see-through Saran Wrap. That's her costume. What *is* that?"

"Maybe she's someone's leftovers," Kaylee said. Kaylee's mouth was painted stitched-shut and she spoke as if in character, which is to say rarely. She had neck-length bobbed hair, sleepy eyes, round cheeks, and a button nose. She looked sullen but polite in a possibly not-a-costume Goth outfit. Maelynne made up for Kaylee's silence and then some. She spoke enough for all four of us, and her cat costume was appropriately catty.

"I think we can all agree that it's pretty clear she's a fashion mummy," I said.

"Fashion mummy!" Maelynne said with a big smile. "What is that? Mystery guest is funny!"

"Seriously, Mae, how can you even be judging fashion mummy

right now when you're in a slutty cat costume?" Naomi snapped back, accurately.

"It's just a regular cat costume," Maelynne said with a shocked face. She stroked her tail. "I can't help it if cats are naturally slutty!"

"So is no one going to mention my slutty Goth costume?" Kaylee deadpanned. She presented her costume. "It's not skimpy," Kaylee said, and then smiled. "But you don't know what my Goth is doing behind closed doors."

"Tell us, please," Maelynne said, clasping her hands together. "What *is* your Goth doing behind closed doors?" The girls all laughed, bumping into each other. I might have missed the joke.

"Oh," Maelynne continued, and put her arms around Naomi's shoulders. She turned her toward the kitchen and pointed at a tall, dark man with a large Afro who was standing by the sink, sweatpants on and not a ton else—he had the body to pull it off. "Who is *that*? I'm honestly in love with him, and I need his name and phone number."

"Never seen him before," Naomi said. "And I hope you didn't ask me just because he's black."

"Um, you know what his costume is, right?" Kaylee asked them. Maelynne shrugged. "He's white. His body is, like, painted brown. I know that kid."

"Get the f—" Maelynne started before all three broke out in laughter. "Well, I don't care if that guy is racist. I'm taking him home," Maelynne said.

"We're nothing if not socially responsible here in East Bridge," I said to some laughs. Life of the party, that's me. I was good for an occasional one-liner.

"And what are you dressed as?" Maelynne asked. "Dick Tracy?"

"I'm a slutty detective," I said.

Maelynne laughed, maybe a little too hard, and she took my fedora and put it on her head. "Really?" she asked, as if I were flirting. "Are you in the market for a cat?"

"Not in the cat market," I said. Kaylee touched my forehead hair curl.

"So are you two . . . ?" Maelynne inquired, pointing at Naomi and me intermittently. It was cool to see who Naomi hung out with, what her friends were like, and it was especially cool that she was introducing me to that part of her life, but these girls were going to require a high adjustment period from me. If Naomi spoke with reckless abandon, these girls made an art of it.

"Walter's my husband, if you must know," Naomi said. "We eloped, whirlwind romance . . . you know, the works."

I shook my head. "No, you

didn't pay enough for husband," I said. "You paid boyfriend prices. This is in strict violation of our agreement."

Naomi played along. "Well, that's unprofessional, not to mention crazy embarrassing," she said. We had a future in improv. "Obviously I was going to pay you the difference after the party, but now you aren't getting any of my money."

"That's fine," I said. "You can expect a visit from my cohorts Johnny and Jimmy, though, and good luck not paying them."

"I'll let Johnny and Jimmy be my boyfriends," Naomi said.

"Okay, so you two are definitely an item," Maelynne said, and took off my hat. "So I'll just put this back on you, then."

The night continued on like that, the four of us stuck together with Mae ready to ditch us for cute guys at a moment's notice. We made our way to a snack table, and we sat on the floor in the living room for a while. I was on the periphery of the group at first. Mae talked about her crushes; they talked about classes. I mostly chimed in with jokes or answered direct questions. Naomi and I continued to dodge any labeling of our togetherness. Eventually the bodies shifted around, and I was part of the circle. It was all going smoothly. Then Naomi left us.

"I'm not sure I can afford much more escort time," Naomi said around ten or so, "so I'm going to mysteriously excuse myself and use the restroom." Naomi got up and left me with the cat and the Goth. With Naomi gone, there was nothing to talk about but me. Or at me.

"You really like her, huh, Walter the escort?" Maelynne asked. She had a gaze that felt like she was picking apart every detail of her surroundings. I didn't think much got past her. It felt like she was looking at me and simultaneously browsing through a cache of my deepest thoughts.

"Yeah," I said. "She's really cool. Of course I do."

"She's the best, isn't she? She's perfect. She's the bomb," Maelynne said, sprawling out a bit on the floor. She had a very casual way about her. "I've seen you around school. I'm going to bother you every time I pass you. Hope you don't mind."

"Yeah, are you kidding?" I asked. "I'm always looking for more people to bother me. Please do." I twirled my shoelaces around my finger—back to the fun guy I was without Naomi present.

"She's never had a boyfriend, you know," Maelynne said. "This is new—I'm so intrigued." She looked at Kaylee, who was leaning back, watching the party, possibly not entirely present in this conversation. How I would usually be. "Kaylee, can you see them together? I can see it. You're a good couple."

"We're not a couple," I said. "Not really, not until she pays me, anyway."

"You will be—I can tell," Maelynne said. "And then there's no time for Mae and Kay. We're gonna get along great, okay, Walter?" She nodded. "We're pro-you, okay?"

I smiled and gave a thumbs-up.

A few more minutes passed. Kay was feeding Mae potato chips for some reason, and I had little to do but watch the clock and wait for Naomi. That was when I saw Lester Dooley, and he had Naomi cornered near the kitchen. I'd seen Lester with Jason before, so it stood to reason Naomi could know him, but he looked aggressive to me, leaning in a little too close.

Naomi was laughing at whatever he was saying. I figured the cool thing to do would be to hang back here, but if he was flirting with her, or if she was uncomfortable, I should probably step in. I was cool with Lester now; I could approach him. But I didn't want to come across as jealous or possessive. But then I was a detective for the night. The indecisive detective.

"Is it awkward if I go sit on Brownface's lap?" Maelynne asked. "I am a cat. It's what I do, right?" This seemed like as good an excuse as any to check on Naomi. Naomi and Lester both smiled when I approached.

"Wally Wilcox, the cop's son," Lester said as I reached them. He nudged Naomi and pointed. "This kid's cool." He must not have seen us come in together.

Naomi smiled. "Hey, Walter."

"Hey," I said. "Hey, Lester. How's it going?"

"I'm all right. You get home okay the other week?" Lester asked. And to Naomi, "He got locked up in a cop car walking home from school."

"Sorry about that," I said, remembering Dad's full-on interrogation of Lester. "That was embarrassing."

"That's cool," Lester said. "I'm sure you told your dad I wasn't trouble when you got home, right?" He flashed his bright smile; I flashed my trademark half-committal semigrin. "You know his dad's a cop?" Lester asked Naomi. "Officer Wilcox, Wally Wilcox's dad. I don't even think he recognized me. He pulled over when he saw his son with a black guy."

"That's not what happened," I said. It made sense that he might have stopped regardless of who I was with. And he clearly knew Lester, who didn't exactly blend in, with his massive size.

"I'm just playing, Wally, you'll get used to it," Lester said, reaching out toward my face. "Let me see those glasses for a second. These big, thick frames, I gotta see how I look in these."

Lester pulled the glasses off and put them on himself. Naomi stood uncomfortably, and we shared a glance. Lester looked around the room. "*Whoa.* These are not fashion glasses. Dude has some real eye problems. How do I look?" Lester leaned like a model against the wall. "How's this look? Do I look good? Handsome? You'd go to homecoming with me in a pair of these, right?"

"Funny, Lester," Naomi said with just a hint of more patience than I had. "Give him his glasses back."

"Hey, Jake," Lester said calling out behind him. Apparently Jake was Brownface—perfect. "How do I look, man? Do I look smart in these? If you were police, would you let me walk by?"

"You pull off the hipster look about as well as I pull off brown," Jake said, and Lester cracked up.

"Hipster—I love it. You got balls, Jake," Lester said, cracking up. And to me, "Wally, is that what you are, a hipster? That's great; that's perfect."

"I don't think so," I said. "Just a little blind."

Lester took out his cell to take some selfies with my glasses. "I need to listen to some indie music, play a guitar. This could be my new thing," he said, posing for his pictures. "Naomi, you like hipsters?"

He was having fun at my expense, showing off for his friends. Trying to impress Naomi and definitely too concerned with what she thought of him. I did not like parties.

"Lester, seriously," Naomi said. "Give him his glasses back. That's not funny."

"I'm sorry, man," Lester said, handing the glasses back. "I had to try them on. Here you go, good as new." I put them back on.

"Yeah, you look sharp, man," Lester said, giving the okay sign with his hands. "Both of you, good-looking couple. Have fun."

"See you around, Lester," Naomi said, rolling her eyes. Lester joined Jake, and Naomi turned back toward the living room and I followed her. A couple came into the living room from the fire escape.

"Do you want fresh air?" I asked. It looked like a good idea. "I feel like I could use some fresh air."

"Oh god, yes," Naomi said, nodding.

"So you know Lester," I said, eyebrows raised. The jury was out on how friendly he was, but friend or foe, he was intense to be around. I was sweating.

"A little. He's like a family friend," Naomi said. "He was arrested the summer before high school for throwing some upperclassman through a door at a house party. He's got some anger issues, poor family, this and that. He did this mentoring program and my dad kinda took him under his wing. So he was around a lot this one summer. He's not a bad kid, just dealt a real bad lot in life."

"I kinda feel sorry for him," I said. I swayed my body a little, unsure how to stand or what to do with my hands. "Just a little, though."

"I know, right?" Naomi said. "He's like a tiny, soft turtle in a big, giant shell. With spikes."

Naomi shrugged, and it looked like a cold shrug to me. I took off my jacket and put it around her. I took off her hat and spun it around so it faced forward. Naomi smiled.

As we leaned on the railing, I moved my body a little closer to hers. I wished we could stay outside on the fire escape. I wished that was the party and the rest wasn't there. And everyone else would be gone by the time we went back in.

"Sorry about that, anyway," Naomi said, glancing at me. "I kinda hate parties."

"I'm not a huge fan, either," I said. I played with my hair curl. "But I'm so popular, it's just a thing I have to do."

"I have this social-anxiety thing," Naomi said. "My parents keep me locked up, which I'm always grumbling about, but I kinda like it. I never know how to act. Hooray, party." She pumped her fists up a bit. "I thought it might be fun if you were here, and it wouldn't be, like, a 'party' and it'd just be—I don't know—more fun or something. I'm not even sure what I'm talking about."

I could have turned her face to me and kissed her, right there with the lights of the city and the hat and my coat, and it would have been perfect. Instead, I chose option number two: doing nothing. The Walter Wilcox regular.

"It was fun," I said, and we both laughed knowing it really wasn't. Neither of us was enjoying the party. But that's the Awkwardness of What's Next: it's always awkward—it has to be. That's the stage. "But it was. It is."

"Yeah, it is," Naomi agreed, still looking forward at the city but turning her eyes to see me. She copied my patented semigrin.

"This is a really nice view," I said, looking around. A view I was aware I wouldn't have, standing right beside Naomi Mills, if I'd stayed home and had a traditional Walter Saturday night. "I want to pack it all up and stick it outside my window."

"This is nothing," Naomi said, shaking her head and squinting her eyes. "You ought to see where my sister used to take me some nights. You can see the whole city. I'll show you. Remind me. This is just a warm-up."

So that's what's next, I thought.

Naomi kissed me, a peck really, on the mouth. I hadn't expected it, and then it was over, my brain scrambling to grab the details.

"That was terrible," she said, laughing at herself and backing away. She took off the hat and pushed her hair back with her

111

hand. "I just kissed you like I kiss my aunt. That was like a three-year-old's kiss. I'm gonna jump off this fire escape, okay? I'm so embarrassed. Don't try to save me."

"It wasn't bad," I said. "Any kiss is a good one with you. But . . . I mean, if you weren't happy with it . . ."

I stepped closer and we kissed again, longer. This was better than the kiss after the concert. It wasn't a passing flash of a spark. I was able to savor it. I hadn't ever kissed another girl besides Naomi, but I found it hard to believe any girl kissed softer or sweeter.

She pulled away, put her hat back on. "Should we go back in?"

I nodded. "We need to get Maelynne off Brownface's lap."

"They're so wrong," Naomi said, and shook her head. "Everyone is so wrong."

* * *

I didn't get home till almost midnight. I fell asleep right away and woke up after what felt like half an hour, though the sun was up, to an odd smell: breakfast being cooked. And there were sounds—clanking in the kitchen. This hadn't happened in years. Dad hadn't cooked breakfast since the whole family was still living together. Eggs were his specialty, fancy eggs with lots of stuff in them—cheeses and meats. Back then, he'd do it all the time.

"Where were you last night?" Dad asked as I shuffled into the kitchen.

"What's with the breakfast?" I asked him back, although I wasn't about to turn down any Belgian waffles.

There were smells of happiness and sunshine streaming in through the windows. I couldn't remember waking up feeling this good, this open to possibility. I had, like, 74 percent of a girlfriend. I still had to ask her out, but that was just a technicality.

I mean, someone was out there in the world waking up this morning, feeling the same sun, maybe smiling, maybe thinking about me the way I was thinking about her. That was amazing.

"You still in your clothes from yesterday?" Dad said quizzically.

"What are you so happy for?"

"Is that lipstick on your collar?"

"Nice try, Dad," I said.

"You win, I'll go first," Dad said. "I had an interesting evening." He bobbed his head a bit. This was proud Dad. "I'm on duty, around eight p.m., driving south down Broad Street, and see a car with a taillight out. No big deal, that's routine. Car's driving slow, though, so that's a little suspicious. I pull him over."

Dad told me the story, how he pulls the kid over; the kid's nervous. He checks around the car and sees all the stuff that Rosie had tipped him on. The kid says it's his dad's. He brings up Rosie, what happened to her, mentions the details he knows, the stuff he's looking for, and the kid cracks and admits to everything.

"He's just a scared little punk," Dad said, wrapping up the story. "I take him down to the station. I'm out by nine thirty—easiest case I ever solved."

"Congrats," I said. That was breakfast-worthy, I agreed.

"Yeah, this could be good, really good for me at work. I'm hoping," Dad said. "And you? Good party?" He set down our food on the table, and we sat. I nodded. He gave me a suspicious eye, but Dad was feeling hopeful, and I was going to enjoy my waffles, because I felt hopeful, too.

Chapter Six

We still hadn't named this, whatever our relationship was. It was all new still. We'd kissed twice, so there was a closeness, but it was all unofficial. We were just a boy and a girl who kissed and liked each other. The next logical step in this budding romance was to meet up between every possible class, when we weren't on complete opposite sides of the school. A few times a day we could spend most of the two minutes allotted between periods to walk to one of our classes together.

"Uncle Dave says hi," I said to Naomi when I found her in the main hall after lunch.

"Tell Uncle Dave I want to make out with him," Naomi said. "Just kidding. That's horrible. I say stupid things."

For three days now, we could find each other between some classes, but I wasn't sure how long I could keep it up, as I'd get to those classes late. This was a fairly new occurrence for me, and I don't think my teachers had picked up on it yet, or else they didn't view me as a potential troublemaker, so for now I was good.

How we used this time differed. We'd count down the time, usually. "One minute and forty-five seconds. Minute and a half." This was in between whatever small banter or school discussion we came up with. "Thirty seconds left," Naomi said on Monday, and came up with an odd send-off. "Quick, say something profound. I'll ponder it in class."

"Thirty seconds till class," Naomi said on Tuesday. "Quick, compliment me on my outfit."

"That's an amazing color combination," I said. "You must really know your color combos."

"Thirty seconds left," she said on Wednesday. "Let's touch pinkie fingers."

We pressed our pinkie fingers together, definitely our most out-there public admission of feelings of some kind. Thirty seconds felt longer than usual.

"Can I get your phone number?" I asked. It was forward momentum from sharing funny memes on Facebook, and the brief visits between classes were feeling shorter and shorter.

"Huh?" Naomi said. "Oh, yeah. Of course." We broke the pinkie hold, and Naomi spun her backpack around and fished out a pen. She wrote it on my palm. "Are you going to call me?" she asked.

"Yeah," I said. "That's what I was thinking." If my sweaty palms didn't wash away her number first. "Is that okay?"

"Yeah, just maybe after seven, or eight, when I'm in my room," Naomi said. "Of course it is."

I walked backward, keeping eye contact like a smooth movie star until I bumped into a girl who told me to watch where I was going.

Naomi wasn't the only one to find me between classes. I was on my way to my last class when I passed Lester at his locker. "Wally!" he called out. I was going to be late, but Lester had a bark that made you stop in your tracks. He'd make an excellent football coach or drill sergeant.

"Hey, Lester," I said, turning around.

"I have something for you," Lester said, and reached into the top of his locker. He pulled out a CD in a square envelope. "You could probably get all this stuff pretty easily anyway, but I burned some music for you. The new Pusha T I was telling you about, some ASAP Rocky, Ferg. Give it a listen."

He handed me the CD. I never thought Lester Dooley would be talking to me in a populated hallway, let alone burning me music. This had really been some year already. "Thanks," I said. "That's awesome, I'll check it out."

"So, listen, none of my business, but what's going on with you and Naomi?" Lester asked. Deflated the gesture a little. "Are you guys, like, a couple or what?"

"Uh . . ." I said. If I told him no, it sounded like she was fair game, which I guess she was. If I said yes, I'd be lying. And I didn't know Lester well enough to tell him what I actually felt for Naomi. "Not really, I mean, not right now, no."

"But you like her, though," Lester said and didn't ask. He smiled like he was saying "good for you," but he wouldn't be bringing it up unless he'd hoped the answer was no. "That's awesome, man. Good luck. Keep me posted."

"Yeah, sure," I said.

Lester closed his locker and grabbed his book bag. "Hey, let me know if you need any advice," he said, and went on his way.

•   •   •

My first phone date with Naomi was on a Thursday evening, and we watched *The Biggest Loser* together. I called her shortly before eight, with not much in the way of conversation prepared. Little did I know that Naomi could have filled a few hours just talking about the show.

"I need to get on there someday," Naomi said. "I'm thinking maybe when I go to college, I'll put on a lot of weight so I'd have a decent amount to work off. I'd be so good at it, but I couldn't be too good, because I want the trainer to get in my face and yell at me and climb on my back and stuff."

I couldn't see exactly why she wanted to be on the show so badly. There was a lot of crying, screaming, and falling over on my TV. "Losing weight is terrifying," I said. This guy was ready to pass out on a treadmill, and this lady was ready to deck him in the face. "Why won't she leave this dude alone? He's going to die."

"He just needs tough love," Naomi said. "He probably doesn't have anyone back home to yell at him like this. Watch, in three months, he's going to look like a model. You know, if you gained the weight, I could be like Jillian. That might actually be easier for me."

"I may never eat again," I said. In the next scene, this girl was ready to quit—finally, some common sense—and Jillian flipped her lid. Then the guy trainer overheard and pulled the girl outside, and he was flipping his lid, too. Then my phone buzzed. I pulled it from my ear and saw a text from my sister Mel that just said *Check your email.*

I sat up in my bed, pulled my laptop in front of me, and signed in to check my e-mail. I had a message from Mel with the subject *dinner.*

Mel lived in her dorm at college a state over about an hour or two up north, and every few weeks she'd come down to stay with Mom and my mom's boyfriend, Seth, and she'd take me out to eat or we'd go to a movie or something. That's the kind of invite I was expecting when I opened her e-mail. But it wasn't quite that.

Hey four eyes, you free Friday? I'm going to mom's, I've been

120

thinking about it and I want you to come with me. I know it's weird for you but I'll be there. I think it would be good for both of us. I'll take you out for ice cream after. Let me know? ~Mel

Seeing Mom became more difficult, it seemed, with each month that passed. At first, the idea was to spend time at Mom's and live with Dad and we'd all still be together, but it didn't work out that way, and the further we got from that time, the less I wanted to go. I'd seen her maybe twice since Dad and I moved, and not once since she moved in with her boyfriend. That made it worse. Sooner or later, I had to get it over with. I didn't want to sever ties indefinitely, but she wasn't on my immediate to-do list, either.

I did want to see Mellie, though. And it would be nice to get out of the city for a night, and especially nice to eat something good. Dad and I cooked sometimes, but it was nothing I'd brag about.

"*Auuugh!*" Naomi yelped.

"What happened?" I asked. "Did Bob smack that lady yet?"

"Huh?" Naomi asked. "No, they talked it out and hugged. But Tracy fell in the water, so Red Team only has, like, two people now! Are you watching still?"

"I still have it on," I said. "I got an e-mail from my sister. She wants me to go to dinner at my mom's house. I don't think I'm going to go, though. It's a little weird, still."

"You should go," Naomi said. "Family's important. Think about Disney World and the fireworks."

"That was a long time ago," I said. I thought of Naomi and the party, and how she went even though she didn't like parties. She said it would be more fun if I was there. I wondered if she'd consider returning the favor.

"I have a bad idea. This is, like, the worst invite you'll ever get," I said. "There's basically no way you'll want to do this. But here goes. Do you want to come with me to the world's worst family reunion? I'm basically at war with half of my family, so it promises to be an unpleasant time."

"Yeah? I'm always up for some unpleasant family time," Naomi replied. "That's my area of expertise."

She barely took the time to think the question over. She legit wanted to spend time with me. The time was going to suck—there was no way around that. But seeing Naomi outside of school again was going to make it at least somewhat worthwhile. In the meantime, a huge fight was about to break out between the last two Red Team members. I had no doubt big hugs and tears were just around the corner.

• • •

Mellie picked Naomi and me up Friday night in the city in the same Honda Civic she'd been driving since she got her license, and it had been getting old then. She always looked shorter to me each time I saw her. Her arms were covered in ink, nearing sleeves at this point. She had them mostly covered tonight, though, wearing a thin sweater with the sleeves rolled up a bit. Her pitch-black hair was cut short and pulled around her face. Mel's iPod was hooked in and playing loud enough that we couldn't actually talk. She was really into classic rock, Led Zeppelin, AC/DC. So we started singing along with noises replacing the majority of words we didn't know. That was the fun part of the night and helped mask the nerves I was feeling. That was the easy twenty minutes. Naomi sat in the back with me, closer to the middle than her own seat. She still managed an impressive posture.

I knew having Naomi with me would make everything a lot easier in terms of seeing my family, but this was going to be a disaster and I regretted it already. We hadn't even officially called ourselves a couple or really told anyone we'd even been seeing each other, and here she was, meeting my estranged mother and sister. She was going to learn too much about me too fast, and I couldn't see anything happening that would bring out my charming or romantic side. This was definitely a mistake.

The longer we stayed in the car, the fewer other cars we saw. Off the highway we could even see the stars multiply. Pulling up to Seth's house, or "Mr. Spencer" as I'd known him growing up, did not feel inviting or like coming home. It felt like I was descending into the enemy's lair. Like knowing that on the other side of the front door, giant spiders would lower and cover me in webbing. It was a hard thing to look forward to or even pretend to be interested in.

This was the large house up the street from where we used to live; the house we used to live in was now inhabited by people I

didn't know. They'd put up a fence and made the lawn look better.

It was a big place with three floors and a long driveway, and it was nice and clean, but it was big and nice in a different way from Naomi's house. The Millses' home was lived-in, filled with comfort and warmth. This place was just filled with stuff. I'd never even seen a TV the size of the one in the living room. Everything felt painted-on, and staged. Dinner felt staged.

"You've gotten so big, Walter," my mom said with doting eyes. I guess teenagers grow.

Mom seemed different, but I didn't really have time to analyze it. Her hair was shorter. She was smiling too much for what we'd all been through. She still had big, doe-like eyes, brown hair that receded a bit. She was still tall and kind of lanky. I didn't know how we were supposed to be acting. I wasn't just a dinner guest;

I was her son. It felt like she was applying for a mortgage loan or inviting her boss to dinner before asking for a raise. I don't mean this in a bad way, but Mom was more sour than this. She used to make fun of the neighbors, she was a little mean, but that was okay. We'd laugh about it, when I was too young to really get it.

Seth gave a distinctly fatherly squinting smile, which was off-putting. I guessed he looked like your traditional TV show father. Dressed expensively, brown hair that sat up on its own. Wristwatch. I wanted to tell him not to look at me or address me in any way. The whole scene was making my stomach turn.

Mom's cooking took me back to a bad time. Meat loaf, mashed potatoes, veggies. There was a basket of rolls. The smells fit our old house, not this place. I was in no position to enjoy food anyway.

"Dinner's very good," Naomi said, and smiled. She was trying—I had to hand it to her. I was having trouble even doing that. Naomi was the perfect houseguest—her smile was sweet and her voice was soft. She could pull back on the biting jabs and "stupid things" without an issue. Which was great, so long as she was just saving it all for me and her family.

"Thank you, Naomi," Mom said. "Walter, tell us a little more about your friend."

She's gorgeous. She's sweet and smart. She likes me. She wants to be around me. She came to a creepy broken-family dinner just to spend more time with me. But Mom wouldn't get it. What could I say anyway? I hadn't even told Dad about her yet.

"This is Naomi," I said, and kept it simple. "She plays the harp."

"I run cross-country, too," Naomi said, filling in the gaps for me.

"Her dream is to be a contestant on *The Biggest Loser*," I added.

"Well, we're glad to have you here, Naomi," my mom said. Everything felt so phony, as if a tap with a mallet would shatter it all. I decided to test it.

"Has anyone read the paper lately?" I asked. Things had really turned around for Dad ever since he'd caught his neighborhood thief. It ended up being some kid we went to school with, Calvin, someone I hadn't heard of. It really was a big deal, at least in our part of the city. The newspaper covered the case, and sent a reporter and photographer over to interview Dad and take pictures. Rosie made him a cake, which I ate most of, and he had a spring in his step that was nice to see.

Mom nodded as she chewed her food. "I did. I see your father's made some news. That's great for him."

He was doing better without her. We were both doing awesome now. It just took us a little while.

"It's a pretty big deal," I said. "This kid was a menace in the neighborhood. Nobody else could catch him. There was a whole chase. Dad had to really push on him, get him to crack. It was this whole high-pressure thing." I embellished a detail or two to keep it impressive in story form. That was how the best legends are built.

"So when's graduation?" Seth asked, smiling. Changing the subject. "Looking at colleges yet?"

"No," I said. *I've been busy surviving, trying not to get my butt kicked in school. Trying to keep my dad out of the hospital. Honestly, I couldn't care less about college, grades, nice clothes, or home-cooked meals, you walking sitcom-reject cretin.* "I could always stay back a year if I run out of time."

"Ooh, we could be seniors together," Naomi said. She got it. That was what was important to me. Her.

126

"Walter," Mom said after putting down her fork, "did you make a costume for Halloween this year?"

"Not really," I said, although my and Naomi's costumes were fairly homemade, even if the actual elements were all store-bought. "Naomi and I went to a Halloween party. I was a detective and she was a gangsta bitch."

"Kind of a femme fatale," Naomi said. "Sort of."

Without an acknowledgment, Mom went right to the ninja turtle story. How when I was a kid, I hated the store-bought ninja turtle costume so much I insisted on making my own version. Not a year goes by that the pictures don't get dragged out: me with my painted green face, my green pillow shell, my shirtsleeve headband. I was already regretting Naomi's presence at the table. Every year after that, my mom and I would make my costume, and it became a family tradition.

"Oh, how about that Fourth of July?" Mom rambled on, pointing at me with her fork. Not buying into my and Naomi's awesome repartee. Of course I remembered; she only told the story to everyone. "You came running inside crying because you picked up your sparkler on the wrong end. We rinsed your hand off and you'd already forgotten anything had happened—you wanted another sparkler. Oh, and then there was Aunt June." Aunt June, my dad's sister-in-law, would get fall-down drunk at those family gatherings.

"Let's not forget the hike that never ended," Mellie said, bringing up another Walter Wilcox classic—the time we got lost in the woods and didn't find our way out until night. I'd gotten tired of walking and was slowing Mellie down. I was supposed to stay by a tree until she found help and would come back for me. But then I got scared and got even more lost. There had to be one story where

I was somewhat heroic and saved the day, but it seemed that, no, there wasn't.

The stories continued, and the laughing continued, and Mom looked at me like her silly little boy and Mellie gave me loving-big-sister looks, and Naomi laughed with them. And they told the stories to Naomi because she was the one hearing them for the first time, and she was learning a lot about me, and it was all wrong. The laughing and the happiness were all a hundred percent incorrect, because Mom had left us and the family was broken, and that ruined the memories, that tainted them all.

My legs were jittering. The memories I had involved furniture flying across the room. They involved ugly words and name-calling; they involved the man up the street. My memories included waking up at two in the morning to screaming fights. Needing earplugs to sleep through the night so I could go to school in the morning, earplugs I couldn't sleep without today.

"Walter was so clingy," Mellie said, holding a glass of wine. "I couldn't even go to the movies with my boyfriend without Walter tagging along. Remember I used to call you my shadow?"

I offered a weak smile. I wasn't her shadow anymore. We saw things differently. She thought Dad had had it coming, that Mr. Spencer was a better match for Mom. She thought Dad was cold and aloof, and Mom had been suffering. What I had seen was Mom depressed, all the time, and when Dad wasn't working, he was trying to cheer her up, and it never worked. And then our neighbor started spending way too much time here, making everyone uncomfortable. Mel hadn't been there when Dad and I moved out, at five in the morning so the neighbors wouldn't watch or talk to us. She didn't have this image burned in, of Mom watching us drive away in a U-Haul truck from the window, drinking coffee. I'd been sure Seth had already been on his way over.

Seth was telling everyone about his big splurge, a sailboat. This wasn't just any boat—this was going to be the envy of the sea. "You've gotta come see this thing, Walter. It's a work of art. What do you think, sport? Maybe in the summer? We can bring Naomi, Mel, your mom."

"You and your toys," Mom said with a laugh. "What are the neighbors going to think?"

"What *do* the neighbors think?" I asked. Naomi's eyes were wide and everyone was quiet, but it was such a good question that I hadn't thought of. After all, I moved away, Dad moved away, but Mom did not. What did the neighbors think? "What do they think of Seth and his ex-wife? What do they think about Dad? Do people actually like this? Do the neighbors all think you're a cute couple? Are they happy for you? They shouldn't be. It's not cute, or sweet or romantic. You basically have the worst how-we-met story in history."

"Oh," Mom said, and her body sunk.

"This isn't appropriate, Walter," Seth said, pushing his plate away. "And it's really disrespectful to your mom and your company."

"And who says 'sport'?" I asked, choosing to ignore his comments about Naomi. "What is that? Is that, like, a British thing? 'Cause you're not even British. You don't break up a kid's family and call him sport, you just don't do that."

Mom got up and left the table, and for a second, my heart broke and I didn't want to feel that way when I was right. So I shoved my chair out from under me and stood up myself. "It's better to not be here, and not think about this," I said. "I was doing fine before. I was doing really good."

There was nowhere else to go but outside, so I went there. I left Naomi at the table. I don't even remember walking to the door or closing it. I just remembered Naomi's shock and my mom withering away, and then I remembered the blankness of standing outside. I was looking at the dark outline of the woods and the light from inside that reached the trees by the street. And the moon. I didn't have my license or the keys, so I couldn't just hop in Mel's car and head off. I couldn't leave Naomi behind, either.

"Are you okay?" Naomi asked from the back doorstep. That was a relief, as she was the only one I wanted to see. She was trying to play it cool. "It's okay. You warned me," Naomi said. "Really I'd have been let down if everything went nice. I was expecting fireworks."

"I told you this wasn't Disney World," I said. I wondered if that could be a Bogart-cool line. "It's a crappy situation. Not good at all."

Naomi walked to where I was and ran her hand up and down my back. I took a deep breath, exhaled, and watched my breath swirl into the air.

I heard Mel tell my mom and Seth that she'd take us out for dessert, and before I knew it, she was grabbing me by the arm and pulling me to her car. I opened the back door. "Front," Mel barked. She was not happy, but I wasn't, either, so that didn't bother me. I slammed the back door shut, got in the passenger side, and slammed that door. Naomi followed behind, wide-eyed, and got in the backseat. Mel got in the driver's seat and slammed her door, too.

"That is not fair to Mom, what you just said." Mellie turned on the car and turned off the music and sped onto the road. She was driving a little faster than I was comfortable with. She was never a great driver. "I know you want to sit there and be quiet, but I'm talking. I know you're mad at Mom for what happened, but it takes two. You're letting Dad off way too easy. He has some blame in this, too. He could have done more. Mom was depressed—you know she was, and he did not want to deal with it."

I regretted Naomi seeing all this. I had no way of knowing what she was thinking. I looked in the mirror and saw her eyes darting around. I let my head tilt, looked out the window, and watched the streetlights hover past.

"If you don't want to put any blame on Dad because he's not the one who cheated, I get that," Mel said. "Just know that adult relationships don't always work out. Everyone has their own path to take, and they don't always line up with their partner's. Things don't always go the way people want or expect. That's something you just figure out when you're older."

What had she figured out? She hadn't even been around for the worst of the fighting. She saw some of it, sure, but then she got out of the house. It was easy to have a levelheaded response from that distance. She hadn't even been around when Mom essentially had a boyfriend over at the house all the time.

"What makes Seth so special?" I asked. "I can't stand how Mom acts around him. I don't think she ever acted like that before."

"It's called taking her meds, Walter," Mel said. "What planet do you live on? Mom was sick; Seth helped her get better. And you're going to ruin all the progress she's made with outbursts like that."

I hadn't thought she was sick. Things hadn't been great, but she'd just seemed bored, or cranky. I could always make her laugh, and things were usually okay before long.

"Seth isn't a doctor," I said. "I don't see why she needed him in any way."

"Dad completely ignored it," Mel said. "Seth noticed; he talked to her. Jesus, he didn't have to write out a prescription to help. She's bipolar." Mel let out a frustrated groan. "I know it wasn't easy for you. Believe me, I have a lot of guilt for leaving you there. I thought maybe we could start some kind of repairing process. I guess not. Naomi, I'm sorry you're hearing all this."

"It's okay," Naomi said. "I have plenty of family drama myself. I've seen it all."

Her family had seemed so warm and together when I saw them. She did mention that sister, though, the one she went to the concert with. I had a lot to learn about Naomi still.

Mel started talking to Naomi because I was quiet. "Our dad would be out working, or upstairs sleeping, and Walter would tell Mom all these corny jokes. I don't even know where you got those bad jokes. Or he'd tell her everything that happened on the TV shows we'd watch. He'd do anything in the world to make her smile."

"Now you're just talking to talk," I said. We were close to the ice-cream place anyway.

"Walter, you can't be mad now because she finally is happy. That's not fair. You should know more than anyone what Mom was like," Mellie said, facing away from the road. Why did she have to turn her head? *Watch the road, Mellie.* "You were *always* trying to cheer her up."

I leaned my head against the window. I could see Naomi in the passenger-side mirror. She lifted her hand to wave. She gave me a soft smile. It wasn't that long ago that I didn't have that smile in my life. It was a major improvement. I guess I had some other improvements, too. Dad was happy, finally. And Mom was happy. Maybe this was a key moment, or I could make it one, a conscious decision to let go.

• • •

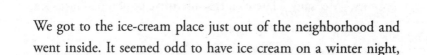

We got to the ice-cream place just out of the neighborhood and went inside. It seemed odd to have ice cream on a winter night, but there we were. I got a hot-fudge sundae. Naomi had mint ice cream. Mel got her usual vanilla milk shake.

"Our mom was babysitting the kids next door once," Mel said. "Walter ran over there with a bunch of flowers he bought for her. He missed her so much, right next door. 'Mom! These are for you!'"

"I didn't buy them," I said. "I pulled them out of our own garden. That doesn't even count. I didn't have any money."

"Oh, it counted," Mel said. "She told everyone about that for months. He's a romantic, Naomi."

"Not anymore, apparently," I said. Regret was starting to sink in. "I probably shouldn't even go back there. I'll give it some more time."

"My sister used to say there's millions of colors in the world, but most people only see a few shades of gray," Naomi said. "She'd say everyone has their own story and something to offer. Basically don't think *do* or *don't*, *good* or *bad*, because life's always more complicated than that. So I think you should talk to your mom and just work with what's there. What's done is done."

I nodded. I would do it for Naomi.

We talked more as we finished our dessert, about the board games Mel and I would make, our crowning achievement being the Piggy Police card game. The famous photos we'd re-create with Mel's stuffed animals. We told Naomi about how we drove Mom and Dad crazy. We'd hide in clothing racks at department stores and drive Dad nuts; he'd hated shopping enough already.

Mom and Seth were in the TV room when we got back. It was an addition to the back of the house with a huge TV, giant windows, and a sprawling couch-and-chair setup. "I'll take Naomi upstairs," Mel said. "There's a treasure trove of photo albums she needs to see if she's going to spend time with my little brother."

"Ooh, yes, please," Naomi said.

I'd been through the albums more than a few times. Family vacations on the coast, camping trips with Mom and Dad, cousins, friends, our one trip to Disney World. It seemed crazy to think we'd done so many things and had so many memories.

I took ten long steps to the TV room. "Hey," Seth said. To his credit, he was still friendly after my outburst. "How was the ice cream?" he asked. Not snarky or sarcastic like he could have been and I'd have understood.

"Can I talk to . . ." I started to ask, and Seth was already up. He put a hand on my shoulder as he passed me on his way into the kitchen. I sat down on the soft couch next to Mom and sank right into it. This room was really amazing. They were watching an episode of *Parks and Recreation*, Amy Poehler's close-up seemed to fill the room. Mom crossed her legs and clutched a sofa pillow.

"Nice couch, isn't it?" she asked.

"It really is," I said. Maybe Mel made the right choice after all, staying with Mom. "I'm sorry. That was really rude, what I said before."

"Me too," Mom said, even though she hadn't done anything. I was the one who'd spazzed out. "You have to apologize for an outburst, but I have to apologize for a half decade. Or more—I don't even know."

I placed my hand on the pillow Mom was holding, and she gave my hand a squeeze. It took me back in time for a second, when tears and laughing and embracing were common. I felt a tear coming on, and I looked up at the ceiling.

"It's okay," Mom said, and smiled. "It's nice to hear your dad is doing well. I was worried about him." She looked exhausted or relieved. It didn't feel like talking to my mom still. She truly felt like another person. Whether it was the meds she was on or the time that had passed. She had a new life. "I want to know how you're doing."

"I'm all right," I said. "High school is pretty different—the city is different. There's a lot of fighting and stuff, but I'm okay. I stay away from it. I met Naomi and she's really cool—that gives me a lot to look forward to every day."

I hadn't planned on talking about Naomi; I still hadn't told Dad about her, or anyone, really. I hadn't talked to my mom in years, but there I was, thoughts pouring out of my mouth.

"We went to a Halloween party last week," I said. "We were supposed to go as a detective and a femme fatale. I don't think she knew what that was, though. She still looked way better than me. I'd never been to a party, really, before that. It was lame, but it was fun going with her."

Mom smiled.

"We're not dating or anything," I said. "I mean, maybe it'll happen at some point, but I'm not really sure how to go about that. It's kind of stressful."

"You'll get there," Mom said. "I think she likes you. Why wouldn't she? Just enjoy the ride. Don't stress it."

Why wouldn't she? Such a simple question, but *Why would she?* was just as simple, and that was my default question. Other people must think *why wouldn't.* I wished I could.

After talking to Mom, I looked at more pictures with Mellie and Naomi before Mel was going to take us back to the city. I lay on my stomach and elbows as they passed through the pages. School pictures . . . myself in ninth grade, just a few years ago. Eighth grade, sixth, elementary school pictures.

"Aww, look at that hair!" Naomi said. "And those glasses!"

Pictures of Mellie and me as kids in the summer. Mellie hitting me like a grown adult—you could tell from the tears on my face. "You deserved it," Mel said.

Pictures of me in a baby stroller. Me just as I was born. "Little baby Walter," Mel said.

Mom and Dad getting married, as a young couple. Their moms and dads. My mom's family, in their big country home, somehow both clean and messy, full of food. Mom's family was right out of *Leave It to Beaver.* Mom's older sister. And Dad's family, all his brothers and sisters. They were louder, always laughing. And Grandpa Wilcox—Dad idolized him. He always had a story, knew all the people in the neighborhood. He was Dad's inspiration to be a cop. Kids loved him.

"What a sweet smile," Naomi said.

Mel drove us back home, and we both fell asleep in the backseat. I woke up to Naomi's head on my arm, a few blocks from her home. I leaned my head on hers for the last few minutes, mad I'd slept through the ride.

Chapter Seven

I woke up to a voice mail from Mom.

"Hi, Walter," she said. "It's your mother. I'm just thinking about you, how much you've changed. All in good ways, better than I could have hoped for. I'm so glad you came over, and I hope we can do it again. And I'm glad you brought your friend over. She's really a sweetie. I feel like a huge weight is off my shoulders. Do you feel that? I was really sick and really worried for a long time, and I want you to know how much better you made me feel. Anyway, I should get to bed. I love you. Talk to you later."

I didn't know where things stood, and we couldn't go back to where things were before. I didn't think any of us could—me, Mom, Mel, Dad. We were all in different places now. But we could pick up from here and see how it goes. She wasn't the only one with a weight off her shoulders. That had been a lot of baggage to carry around.

Ricky came over in the afternoon. I was doing homework in my bedroom, trying alternately to ignore and eavesdrop on his and Dad's conversation. Dad was pacing back and forth. He was the pissed-off one and Ricky was trying to calm him down.

Dad drinking in the afternoon was rare. He didn't normally drink at all, so when he did, it meant something was different.

Either he was celebrating and had company or he was especially depressed. Even when he was depressed, though, like right after the divorce, he didn't drink much. He turned to food more than anything. In this case, he was drinking angry.

From what I pieced together, everything that was going good for him was possibly out the window, just a week later. The confession was gone, his popularity at the precinct was gone, and he was back to square one. Or maybe worse.

"There's too many people involved," Ricky said. "Too many loopholes. It's supposed to protect the innocent, but it protects the guilty—the system is flawed. The courts are flawed and they don't work one hundred percent of the time."

"It doesn't work even fifty percent of the time," Dad said. "It's not flawed; it's corrupt. These kids that go down to fight in the old basketball court have it right. You go there, state your business, and you settle it. Done. I'd thrive there, Ricky."

"I know," Ricky said. He was just listening and agreeing. Sometimes that was the best you could do.

"Since when is an outright confession not good enough?" Dad said. "I had the confession, the kid admitted to the crime, case closed, right? Red hat and everything, just like my neighbor had said, same kid. Not only does the punk take away the confession, he makes me out to be some monster. Profiling, assault. I'm a goddamn honest cop, straight up and down—all there is to it."

"I hear you," Ricky said. "I know it doesn't look like it, but it really does happen to all of us."

"Well, that's a problem, then, isn't it?" Dad asked, and I heard his bottle hit the table. "The truth will prevail—that's what they say, right? It'll turn around again."

One of our good-luck swings was tilting, but this could still work in my favor. It was getting difficult to be around Dad, ever since the Halloween party. He'd figured something was up, that I was a little more secretive, a little quieter. He asked outright if I had a girlfriend I was hiding and I said no, which was true. Naomi was not my girlfriend, much as I wanted her to be. But Dad knew something was up. I was on the phone more, not that we shared a phone, but he could hear me talking to someone through the walls for sure. I'd been grooming a little more, and I might have asked to borrow his weights, which certainly raised suspicion. Seemingly anytime we were in the same room, he found a new way to ask the same questions.

Like when I finally stepped out into the living room.

"And then there's this guy," Dad said, holding out his arm toward me. "The case of my own son. Suddenly he's got places to be. Mr. Popularity over here."

"There's worse things to be," I said.

"He's a good-looking kid," Ricky said, and gave me a tap on the shoulder. "He's coming out of his shell. It was only a matter of time, pops."

"Did something happen with the burglar?" I asked Dad.

"Listen to him—he changes the subject," Dad said. "He's a master, but I'm better. I'm gonna figure you out. I've got people all over the city. You can't hide anything from your old man. This is what I do."

"Did something happen?" I asked again. Maybe I was a master.

"You really want to know?" Dad asked. He gave me a loose recap, holding up a finger for each item. "Half the crime in the city we can't even catch. We're hiring these young kids that don't know anything and cutting training time in half. People are working ten-hour days. Our city has a legitimate problem and I can help, but guess what? They don't want my help."

"It'll turn around when this whole case dies down, right?" I asked. "They're probably just being careful because of all the attention it's getting."

"Yeah, I think so," Dad said. "Where are you off to?"

"The park," I said.

"See? This is what I'm talking about." Dad clapped sarcastically. "Can I get her name at least? Is she a criminal? Is that what you're hiding? Are *you* a criminal?"

I laughed at the jokes and grabbed my coat. "Just friends from school," I said, a little white lie.

The plan was to meet Naomi, and that was about as far as the plan went: meet Naomi and let the day take over.

It was November and the leaves were half on the ground, shuffling and crunching beneath the foot traffic. The slums my dad would go on about after work were nowhere in sight, the people were smiling, and the colors were out of a Disney cartoon. The park was at the edge of High Hill, where the buildings got taller. We were surrounded by buildings on all sides, the center of a wall of giants. There was us in the park, and outside of us, there was the world.

Naomi was standing on the sidewalk. She had her hair pulled back and large sunglasses on, and she had a backpack with her, which I was used to, since I mostly saw her at school. She spotted me and waved. I was getting more comfortable around her in general, but she still made me nervous every time I saw her. My breathing rhythms changed. Every step closer to her I felt a little more light-headed. I hoped today wouldn't be the day I finally blew it.

"Ready?" I said as I approached. I took a deep breath and buried my hands in my sleeves. "Let's find the biggest pile of leaves and jump in. We'll just run and dive."

"Okay, let's do it," Naomi said. "I can't wait to get all those bugs in my hair."

"I hope I land right on a rat," I said. "The biggest, fattest rat in the city."

We started walking in no particular direction with no mention of where we were headed or how long we had. We walked and talked, and I looked at her, and down at her feet, and back at her. And she looked at me. Which isn't to say there weren't a million other things in the periphery of my vision: a lady with four or five dogs pulling her like a bobsled team, a food truck with a long line, traffic starting and stopping. But mostly I saw Naomi. We came to a section of the park I'd been to many times; in fact, it was my personal tree.

"You have your own tree?" Naomi said. "This is a Walter Tree?"

"This is *the* Walter Tree," I said. "There's my comic-book store across the street. Sometimes I'll go there and then sit down by this tree. I like it because I can be alone and sit there and read, but there's always people all around, so I'm not alone-alone. Just regular alone."

That was when I wasn't there with Jason, but I didn't mention that part to Naomi. I imagined him walking out of the comic-book store, seeing me on a sort of date with his sister. I'd dodged Shadows for three weeks now. I was officially avoiding him. I hadn't said a thing about Naomi and me to him. There was nothing to say. Except that I liked her a lot, but he wouldn't want to hear that and I didn't want to say it.

"Walter Tree, I love it," Naomi said. "I'm going to show you my special place, too. But it has to be dark first." Naomi leaned against the tree. "You need to carve your name into it or something so everyone knows it's your tree."

"I pee on it, like, once a month," I joked. "That's how I mark my territory."

"All right, I won't lean here, then," Naomi said, pushing off the tree. We crossed the street and headed into the comic-book store. There were seven or eight people in there, which was about average whether it was a Saturday afternoon or a weekday morning. "So you read comics? Like X-Men, Batman?" Naomi asked.

I showed her around the store. "Yeah, there's so much more than that, though. There's the mainstream comics, the just-right-of-mainstream comics, like indie superhero stuff, and the real indie stuff."

"Do you read regular books?" Naomi asked.

"Yeah," I said. "I like comics because I can read them in one sitting and feel like I accomplished something, but I read all kinds of stuff. Stephen King. Nick Hornby, I just finished reading *High Fidelity*. I have a lot of free time, you see."

"Well, I'm gonna take up all your free time," Naomi said. "I'm going to make you quit reading."

Please do.

"So where is this special place of yours?" I asked when we headed back outside. The sun cast a golden light on the storefronts. "I'm getting curious."

"It's where my sister would take me when I was a kid," Naomi said.

"The invisible sister nobody's seen," I said.

"Oh, she's real. But no one sees her anymore," Naomi said. "Drugs and boys, man."

"Been there," I joked before I knew if it was okay to joke.

"I love my big sis, though. She taught me all about capital-*L* life," Naomi said. We walked a slow pace along the street, contently aimless. "She was smart as anyone but such a mess, too. She made every bad decision she could like it was a contest. She got involved with this boy my parents hated, and they were right. I mean, even as a kid I knew he was the bad guy in the movies, right? But he was a charming, good-looking kid, and Mom and Dad were Mom and Dad, so you can guess which side Alicia took. She ran away when she was seventeen. I was just twelve then. I saw her once or twice after that. She was kinda messed up on stuff. She wasn't the same person at all. I hope she's better now, but I almost don't want to know."

"Wow," I said. "That's some story."

"Yeah, so I get screwed over from all that because now I'm the *good kid*," Naomi said. "So they need to keep me on the straight and narrow, but they don't know I'm secretly a *wild child*."

"I thought you were," I said. "I wasn't sure, though."

"Come on, Walter. I get out of the house, and ten minutes later, I'm jumping in piles of rats and garbage," Naomi said. "Wild child."

"I'm taking the blame for that," I said. "That was my idea. I'm the bad guy. Don't tell your parents."

We walked past the storefronts, an electronics store, a nail place. We went into a music store at the end of the block and combed through the CD bins. Nicki Minaj was blasting from the speakers even though the store was empty aside from an older guy who worked there.

"It's kind of weird stores like this are around still, right?" Naomi asked. "Everyone downloads stuff. You wonder how they stay in business. It's like a relic."

"Where are we going to waddle around once they're all closed, though?" I asked.

"Maybe it'll be like those apocalyptic shows," Naomi said, "and all the trees and grass will consume the buildings, and wild cats will be everywhere."

"Damn, I don't want to fight off beasts just to get my Nicki Minaj fix," I said. "Can you imagine if this store went out of business? We wouldn't even be standing here right now. We'd be bored and lost, probably turn to drugs and alcohol. If this store wasn't here, an hour from now our entire future would be lying in a gutter."

"Then we need to buy something," Naomi said. "To keep them in business. This is going to be *our* album, so I'm going to say no rap."

"No rap?" I asked. "Pressure's on."

"So how'd you get into all this rap music, anyway?" Naomi asked me as I flipped through the CDs. We were stationed under a vintage poster of Stevie Wonder in some dapper shades, promising an electric night, live in concert.

"How *did* I get into rap?" I asked back, thinking about it. "I just really like discovering new stuff. One thing leads to another. Pop music led me to older pop music, the Beatles were a gateway into Motown, which led me back to modern R&B, and some rap, which I really settled on and devoured."

"Top five rappers," Naomi said.

"Just five? I thought you didn't even listen to rap," I said. I was flipping through the pop section, which seemed to encompass pretty much everything under the sun that wasn't rap.

"I listen to *some*," Naomi said. "I just couldn't have you thinking I'm like Jason or anything. I listen to a *little*. Top five, let's hear it."

"All right, this isn't too bad," I said. I'd had this conversation with Jason before. "It's probably the same basic list everyone has, but I'm gonna be a little outrageous. First off, I'm going to use one slot and put the entirety of the Wu-Tang Clan in there. Solo Wu-Tang rappers would be its own top five. Eminem would be on the list. Nas. Tupac. And then that leaves me one spot . . . Can I split it between A Tribe Called Quest, Kanye West, and Biggie? Otherwise I have to bow out."

"No way," Naomi said down the aisle from me now. "This is, like, your top seventeen already. Let's pick out a random CD from the rap section. That'll be your number five."

"Good deal," I said. My number five pick was Positive K, *The Skills dat Pay da Bills*. The cover was hella nineties, featuring the hit single "I Got a Man." "So what do you listen to?" I asked.

"Oh gosh," Naomi sighed. "Nobody ever asks me that. I'm embarrassed."

"Don't be embarrassed. I'm apparently a huge Positive K fan," I said. I had to find a good CD that would make her think of me, us, and this moment. So far I was blanking.

"Here's one—this was pretty good," Naomi said, and handed me a CD. Janelle Monáe, *The Electric Lady*. "I like Esperanza Spalding, too, but you won't know her. Uh, what else? Some jazz, some classical. Some harp stuff you'd probably leave the store if I put on."

"I'm sure it's good," I said. "I like the stuff I've heard you play. You have good taste."

"I do listen to a lot of R & B, too," Naomi said. "That freaky sex music. *Oh, shut up, Naomi, you're not funny.* I'm so sorry."

I laughed.

"You want to know what really got me into harp?" she asked me. "I can't believe I'm even admitting this—I'm such a dork. But video games. My brother used to play these fantasy video games on his PlayStation, and they'd have this cool harp music, and I wanted to learn to play."

"That's kinda funny," I said. "When I was over a few weeks ago, Jason said it sounded like Final Fantasy music. He was annoyed with it and had no idea he was the inspiration for it."

"He'd flip out just knowing we're hanging out right now," Naomi said. She felt that pressure, too. He was a ghost on our maybe-date. "I don't even know what to tell him. I can't handle it right now. I love him—he's my brother—but he's such a punk, too."

"He *is* kind of a punk," I said. "But that's just Jason."

"*That's just Jason*—it should be a friggin' sitcom," Naomi said, nerve exposed. She rolled her eyes. "Everyone says that. He's the golden child of the family. He gets into all this trouble, he gets to do whatever he wants, messes up all the time, but he's the golden child. He can be out as late as he wants, he can date whoever. But my older sister gets in trouble and somehow it all falls on my shoulders. Because Alicia was a girl and I'm a girl, and Jason's just Jason. It's crazy."

"That's what it's like at school, too," I said. "He has a charm that wins people over. He's untouchable."

"It's Jason and girls. That's the issue when it comes to me," Naomi said, her eyes in an angry squint. "He dates these skanks and then he gets all defensive of me because he doesn't want me to be like the girls he dates. He's such a hypocrite. My family is nuts, Walter."

"Not to change the subject or anything, but I've got it," I said, once I'd spotted the Maltese Falcon of CDs. "This can be our album, and with this purchase, we save the record-store industry."

I handed the CD to Naomi. I'd chosen the first Stevie Wonder album I got into, *Talking Book*, in honor of our conversation under his mug. It had two of my favorite Stevie Wonder songs, "Tuesday Heartbreak," and "I Believe." If only it'd had "Knocks Me Off My Feet"—I would have put Naomi in a perpetual swoon.

We headed back out as the afternoon was fading. Shadows were flooding the buildings up to the bright tops the sun could still reach. My mom had given me money when I'd visited to take Naomi out, though I didn't tell Naomi that. I gave my mom a hard time over the money concerns and the priority she puts on it, but the truth is it felt good to have money to take Naomi out and spend the day in the city.

"What's next?" Naomi asked.

I didn't have a plan, and Naomi was looking at me expectantly. I could dodge it for a bit, but at some point she was going to realize I was dreadfully boring.

"We can visit my mom again," I said. At least I had jokes.

"Oh no," Naomi said, waving her hands. "I think we've had enough of that for one week, or month, or year. I'm kidding, I love your mom."

"Are you hungry?" I asked.

"Always," Naomi said. That was good, she'd never figure out how boring I was as long as I could keep her fed.

"We could have a dinner adventure," I suggested. "Let's get something neither of us has ever had before. Like, I've never had Thai. Korean barbecue. Sushi. Basically anything that isn't McDonald's is going to be an adventure on my end."

"Let's do sushi!" Naomi said. "That's exciting."

There was a sushi restaurant farther into the city, Sushi Palace Ai. The palace was down a set of stairs, through a few tight hallways. It was a little claustrophobic and dim, with strung lights hanging along the walls and ceiling and neon signs for color. The restaurant was about half full, and seeing as it wasn't even five yet, we took that as a sign that this was a good place. They sat us at a small table in the middle of the room. We didn't know what to order, so we chose completely at random. Oysters looked gross. The sushi rolls all had bizarre ingredients, fish and fruit and things I didn't know what they were. But I wanted to go really random. I chose the monkfish.

"It's probably all good, right?" I asked. I took my phone out after we'd ordered. "They wouldn't sell it if it was gross. I'm not ignoring you—promise. I'm looking up my dinner."

Apparently I was about to eat a fish that was large enough to eat lobsters, giving itself a lobsteresque flavor. My dinner was science fiction. "Oh, I'll pay for dinner," I said. "I actually have money and everything."

"Are you sure?" Naomi asked. "I can pay for my half. I don't want you to think you have to or anything."

"I got it," I said. "I'm going to get you that Positive K CD, too, so you can hear what all the buzz is about."

"This is going to sound crazy, but I kinda hate sitting in the middle of a restaurant," Naomi said, hunched in on herself. "This is the crazy part. I feel like I'm being *watched*. I know nobody actually cares what I do, but what if I have to use a fork instead of chopsticks or something, right? And then they'll laugh or get us kicked out or something."

"If anyone laughs, we'll stab them with our forks," I said. When the waiter walked by, I asked if we could have a more private table, and he led us to an elevated booth area in the corner of the restaurant. We had a candle and some yellow flowers in our new spot.

"You're so sweet. You actually entertained my neurosis," Naomi said, sliding into our new booth. "You didn't have to do that."

"No, I was thinking about it, and you're definitely right. They'd kick us out if they caught us using the forks they provided," I said. "I can't believe I ordered the Godzilla of the sea. This thing eats *lobsters*, Nay. Can I call you that?"

"Nay." Naomi shook her head.

"What if it springs back to life and tries to eat me?" I asked.

"I'll stab it with my fork," Naomi said, clutching her fork like a weapon. People go to restaurants all the time. People my own age go to diners or whatever like it's nothing, but I felt like a kid in

a grown-up's suit in this place. Like Naomi and I were playing pretend.

"I read somewhere you have to have water with sushi because it's offensive to the fish if you drink soda," I said as the waiter brought us two glasses of water.

"That makes sense, since they swim in water," Naomi said. "But they swim in salt water, so . . ."

"We'll have to add salt, then," I lamented. "This dinner is going to be horrible, isn't it?"

"It's so complicated." Naomi took out her phone. "I'm not ignoring you—promise. Want to see something frightening? You're going to hate me after this."

Naomi fiddled with her phone and then showed me a series of photos of her baby sister in various outfits Naomi had made for her—baby superhero, baby English gentleman, baby fairy, baby monster. They were actually detailed and well done.

"This is amazing," I said. "Do you want to be a photographer or designer or something? What do you do with these?"

"This is the first thing I have ever done with them. My mom helps me out with the outfits and gets me materials and stuff. This is what we do in my family. I'm such a weirdo, right? You can leave if you want. I'll pay for dinner. I'm sorry I showed you that." She put the phone away. "But, no, I don't know what I want to do. Is that crazy? I can play the harp all right, but is that something people do? I need more hobbies. I'm going to be a cat lady or something, making outfits for all my cats."

"I doubt that," I said. "But you could probably get really famous if you did."

Our waiter brought out our dinner, and the monkfish wasn't the best thing I'd ever had. Not terrible, but it was no cheeseburger. Naomi, however, fixed herself a small dish of wasabi and soy sauce and dove into her monster roll.

"Don't like it?" Naomi said, reading my face. "You're eating the Godzilla of the sea. You'd think it would be the most delicious."

"It's fine," I said. Naomi pushed her miso soup over to me.

"Try that," she said. "Okay. Naomi confession: I've had sushi before. Like, a lot. I kind of love sushi. My family gets it every Sunday. I guess I'm not that adventurous." She slapped her palm to her face.

"You're such a cute little habitual liar," I said, and finished off her miso soup.

"Tell that to Uncle Dave," Naomi said, and snuck a piece of monkfish off my plate.

．　　　．　　　．

The sun was fully down by the time we were street level again. Naomi rubbed her arms to warm up. Just an hour or two earlier I wasn't sure we'd need coats. I rubbed her back with my hand for a second, sure she'd feel like she was by the fireplace.

"So you still can't tell me about this spot?" I asked. "Are you going to kill me? That's it, isn't it? It's a murder dungeon."

"Maybe, but I can't tell you yet," Naomi said. "You'll have to be surprised. It's a surprise murder."

Naomi took me up the street to a department store where a lady was selling flowers, specifically to young couples. I shrugged. *Lady, I blew all my money on dinner. Leave us alone.* We went inside and browsed casually for a bit, and then Naomi pulled me through a door in the back.

"You have to sneak up. It doesn't work if anyone knows you're here," Naomi said as we went up a bunch of flights of stairs. "This is where my sister used to work, by the way."

"You *are* a wild child," I said, following her up the spirals of stairs and rapidly losing my breath. We finally got to the top and exited a door and emerged on the rooftop.

"So this is where my sis would take me." Naomi twirled. The city lights reached up from the streets and alleys, but up here, the moonlight fought them off. "It looks like a regular old building roof, right? But it's *not*. It's the highest building in the city. This is my spot. You can't help but dream up here. I'm going to take my baby sis up here when she's older so she can dream, too. You can see the whole world from up here."

I could only see Naomi.

"I kind of am a habitual liar," Naomi said. She looked away from me, down at the ground, and sank her hands into her coat pockets. "I should probably go ahead and tell you this, too. I snuck out to see you tonight. My parents think I'm at Mae's house. She's covering for me. I snuck out the other night, too, when we went to your mom's house."

"You didn't want to tell them?" I asked. "Are you going to get in trouble?"

"Not if they don't find out," Naomi said. "I didn't want to give them a chance to say no. I wanted to see you."

"I'm glad you did," I said. "Thanks for hanging out with me today. And coming to dinner. And thanks to your sister for the advice the other night. The millions of colors. I needed to hear that."

"I think everyone does," Naomi said. "I did, too."

"Well, thanks," I said. "I feel really good, like, not just right now, but all the time. Because of you."

We stood near the edge of the rooftop and looked out over the city. She wasn't kidding, the city was even more enormous than it had looked from the fire escape at the Halloween party. It looked like it went on forever. I couldn't imagine what a real city like Manhattan would look like from its tallest building. The buildings shrouded us off from the rest of the world most of the time but you could climb them still and see everything out there, all the world had to offer. We had a comfortable silence, which hadn't happened often. The wind was blowing the few strands of Naomi's hair that weren't pulled back.

"I think about you a lot," I said. "Like all the time. Is that weird?"

"You do?" Naomi asked.

"Yeah, of course," I said. I surprised myself by saying that aloud and wasn't sure how to follow it up. I made an effort to turn off my brain. "You're just so cool."

"I promise you I'm not," Naomi said, and laughed. Not defensive, just self-deprecating. "I promise you I'm the uncool one. You're much cooler than me. You've got that hair curl and everything."

"But saying that makes you the cool one," I said. "I think the less cool, the better anyway."

"Yeah, I like dorky," Naomi said. I couldn't have dreamed up someone like Naomi Mills. Every clichéd feeling, she gave me.

"I'm dorky," I said. "Dorky like a fox."

"See, there's that wit again," Naomi said. "You are really smart, aren't you? C student, my ass. You think fast, you keep up with me, you say the craziest stuff. That's smart. It's kinda hot."

Naomi laughed, but she didn't say what she usually says; she didn't say *I say stupid things.*

I leaned over to kiss her. I still worried she'd pull away, that this whole bond we had going on was actually one-sided, but she didn't. It could have been a second or a minute—time was working some weird magic. I'd climbed the tallest building and my inner cynic plunged to the pavement, ripe for tomorrow's paper.

We held the kiss. I moved my hand to her neck; her earring rested on my thumb. Naomi's lips pulled away from mine. I felt the breeze, heard the cars again, like I was landing back on earth.

"This is the dumbest thing. I'm so nervous," I said. "Are we like . . . ? Do you want to go out? Do you want to be my girlfriend? I don't know how you're supposed to word this kind of thing. Will you go steady with me? Will you be my main squeeze?"

Naomi smiled. She laughed. She nodded. "Walter," she said. She kissed me back.

165

•   •   •

I got home before ten. Dad was in bed already, which I took to be a not-great sign. Then I was lying in bed with the news on, and everything changed.

A clip was playing of the burglar Dad had caught and his parents from earlier in the day. The Channel 3 news guy was in his face with a microphone.

"I'm talking with Calvin Temple," he said. "Calvin, the judge released you today, and there seems to be some confusion. Was there a confession?"

"No, man, no confession," Calvin said. "Just a racist cop, that's all. I didn't even do anything. This guy pulled me over. I didn't even do anything, and then they have me going to jail, interrogating me. I'm in court, and I didn't even do anything! No confession. Just a racist cop."

They dropped all the charges after the investigation and let him off, but his family was pushing for more. They wanted my dad fired.

"This was not an incident," his mother said on the courthouse steps in the same video. "This is a pattern. We know it, they know it, the records show it. It needs to stop."

That was a blanket statement on the entire police department. It painted them like a bunch of harassing racists. That wasn't my dad, that wasn't Ricky, or my uncle Joe, he was a cop, too. I opened my laptop and started searching the news sites. The story was a leading article on our local news page. CHARGES DROPPED AGAINST ACCUSED TEEN INTRUDER was the headline. I saw Naomi online, so I sent her a message.

11/08 10:20 WalterW1014: Have you seen the news?

11/08 10:20 NMillz: ? No, whats up?

11/08 10:21 WalterW1014: There's kind of a mess that my dad's involved in. It's not good.

11/08 10:21 NMillz: Omg, what is it? Are u okay?

11/08 10:21 WalterW1014: Can we talk on the phone?

My phone rang a second later. "Hey," I said. "This is a mess. I feel sick right now."

I did feel sick, I wanted to throw up. This was bad enough for my dad, but it was going to affect me, too. And probably Naomi. This wasn't about some burglar getting caught anymore.

"What is it?" Naomi asked.

"So remember how I told you my dad caught that kid who was breaking into homes and everything—that was all great. My dad was a hero down at the precinct. But the kid changed his story—like, completely. Not only is he taking his confession away, but they're accusing my dad and the whole police force of all this stuff—like, sick stuff." I paused. "Race stuff. I'm not even sure what's going on. I mean he's not—"

"Oh my god," Naomi said.

"I don't even know what happens next," I said. "This could be really bad. Listen, I know what we said tonight, but honestly, if you want out, I don't blame you at all. This can be really messy, and I don't want you to be a part of it if you think—"

"If I think what?" Naomi asked. "Why would I want out?"

"Because," I said. The rest of the sentence got stuck in my throat.

"Because I'm black?" Naomi asked.

"I'm just saying you don't have to deal with this if you don't want to," I said. "Of course I don't want anything to change."

"Walter, I'm not going anywhere, okay?" Naomi asked. "I agree this is awful, and I hope your dad clears his name, but that's his thing, okay? We're fine. Don't waste any energy on that. I just hope your dad's okay."

"Thanks," I said. "Me too."

We sat in silence for a moment before Naomi spoke again. "You're gonna get through this."

Chapter Eight

The hallways were claustrophobic on Wednesday afternoon. One of the football players gave me a nod and a "'sup," and I didn't know him from a hole in the wall. Maybe he was nodding to Nate, who was right beside me—he knows more people than I do. But he was looking at me—I was sure of it.

This had been happening the past few days. I could have sworn everyone was staring at me in the halls. I was more inclined to watch my feet than make eye contact on the average day, so this could have been normal. Maybe people just looked at you when you passed them in the halls. It was either that or they knew.

I wasn't aware if everyone at school knew that my dad was a police officer. Maybe they did. Maybe they saw the news. Word could be spreading and I wasn't just being looked at but talked about. Maybe I was being paranoid. But maybe not. It was like when Daredevil lost his vision but could suddenly hear every little thing. But if my newfound supersense was an awareness of everyone staring at me and whispering, it was a terrible power to have.

"Walter, you there? I've got another one," Nate said, walking far too casually for my taste. "Another joy of being single. Kate and I would take my truck to school every morning, and I had to get to her place by six thirty so we could have breakfast together.

Do you know how early I had to get up for that? Now I skip first period if I feel like it."

Nate and I hadn't discussed Naomi since the first time I kissed her. He would be the easiest person to tell. He didn't know Jason or anyone connected to Naomi. I had to run it by her first, though. We still hadn't told anyone what was going on with us, and I didn't want to be the first one to do it. For all I knew, any wrong action at this point could put me right back to where I was a month ago. Alone, trying to memorize all the lyrics to Tupac's "Me Against the World."

"I could even skip class right now," Nate said, proud of this thought, convincing himself his single life was truly that good. "What say you, Walter? Care to skip eighth period with me and check out the furniture store for soft new chairs?"

"Are you looking for a new chair?" I asked.

"Absolutely not." Nate beamed.

"You know I don't skip class," I said. "Besides, I've got a test to take." My actual plan did involve skipping, but it was a first for me, so that wasn't a full lie. Naomi and I were going to meet outside on the steps, so I had to ditch Nate, who had become somewhat clingy since he and Kate decided to spend more time apart.

"You sure, man? You seem like you could use some downtime," Nate said, branching away. Guess I was wearing my anxiety on the outside. "Hey, good luck on your test."

I needed Naomi like I needed a handful of Advil and a glass of water.

•　　•　　•

We'd tried to find time to be together during the school day, but it wasn't enough. After school was a possibility, before school was less tantalizing. We were, as weird as it was to say, a new couple. There was no map for us, really. We had no idea where this was headed or what it should be or feel like. Neither of us had ever dated anyone else before. It could be argued that it was a bad idea, that we'd do it all wrong. We saw the other couples, clinging to each other's sides, kissing, but that didn't feel right. Yet, anyway. That was what we needed time to figure out.

I could jump in the air and kick my feet together. Naomi was just feet away and some time alone was well-earned after dodging so much to make it happen.

I was on the third floor, passing a stretch of lockers and heading toward the stairs outside. The sun was beaming through the door windows and pulling me toward it, and outside, alone apart from a few freshmen on their way downstairs, was Naomi. Bathed in sun and the blue of the sky.

I opened the door with thoughts of hand-holding and eyes and lips.

"Bro, Walter," Jason said, way too in-my-face, way too from-out-of-nowhere. He must have been right on the other side of the door. I quickly adjusted my attention to him. "You going to Shadows later? I've got a backlist now. It's been weeks."

"Yeah," I said. "I'll bring my book bag so we can carry it all." Stupid Wednesday routines. I had no excuse planned. It was potentially good, though. Things had felt off, but I was the one with the secret. It'd be a good chance to feel things out. Eventually he was going to find out about Naomi, and it would be better if things were good and normal between us first.

"Bye," Naomi said to us, or maybe to Jason, or maybe secretly to just me, and jetted down the stairs.

"Oh, I gotta go, too," Jason said, looking at his watch. "I'm late. If I'm not at Shadows, come break me out of Colfer's office. I'm probably in detention."

"I'll bring a saw in a birthday cake," I said. Nervous laughter. I was bad at this. My best bet was to get a few comics and get out of there fast after school.

The bell rang and rather than run to class, I went down the stairs to see if I could find Naomi, to see if she'd waited for me or if the plan was off. Maybe I could still go to that furniture store with Nate. I reached the bottom of the stairs and a pair of hands grabbed my arm and yanked me under the steps in a dark, shaded, secluded spot. We kissed.

"That was weird, huh?" I asked, waiting for my eyes to adjust.

"Yeah, it was. I never lie to Jason," Naomi said, looking at her gloved hands as they picked up my bare hands. "Of course, I never skip class, either."

"Never?" I asked. I rubbed her glove fingers and gave her hands a squeeze. "Me neither. Do you want to skip skipping? I mean, we're late already. So we may as well. What do you want to do?"

"Let's get out of here," Naomi said. "Go for a walk or something."

We started heading west from the school, toward the bridge that gives East Bridge its name. It was just a few blocks away. It didn't feel like we were doing anything wrong, cutting class and leaving school. Naomi and I shared a bubble in which regular actions, thoughts, laws, and principles did not apply. Not that anyone else would agree.

"We're two bad seeds," Naomi said.

"Absolutely rotten," I said. "You're a wild child. We've established that." Two bad-seed, wild children carrying their guilt as they skipped a class for the first time. The sun was bright and inviting, leading us away from the school, promising this was the correct path to take. The roads were loud with construction; East Bridge was in a constant state of rebuilding, or possibly debuilding, as it only seemed to get messier and louder.

"What's the worst thing you've ever done?" I asked Naomi, and pulled her body closer to mine.

"Is murder off the table?" Naomi asked. "Other than the murders, let's see," Naomi said, lifting her face and looking upward. "Okay, well, I told you I used to hang out with my older sister on top of the store, right? Well sometimes she'd drink alcohol up there, and she'd share it with me."

"That's your bad story?"

"I was, like, ten years old!" Naomi exclaimed. "Up there getting wasted, saying swearwords. I'm a bad kid."

"Did you like it?" I asked.

"No!" Naomi said. "I didn't like it at all, but I thought I was being cool. That stuff tasted gross. Okay, your turn. What's the worst thing you've ever done?"

"I branded my mom with a scarlet *A* and bolted from dinner," I said, and laughed. "That was kinda bad. This one's dark and you're going to like me less afterward, but this is real. This is a deep regret. I hit my sister once."

"*No!*" Naomi exclaimed. "You're a woman beater? Mellie's so nice, too . . ."

"I'm not a—no. Here's the story," I started. "We had a dog named Murph. And Murph would get away sometimes, and we'd spend all day chasing him around the neighborhood. He'd run away and we'd get close and he'd run again—it was a game. To him. So one day, the sun had gone down, we're missing dinner, we've been out there for hours already, we don't even know where he is anymore.

I'm about that age, around ten, I'm cranky, Mel's cranky, I'm whining, she's telling me to shut up. We get into this huge fight, and Murph had this chain leash Mel was holding that she balled up and struck me right in the face with, and I hit her back. We're both crying, Murph can tell we're upset, comes running up to us. We all go home."

"Oh my god," Naomi said.

"Yeah, so I've got a huge bloody gash across my nose and Mel's got a bruised cheek. We told my parents Murph ran into us both. I don't think they bought it for a second. I felt awful. I still feel awful. But she kinda started it."

"Aw," Naomi said, and slid her gloved hand along my nose. "We were some bad ten-year-olds. I can't believe you sold out your dog."

"And then there are the murders," I said. "But those don't count."

• • •

We got to the bridge and sat down by a wall one of the bridge legs formed, on a small gravel hill pushing up against it.

"Truth time," Naomi said, placing her hands on her lap. She slid closer to me, and we huddled together for warmth. "I think we should go ahead and tell everyone. I don't want to be sneaking around and skipping classes just to see you. And I'd prefer not to lie to anyone. That was way too close with Jason."

I had already lied to Nate and Jason in a five-minute stretch. Naomi had lied about where she was on Saturday. "It's not the best time to tell my dad," I said. "Maybe a week ago, it would have been, but now he's stressing himself sick over this lawsuit stuff. He's busy with lawyers and media requests and work problems all day. I think he's at war with his boss." When he wasn't running around with that stuff, he was home eating junk food, drinking with Ricky, sleeping, or watching old movies.

"I'd like to at least tell my parents," Naomi said.

"That's a good idea," I said with a nod. "When are you going to tell them?"

"Not just me," Naomi said, alarmed. "*We* have to tell them. And Jason, too."

This wasn't exciting news for me as I was missing Naomi's flair for drama and big scenes. Or at least her ability to speak first and think after. We handled secrets differently. For her, a secret was a lie. She needed to talk and be open and free with her feelings. I don't think she could hold back if she tried. Myself, I was a loner. I was used to keeping things in my head. I didn't always need to talk, I didn't think of it as a secret or a lie so much as it was just my business. I was just getting to know the Mills family, too, so the idea of a big reveal was enough to tie my stomach in a knot or two. Confrontation made me queasy and it wasn't something I looked forward to. I was definitely going to develop an ulcer by graduation at the rate things were going.

"Don't you think it'll seem like a bigger issue than it is if we make a big scene out of it?" I asked. "Are you sure it's the right time for that?"

"Stop, you're making me nervous," Naomi said. "This is new to me, too. Besides, you don't know my family. They'll say no if I just bring it up or ask myself. They'll find some excuse to keep me locked up playing harp all day and night. Jason will throw a fit. You need to be there or all this is going to go away." She took my hands in hers. "And I'll feel better if I have you there."

"All right," I said. She didn't have to twist my arm. I'd have run out into traffic if she asked me nicely. "When do you want to do it?"

"Tonight," Naomi said. And when she kissed me, my heart beat heavily like the first time she touched my hand, but for all kinds of reasons now.

I understood where Naomi was coming from but it also felt so formal and mature, like I was asking her hand in marriage. Keeping it secret felt like we were doing something wrong, though, which we weren't. And the longer we kept the secret the more it seemed to imply this was something we shouldn't be doing. I wanted to be Naomi's boyfriend, and if talking to her parents was what it took to make it happen, that was what I was going to do.

Naomi picked up a discarded spray can.

"Think there's anything left?" she said, and shook the can. She sprayed a little spot on the ground next to her, a bright orange spot. "Works! Tag something!"

"I don't know how to tag," I said. "Listen, I'm no ten-year-old misfit anymore. I've matured."

"You just write something," Naomi said. "Put our names together. Wallomi."

"Wallomi?" I said. "Is that what we are, Wallomi?"

"Yeah, it's like a wallaby," Naomi said. "Like Rocko. Draw that."

"What's a wallaby, and what's a Rocko?" I asked, and Naomi laughed.

"You don't know anything!" Naomi tossed the can, and we kissed. Then she added, with disappointment, "I guess we're good kids after all."

Not two seconds after that, a cop walked by and looked at us, two kids kissing under the bridge in the middle of a school day, inches from a can of spray paint.

"Shouldn't you two be in school?" the cop asked, turning to face us, looking authoritative. But before we could respond—not that we had a response—he said "I'm just kidding!" The cop went on his way, protecting the city, or possibly ignoring crimes.

"Should we head back?" I asked, a nervous rock still sitting in my stomach.

"Yeah," Naomi said, and we got out of there.

• • •

"Finally, my man Walter returns to Shadows," Jason said, waiting for me outside as I walked toward the store. The buildings formed a wind tunnel and a frigid gust shoved us in through the door. I hadn't spent any real alone time with Jason since I started seeing Naomi, so I wasn't sure what to expect. As far as I knew, he'd figured it out already and was just waiting for me to announce it.

"I was starting to think you'd grown out of comics or something," Jason said. "Got into girls, started sowing those wild oats."

Jason picked up three comics fast. He hadn't missed a beat.

"I'm not like that," I said. He didn't need to think I was some horndog when Naomi and I told him we were dating later. I needed to steer as far from that narrative as I could. "I mean the wild oats. I have calm oats. Where'd you get all this money?"

"Don't worry about my money," Jason said. "I haven't come here in, like, four weeks. I have a lot of catching up to do."

"You can get comics without me," I said. "Anyway. Calm oats. I'm really not girl-crazy."

I wasn't used to having secrets. Jason hadn't mentioned it; maybe no one knew still. I couldn't bring it up in some casual manner myself. It was too weird.

"Oh, you're not? You trying to tell me something?" Jason asked, and put his books down on a bin of back issues. "Like, something serious? Because I'm cool with it. I guess I'm not totally surprised—"

"What? No, not that," I said. "I like girls, just not in that—never mind."

"I blew it," Jason said. "I was too strong, too macho, I scared you off, damn. You can tell me. I'll be sensitive, I can do that. I'm a forward-thinking man."

I laughed. His energy was as positive as ever. I even wondered if he was capable of being mad. I'd never really seen it. Jason was a happy, goofy guy. I didn't know what fears of mine were legitimate and which ones I was projecting. I could have nothing to worry about.

Jason tossed the comics on the counter.

"Walter's probably gay, but you're okay with that, right?" Jason asked Romero at the register, nudging me out of the way while he reached for his wallet.

"For real?" Romero asked with a quizzical look on his face. "Yeah, I'm cool, of course."

"Thanks," I said. "I'm not, but I appreciate it."

"Dude, you've got a lot on your mind, and I don't envy it," Jason said, and handed Romero a twenty. "This is the face of a man with the world on his shoulders. You'll talk someday. And when you do, your boy Jason's gonna be there to listen."

It's hard work carrying around these thoughts. When I talked to Mom, it changed the way the world looked. You'd think I'd have learned something. Telling Naomi's family about us would hopefully be the same kind of relief, but damned if I wasn't looking forward to it.

• • •

When I got back from school, Dad was home already and sitting on the couch. The air was tense.

"Walter, have a seat," Dad said. He seemed to be gathering his bearings, leaning forward from his seat like this was something urgent. I sat down.

"What now?" I asked. I knew the big strokes of the story, I knew he was innocent. A sit-down was never good news, though.

"I'm on work leave for a bit while things settle," Dad said. "I want you to hear this stuff from me before you hear it anywhere else, okay? As you know, that arrest I made, they did an internal investigation and let the case go. Kid denied he ever said anything. Politics, legal mumbo jumbo. So his family starts floating some wild accusations about the arrest. None of it's true. You're hearing that right from me."

"What do they want?" I asked.

"Time in the spotlight, a payday," Dad said. "There's plenty of reasons why someone would do something like this, honestly it happens all the time, now more than ever. I'm not worried. I've been a solid, dependable cop for over fifteen years now. This sucks but it happens from time to time, you take the bad with the good. That said, there is more, and I want to be up front about it. They haven't talked about this, yet, but they will. There was a scuffle. Minor. Brought on by that kid's actions, not mine, I can promise you that. He tried to get in his car and leave before we were done talking. I did what I had to within the parameters of my job and the law. That's it. Right now we just have to hope the force does the right thing by me. And we'll be okay."

Dad was put on leave after the investigation. His bosses weren't changing their minds a week later. Dad was going to be home for a while.

"Hey, at least I didn't lose the fight," Dad joked, likely reading the worry on my face. "Now, *that* would have ended my career."

I couldn't muster a smile, let alone a laugh. No amount of joking was going to change the fact that this was actually happening and the worst was still to come. "It doesn't look good at all," I said.

"It's nothing, Walter, okay?" Dad put a hand on my knee. "I've been through far worse. Every cop worth his salt has. It's part of the job. We want things to be nice and clean-cut, but when you deal with people, there will be variables. Every situation gets reassessed with every movement, every sentence spoken. I'm a good cop. I did the right thing. At the end of the day that's what they're gonna look at."

• • •

I walked to the Millses' unsure what I was even nervous about anymore. I was worried about so much it took over my brain and melted together. The feeling of dread slowed me to a zombielike crawl, like a march to my own execution. Too much bad news in the air. What I needed was an embrace from Naomi. For her parents to welcome me with open arms. *This is the best. We can hang out all the time now*—that was what Jason would say. Naomi would kiss me on the cheek, lay her head on my shoulder. I'd put my arm around her.

I didn't know what I was supposed to be doing by the time I reached their front door. Naomi and I hadn't rehearsed a thing, so when Mr. Mills opened the door and asked if I was there for Jason, I froze. It was an odd question that I hadn't anticipated. The only other time I'd been there, it was to see Jason.

"Uh, Naomi?" I asked. This was too much. The door was right there still. I hadn't crossed it. I could say I forgot something, chores, my dad was calling. The Walter signal shone in the night sky; East Bridge needed me.

"I invited him," Naomi said, appearing from the kitchen. "We have something we kinda want to say."

"Come on in, Walter," her dad said, and to Naomi, "Let's kinda hear it."

Mr. Mills stepped aside as I walked into the dark living room where he and Denise had been watching TV. He turned on a light.

"Walter and I have been seeing each other," Naomi said hesitantly, entering the living room herself. She usually seemed nervous through her overconfidence, but now she looked how I felt. I hadn't really considered that her parents did have the authority to end our relationship, to an extent.

"Really?" Denise said, not in a pleased tone. "Let me wrap my head around this."

"Oh dear," her dad said with no more pleasure. He was sitting in his own large chair while her mom was on the couch. "Naomi, I don't know about this right now . . ."

"Mom's wrapping her head around it—shh," Naomi said. Her mom shot her a look she didn't seem to catch. If ever there was a time to tread carefully.

"We do like you, Walter," Denise said, "so don't take any of this personally. No teenager wants to hear this, but you're both very young still, and with that comes a naïveté."

Jason came out of his room, in on the conversation already. *Guess that kills two birds with one stone.* "What's going on here?" Jason asked. "Is this about Naomi and Walter? I knew something was going on!"

"Jason, shut up," Naomi said. She must have wished at times for a button she could press that would just play "Jason, shut up." This was three for three not on board Team Walter and Naomi.

"Hey, I'm part of this family, too. I'm part of this conversation," Jason said. I knew he'd be a complication, but I hadn't thought he'd be *the* complication. He had the energy of a spoiled eight-year-old. "Walter's supposed to be my friend, and you're supposed to be my sis, so where does this leave me in all this?"

"Believe it or not, this isn't about you," Naomi said. "Go away, I'll deal with you later."

"People at school are gonna think I'm cosigning for Walter," Jason said, decreasing in age by the minute. "Letting him date my baby sis. I am not cosigning for you, Walter! You should have come to me like a man, and *maybe* I'd have cosigned."

"Jason, nobody wants your deadbeat cosign," their dad said, and leaned forward in his chair. "Now, can I say something here?"

Everyone quieted down. Jason folded his arms. Naomi was sitting nervously on the arm of the couch by her mom, and I sat down on the floor. This was calmer than I'd seen Naomi's family. A calm before the storm, maybe.

"Walter, your dad's been in the news," Mr. Mills said slowly. "I don't think it's any secret what's been going on in the community here."

"I'm completely separate from that," I said, hoping to avoid the conversation making a turn it couldn't recover from. I still had hope this would end well.

"I understand that," he said. "And I'm not saying there's any truth to anything that's being floated around. Your father's a well-known police officer, and he has plenty of support. I, myself, do not know the man. But with the attention the case is getting, and with the racial implications of it"—he took a moment to collect his thoughts—"things we're just scratching the surface of. This is a very real and potentially dangerous situation that needs to be considered, for a lot of reasons. I'm just not sure this is a good idea right now."

"Naomi, I think it's a no," Denise said, and Jason audibly agreed, nodding emphatically.

"You're just saying that because of Dad! Try having your own opinion!" Naomi said to her mom, rising from the couch like she couldn't be near her. This was not going well. "Maybe I'll just run away like Alicia did!"

"Naomi, you are not helping your case talking to me like that," her mom said with a stern look. It felt like Naomi and I were no longer on the cusp of some grand adventure, but little kids being lectured for walking too far from home. I wanted to add something but didn't know what. I wanted to defuse the situation but didn't know how. I wanted to hold Naomi when she was upset, but I couldn't.

"And maybe I'll hunt down Walter and kill him," Jason said, interrupting Denise to make sure he was being heard.

"Dude," I said. Things escalated quickly here. In my family, I was the one to hide and listen from a safe spot when fighting was happening. I didn't like to be around it, and I definitely didn't like being a part of it.

"That stuff has nothing to do with us," Naomi said to her dad. "And can we acknowledge that nothing you've said actually takes my feelings into account?"

"Here's a tip: don't have feelings," Jason said. "I've been around the block, and a girl with feelings just gets exploited, like Walter's doing to you right now."

"No, here's the issue," their dad said, and placed his palms flat against each other. "My daughter's safety is what comes first in all this. This is a violent world we're living in. Right now, I'm not convinced she's going to be safe. Maybe just give this some time."

"I'll protect her," I said. "I'll make sure she's safe."

"You couldn't protect a peanut butter sandwich," Jason said. "I'll look out for Naomi, Dad."

"I'll protect myself," Naomi said. "Mom, you know I'm not going to just roll over. You know I'm stubborn. But this isn't going to a concert or getting new shoes. This is my life—this is serious. I'm sixteen. I'm *going* to date, and I won't be a kid forever. And Walter makes me happy."

"I understand your feelings, honey," Denise said. "I had the same feelings for your father when I was your age."

"Mom, this is different," Naomi said.

"I had the same feelings," her mom interrupted. "But there's a whole world out there you don't even know about, and believe me, not everyone is going to care about your feelings like your father and I do. You're sixteen—that's true."

Her mom paused for a second and looked at Naomi's dad, and he caught her look and turned his head, lost in thought. Naomi looked at me. Her eyes widened, as did mine and Jason's, too.

"Naomi, I want you to really think this through, and be careful," her mom said. Naomi looked at me again, still wide-eyed.

"Be careful?" Naomi asked. "So it's okay?" Naomi hugged her mom. Then I stood up, and she hugged me, too. This had gone worse than I'd pictured while walking over, and better than I'd pictured just minutes ago. I was glad to have Naomi in my arms.

"Before we bring out the cake and balloons," Naomi's dad said, "I just want to make this very clear, what we're talking about. Walter, you're a white boy, and, Naomi, you're a black girl. I don't have any issue with that, and wish you the best. But what your father is involved with right now involves white and black. Those two words have a lot of history that you kids just don't know about. And that's what worries me."

"That's your generation," Naomi said dismissively. She didn't know when to quit.

"This is messed up," Jason said on his way out of the room. "I don't want any part of it. No cosign from me."

I felt like scum, like a bad friend, and I wasn't entirely sure why. I hadn't picked Naomi over Jason. I hadn't done anything to Jason.

"I should get going," I said, resting my forehead on the top of Naomi's head. I guessed we'd won, but I felt exhausted. I was leaving the house in a relationship with an amazing girl, but we'd lost our steam. We'd been met with warning and caution and, in the case of Jason, flat-out disapproval. No "cosign."

"I'll see you at school," Naomi said. She had a slight smile, at least. We didn't kiss or anything, not in that room. But she touched my hand as I opened the door and left.

The secret was gone. The weight of keeping it had been lifted, but it was replaced with another weight that hadn't been there before. This wasn't going to be as easy as it should be.

Chapter Nine

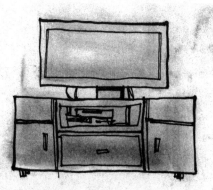

"**C**an you take us through that night?"

"I can try, but most of it would be pretty boring," Dad said, and took a sip from his water.

Dad was on the evening news, 10 p.m. edition. Sitting across from him was hard-hitting news anchor and sometimes interviewer Erika Vasquez, a transport from New York City. She was pretty, in her thirties, Latina. She had a red pantsuit on, red lipstick, brown curled hair. She was very pretty but known for her no-nonsense interviews, which had us all on the edge of our seat as we watched.

"Being a cop is not as glamorous as it looks in the movies," Dad said with a smile. Dad looked relaxed, dressed up in a dark shirt and tie. They sat in two big brown chairs in front of a dark blue backdrop of the city. Bright studio lights gave Dad a glint of sweat. "I'm no Iron Man, although I have been told I look like Robert Downey Jr."

"You have?" Erika asked, disbelieving. She had the more flattering camera angle.

"Really, being a cop entails a lot of sitting," Dad continued, ignoring her question. She smiled. Dad could put on the charm for an attractive lady, but even charm could go any way. He could embarrass himself. "Waiting, observing, all of which takes skill.

But the interesting part of the night in question involved Calvin Temple, who I just happened to pull over during a routine stop, a taillight thing, driving a little slow. I was observing, and certain details I'd heard regarding this thief stood out to me, three things in particular: the red hat, the garbage bags, and the gloves. None of which are enough to make an arrest, but enough to—"

"Were you originally assigned to this particular case?" Erika asked, and tilted her head. There was the setup. Dad wanted to clear his name, but this was too dangerous. This one interview, this one lady in the chair across from him, had the power to make our lives a nightmare. The interview had been recorded earlier this afternoon, and Dad had said it'd gone well, but they could do anything in editing.

"I was not assigned to that case," Dad admitted. She was going to throw him under the bus. "But we're all certainly aware of what's going on in the neighborhood. And of course we're expected to take action when we see something that's not quite right."

"So you ask a few questions, I'd imagine, and there was a physical altercation?" Erika asked. Dad nodded along with her questions. I couldn't tell if she was going for a scoop or what. Maybe the news station worked with the police—maybe Dad had more control than I thought. So far he'd been handling her questions really well, but she could make a name for herself if she played her cards right. We just had to wait and see whose side she was on.

"There was an altercation, although the term is a little misleading," Dad said. "Or open-ended, I suppose. I could pat you on the back, and it's a physical altercation. But what happened was he didn't like where the questions were going. He's eyeing his car, and he walks away. I pull him back because we're not finished."

"He was bruised," she stated firmly and clearly, a slight nod to confirm the fact.

"Kids have bruises," Dad said. "He could have gotten that bruise anywhere. I don't know what he was up to five minutes before he saw me. Hell, I've got bruises I can show you. I've got a wicked bruise on my shin from a car door."

"You mentioned earlier that a cop's job isn't 'glamorous.' I believe that was the term you used," Erika said. "But there's a certain notoriety for solving a case like that one."

"Yeah, well, I've got that, and I can do without it," Dad said, leaning back a bit, comfortable. "Let me sit around and observe any day. It's not about notoriety. It's about safety—I want to make sure the people in my city can get where they're going and feel safe doing it. It's not about the police chasing down bad guys and taking them out. We are the community. We want to blend in and keep everything on the up-and-up, and that's it. We serve you. Some kid breaking

into homes, stealing what we work hard for, invading privacy, making all of us feel less safe, in some cases attacking us? That isn't helping his community. He's a detriment, and we'll see. Personally, I think the burglaries go away."

"Let's hope, James. Thank you for coming on," Erika said before facing the camera and sending to commercials. I didn't know if she sounded convinced or suspicious or what. I guessed she asked the questions, let Dad talk, and left the rest up to the audience. Not the best scenario, not the worst.

"Well? Did I look okay?" Dad asked, getting up and turning off the TV. It wasn't the hatchet job I'd feared. He was funny, self-effacing, but came off like he cared about the city and was doing the right thing. I'd think it was how you'd want your law enforcement to sound. He'd gone over it a hundred times with Ricky, too, so the interview was a big deal.

"James, you did wonderful," Rosie said. She'd come over to watch with us. "I think you'll win over a lot of people."

"Thanks, Rosie," Dad said. "You know what else was cool? I got to meet Brandon Peters when I was in the studio."

"The weather guy?" Rosie asked, eyes lit up. "I love him. He is so nice. He does events in the city all the time. He's so sweet, so good with kids."

"He's great, even off camera," Dad said. "Big poker fan. I tried to get myself invited to one of his games but no dice. The studio is small, too. The weather center is right on the other side of the news desk."

While Dad and Rosie chatted about weathermen, I was sitting at the living room computer to look up the news site and check out the video of Dad's interview there. That was where everyone could leave comments. He did well, but truthfully he could only sway opinion so much. Nothing up yet. Maybe it'd stay below radar still.

"How do I Google myself?" Dad had asked me, standing over me at the computer. He was in a good mood, especially with company over.

"You go to Google," I said. "And you Google yourself."

"Smart-ass," Dad said. "What else can I do? I want to find detailed stuff, time frames, specific websites." He was pretty old-school when it came to computers. He had e-mail, he went online, but he wasn't really "connected" 24-7 like most people.

"You can use quotation marks around multiple words, like a name, to search for exactly what you want," I told him. I showed him how to narrow the results down by time, so we could see stuff posted only after the interview. I showed him too much, probably. Dad was used to being supercop, man around town, but not everything said online about him was going to be good. In fact, with this case going on, I couldn't imagine he'd want to know what anyone was saying about him. *Give a man a fish, feed him for a day. Teach a man to fish, and watch him drown himself.*

"Let me take a look, Walter," Rosie said, and I got out of the seat. "I'll let you know if it's safe."

"I wouldn't do it," I said. Dad didn't grow up with the Internet. He just kind of found it as an adult. He thought the world was his friend online, but of course I knew better. "Who knows what's on there. The Internet's a wasteland."

"I've gotta be online. It's a preemptive strike," Dad said. "These are things you have to think about now. This isn't five, ten years ago. You have to think 'online.' You have to consider your social-media image." Dad sounded convoluted. He really was a mess. I didn't know a single person who used the term *social media* in regular conversation. "People can smile to my face, Walter, tell me I'm doing a good job, but online it's a whole other world, brother. You have to look at your public image and your online profile."

My dad called me "brother."

"Your father's being proactive, sweetie. It's a good thing," Rosie said in her soothing voice. "Now is not the time to sit idly."

"You guys don't understand the Internet, though," I said. "These people are going to bait you in, get you to say something stupid, and then it's all over. It's called troll-baiting, and you're going to play right into it."

"You're assuming I'll say something stupid," Dad said, exceedingly proud of himself. "I'm right, Walter. I haven't done anything wrong, and that's my advantage. There's no slipping, no saying something stupid, because all I have to do is tell the truth, and I win."

I was on an after-school special. Dad was still convinced he was supercop, but he was just the underdog now.

"There's a lot of links here," Rosie said in the glow of the computer screen. "I hope I don't click the wrong thing and give your computer a virus, James."

"I'll click it, Rosie," Dad said, and Rosie wheeled the chair away from the computer. *Such a gentleman.*

"It's a dangerous time, Walter," Dad said to me. "People see a news story like this and they're all culture vultures. Everyone expects that the cop is crooked, the world is racist. And they're hunched over, primed to pounce with fingers wagging, the mob mentality. Once that kicks in, it's over, I'm out of a job, doesn't matter anymore who's right and who's wrong."

"Do you have a plan?" I asked. He had awareness, at least, but it still felt like he was in over his head. I guess that couldn't be avoided.

"Yeah, I have a plan," Dad said. "I need to defend myself and what I know. And I know what happened that night. Have some faith in me. For now, I just need to keep this thing from going viral."

I went to check out what I could on my laptop in my room. Plan or no plan, I could still stay a few steps ahead of him.

Our local news site had some comments on the interview now. They were more revealing than the actual news. Everyone seemed to have issues with the police department. One person said she couldn't get past the bridge without doubling her chances of getting stopped. One person got the same officer pulling him over every time. Another person said they had to deal with three cops for going ten miles over the speed limit. Mr. Mills was right: the race stuff got heated quickly.

Proud Whitey: Uh-oh, it was a black kid? Start the timer! How long before this guy's lynched by the media?

The Real Deal: Lynched? Really, that's the word you're going to use?

Proud Whitey: Waaah. How much does it pay being a professional victim? I could use the work.

Miss Monroe: You're the one making it about race. Sit there complaining and collecting your welfare checks.

I closed my laptop, got into bed, and hoped all this bad-cop business would be gone by morning. I fell asleep to the sound of Dad typing away on the computer.

•   •   •

Dad was glued to his computer the next few days, and I tried to stay out as much as I could. It's a weird thing for me to sneak out of the house and have a secret from Dad, especially a cop dad, but he was so involved with everything going on in his own life he didn't bother to ask where I went anymore. So I was at Naomi's a lot.

Naomi's room was at the top of the stairs, and the next room over was Jason's. Privacy was not an option. We were allowed in there as long as the door was wide open. It was a new feeling to be in a girl's room that wasn't my sister's. It was kind of the same, with the same stuff you wouldn't find in a boy's room—makeup, teen magazines. But it felt a little more dangerous when it was your girlfriend's room.

It was both crowded and clean, full of stuff but organized well. There was a TV, an iPod speaker setup, a desk with her laptop, books and magazines, DVDs, a walk-in closet. Almost every corner of the room had some unique use. Each wall had its own central purpose—the door, the mirror, the window, the closet, and the bed.

Naomi and I were kissing there until we heard footsteps approaching. Then they stopped, and turned around, heading back away. We laughed. Naomi picked up my hand and was studying my hand and fingers, then reached over for a marker and started to draw. The marker tickled my palm.

"This is the only thing I can draw," she said. "I had a book on drawing when I was a kid. The only thing I remember from it is how to make this cat."

"This is my favorite cat," I said. "I'm going to adopt it." The cat was simple and cute. I couldn't draw much myself but had sketchbooks of comic-book characters I'd try to copy. I was okay at it.

"This door was open wider before, wasn't it?" Naomi's dad said, suddenly in the doorway, shoes off. He was finding ways to mask his footsteps.

Naomi had fought for the bedroom use. Her parents were initially set against it, and I was fine with whatever. If they didn't like us being in the bedroom, then I was happy wherever we ended up. But Naomi argued that all her stuff was in her room. Her parents argued she could bring it out into the living room. She argued, "But *you're* in the living room." And they argued that so were a nice big TV and a comfy couch and plenty of room. Naomi insisted not everything she has to say needs to be heard by her mom and dad. But really she just wanted to be able to kiss.

"Put a brick there or something," Naomi said, finishing the cat drawing. "There's a draft from you walking by it every ten seconds." Sarcasm was so prevalent in the house it wasn't even acknowledged half the time. He set off to look for something heavy to block the door open.

"I want to draw you something," I said while admiring my cat.

Naomi reached under her bed and pulled a sneaker out. She wanted me to draw on the shoe so she could look at it wherever she was.

I played with the marker cap while I thought of what I could draw. I thought of comic-book characters, the sea monster I had at the sushi place. I thought of noir movies. I decided on a cityscape. The view from on top of the city. I started by drawing boxes for each of the buildings and a skyline behind them.

Music started blaring from Jason's room. He was listening to Notorious B.I.G.'s second album. Naomi rolled her eyes and pulled her laptop up onto the bed. She opened up Facebook.

"Have you seen this?" she asked. "It's a page about the burglaries and all that stuff. Some stuff about your dad. Everyone keeps liking it, so it's always on my profile." The page was called POLICE AND COMMUNITY IN EAST BRIDGE. It was supposedly about local politics, but it'd been made right after the Temple case blew up, and that was all anyone talked about on it. There were kids from school on there, people I recognized from the neighborhood, some people I didn't know, and, of course, some trolls. I had seen it, but I hadn't gone looking for it. Facebook and sites like it were a clutter for commentary I tried to avoid. I was connected like everyone else, but you lose something in all that connectivity. Individuality gets lost in the noise.

"There's a picture of my dad," I said, looking at the screen. It was a picture from a newspaper article my dad was in a year ago. He's standing by his police cruiser with sunglasses on. He looked a little conceited out of context, when you grouped the picture with the case that was going on.

"You might not want to click it," Naomi said, spinning the laptop to me. "I can't vouch for anything crazy that people write on there. I'm not even allowed to post on this page."

I clicked on the picture.

Fannie Sanchez: Same guy that pulled my kid in for doing nothing. Wrong place, wrong time, I guess?

Darren Harrington: It's a long line of bloated egos, police force is full of em, they just want the badge and the gun so they can play tough guy.

Arturo Morrison: He couldn't handle my gramma.

Ken Palmer: I'm not urging anyone to do anything stupid, but I know this guy's address, DM me.

Naomi pounded the wall with her fist and startled me. "Jason, turn that down!"

I backed out of the picture and spun the laptop back to Naomi. "Yeah, I've seen enough," I said. This was getting unnerving, fast. Was that even legal? I didn't want to look at Facebook again.

Naomi clicked on something. "It looks like your dad is replying to posts on here. That's probably not good," Naomi said. I rested my head on Naomi's leg.

"There is no universe in which that is a good thing," I said.

211

The music was still blaring. "I don't want to look at it. What's he saying?"

"Just defending himself," Naomi said, presumably looking for anything interesting. "He's on, like, every post almost. He's all over this page."

"*Your gonna lose your job*," Naomi read, overpronouncing the misspelling of *you're*. "*They should just start clean with a whole new police department*."

"It's '*you're*' *gonna lose your job*," Dad had replied. He was correcting grammar. My dad wasn't getting trolled; he was the troll. Naomi and I laughed at that. I needed a laugh. Hopefully he could pull some strings and get the address guy arrested before anyone took him up on it.

"A week ago I wouldn't have imagined this would be an actual issue in my life," I said. "My dad on the Internet, riling up drama."

Naomi read one of the other comments. "*My job is to protect the community, so every action I take should be viewed through that lens. I am serving us all*."

"He almost sounds guilty," I said, sitting up. I grabbed the marker and shoe and started coloring in some of the buildings on the sneaker, making them all black with white windows. Other buildings I left the other way for contrast. Her left shoe was going to look empty now, but her right one was decked out. "Who even talks like that?" I asked. "He's going to get ripped apart. Why can't parents just leave the Internet to us?"

"My parents are on Facebook, too," Naomi said. "It's major drama in the Millses' home. Jason won't add them, so they were threatening to ground him, like he must be hiding something on there. Which, of course, he is."

"Your dad friend-requested me," I said. "Should I add him? I didn't know if that was weird or not. I probably shouldn't, right?"

"He's kind of funny. You can add him," Naomi said. "You'll get a lot of requests to play games, though, heads-up."

I presented Naomi her shoe. "Hope I didn't ruin it," I said.

"Come here," Naomi said when she saw it. She pulled me in by my cheeks for a kiss. And her dad was in the doorway. *Knock knock.*

"You know, I think there is a draft," he said. "Maybe we need a doorstop to keep this thing open. Maybe we should just take it off completely . . ."

And he left. "Your dad's the best," I said, and Naomi laughed.

• • •

EAST BRIDGE OFFICER BEING INVESTIGATED HAS HISTORY OF PROBLEMS

Op-Ed by Barry Sharp

THE EAST BRIDGE police officer at the center of the Basement burglaries case is Officer James Wilcox, who the regular readers of the news may be aware of already. All it took was a glance at Wilcox's personnel file from the city to find a laundry list of earlier reprimands, which are very informative for his current and ongoing troubles.

Nearly three years ago, we find Wilcox's first suspension, one he did not fight and served a month of. The suspension was originally for two months. The suspension came about after an internal affairs investigation involving a neighbor who accused Wilcox of threatening him with his gun. In addition to the suspension, Wilcox was required to hand in his weapon when off duty for at least the following year. This is post-LEOSA, the Law Enforcement Officers Safety Act, enacted in 2004, which allows an officer of the law to carry a weapon at all times.

Following that incident, Officer Wilcox was also under investigation for leaving a crime scene unattended. The fallout of this case has been obscured or covered up, and no penalty seems to have been handed out.

Perhaps most telling of Wilcox's character, and most influential on his current investigations involving the alleged "Basement Burglar," Calvin Temple, is a report from only last year in which he referred to an African American man involved in an altercation as a "gorilla." In a police department with a long history of problematic racial relations, that they still have officers calling black men gorillas is ridiculous to me. That they're still on the street and adding to their extensive personnel files is even worse.

"As far as I know, he made his apologies and no charges were ever filed," Sgt. Peter Chandler, president of the East Bridge Police Union, said about the incident.

There were five such incidents contained in the reports, but nearly all ended quietly or unclearly, presumably "swept under the rug." How this case involving the Temple family turns out is anyone's guess, though don't be surprised if by this time next year, no one seems to remember a thing about it.

"Who is this guy?" I asked Dad.

Dad was freaking me out, slapping his palm against the table while he read the column. His face was red, his mouth was clenched shut. He paused a good few seconds before answering.

"Barry Sharp," Dad said with distaste. "Some dirtbag that made a name for himself off the Eric Garner ordeal. He's a professor at the university, thinks he's a civil rights leader, goddamn Martin Luther King. If it were up to Barry Sharp, we'd have a perfect color-blind utopia, and everyone would be immune to the law."

The article had been posted overnight on the news site and linked to on Facebook today. It'd run in the paper too, probably over the weekend. Dad hit the table again and let out a grunt.

"Hey, forget I said that, Walter, all right?" Dad said. "This guy just pisses me off, that's all."

I was looking at the article on my laptop while he was at the table on his. "Did you really threaten someone?" I asked.

"What's a threat?" Dad asked. "To me, if I pull a gun out, say I'm going to shoot you, that's a threat. No. I had some words with that friggin' neighbor; he took them to mean something. This was years ago. It'd been a misunderstanding. We cleared it up."

Seth. I didn't even know this stuff. I didn't really want to know.

Dad slammed his laptop shut and went to his room. I wondered if this was what he was trying to Google himself over, if this stuff was the "social media image" maintaining he had to do. Maybe this is what he feared would make it go "viral." I wondered if this could get worse still.

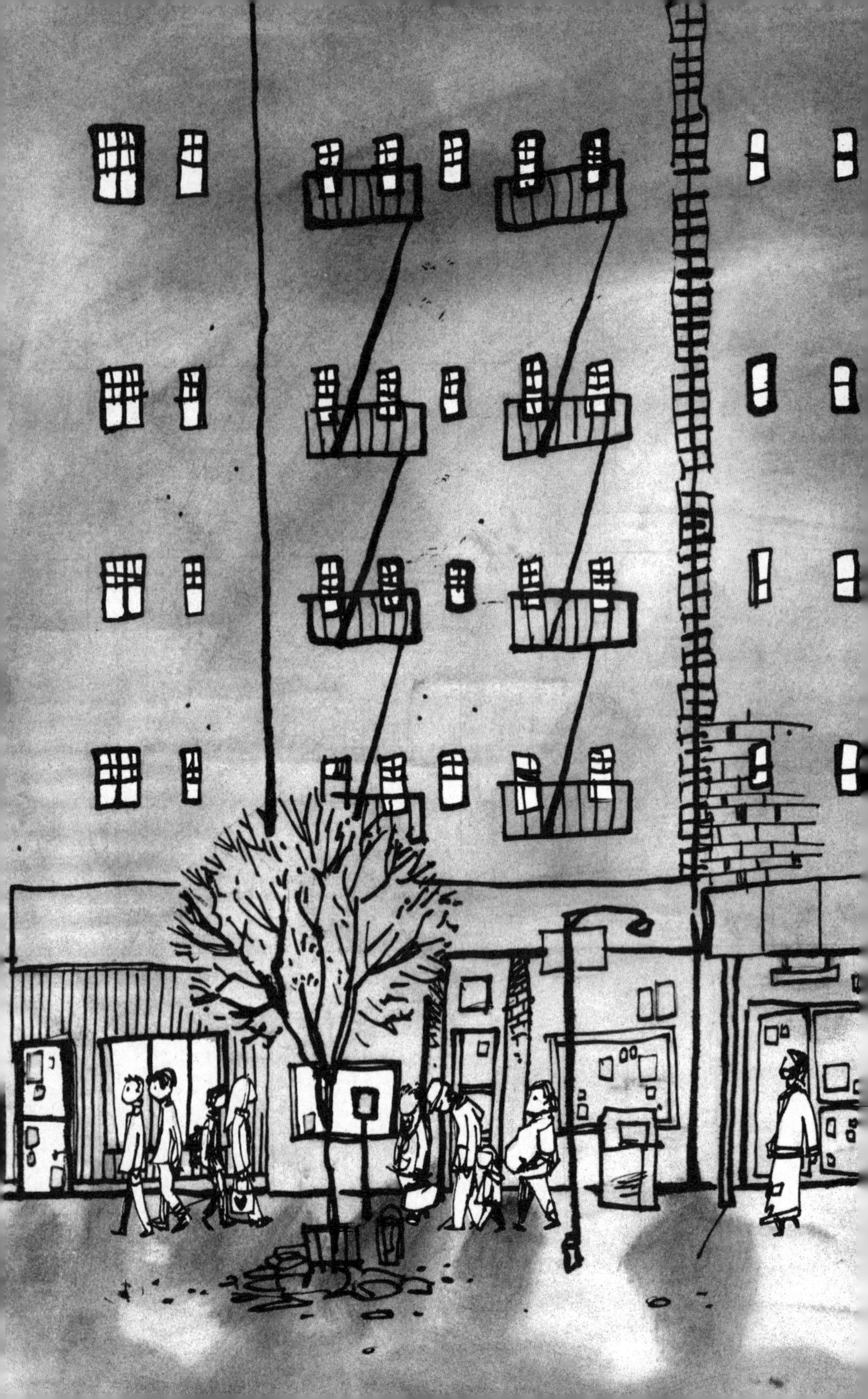

Chapter
Ten

"All right, guys, sorry for the wait. Saturdays are busy," our waiter said in an overly relaxed tone. "You want quick service, come in on a Tuesday around three—we'll get you right in." We followed him to our table.

"Could you put down your phone and act like an adult?" Naomi asked, nudging her elbow into Jason. We'd been waiting for a table at the pizza place uptown for twenty minutes, and Jason had his cell to his nose for the duration of it. We slid into our booth, Naomi and me on one side and Jason and his date on the other.

"I'm the oldest one at this table, Naomi," Jason said, and put his arm around the girl he came with, Jessica Barnes. Small, thin, and, from what I could tell, very agreeable, as she smiled, laughed, or nodded to almost anything Jason said. Sitting next to Jason with her braided hair, they looked a little like Will and Jada Pinkett Smith.

The double date was actually a favor for me. If there was a way to keep Jason from hating me, and especially from hating Naomi, I wanted to try it. We could still bring him in a little, help him feel like he's a part of things. Naomi agreed after a few days of general household nastiness I was only partially privy to. Loud music, hallway snubs, the top secret meeting Jason held with their parents. She was concerned that if we didn't do something, she was going to be ousted from the family.

Dad had long ago stopped questioning my whereabouts. He even gave me some money to go out, his way of showing me everything's fine and to let him worry about Calvin Temple and the case. I would gladly let Dad worry and take the money. I was going to have to get a part-time job soon if I was going to date Naomi. Anything we wanted to do cost money.

"Thanks for coming out with us anyway," Naomi said to Jason, dropping the attitude and remembering why we were here in the first place. "You know, I'm still your sister."

"And I'm still your friend," I chipped in, not that anyone asked.

"Aww," Jessica said, with a smile and a head tilt, beaming for her guy. They were sitting closer together than Naomi and I were, their sides touching.

"No, no aww," Jason said, taken aback. "What is this, an intervention? I'm fine." It was kind of intervention-like, taking Jason out and having him cornered, reassuring him he's still loved. Knowing there's a problem that needs to be fixed, Jason went right back to his phone.

I watched a TV in the corner over Jason. It was turned to ESPN. Naomi and I should have come up with a plan first. Maybe we still could. We needed some talking points, or even an endgame. I wasn't even sure what we'd consider a success or failure.

One of the waiters stopped by our table. "Jason!" The waiter bumped fists with him. At least he was happy to see someone.

"Hey, Reggie," Jason said. "Can you give us a minute? I'm with amateurs, so we still haven't decided."

Reggie shook his head and left. I had nothing, no plan. We were officially winging it.

"We should have gone to Giuseppe's," Naomi said once Reggie was out of earshot. "They have the thick crust."

The pizza places in East Bridge were in a constant war, so we always had that to talk about. There were Giuseppe's and Angelo's in the lead, but King's Pizza, Pizza on Main, and Tony's Place made sure the argument for best pizza never ended. We were in Angelo's, known for their long lines, loud atmosphere, and ginormous pies.

"Who likes thick crust?" Jason asked with his face crunched up. "They do the square pizza, too, I hate that stuff. Everyone knows Angelo's is the best, and keep quiet with that stuff, you'll offend someone. What do we want, anyway? You're going to embarrass me again."

"Sausage, and peppers, and quit being negative, you're annoying everyone," Naomi said. I agreed with her choice. Sausage and peppers. Not just because I was dating her, but because I'd eat pretty much anything on a pizza.

"That sounds good," Jessica said, presumably about the pizza but maybe about Jason. She nodded and smiled at us.

"Damn, get creative, this is Angelo's," Jason said. "They'll put my car keys on a pizza if we ask for it. Bunch of amateurs, act like you've never been in a pizza place before." He nudged Jessica and she smiled.

"Well, since you don't have a car, and that's disgusting," Naomi said, "we'll do sausage and peppers." I got her to come out here with Jason, but I guess asking for civility or kindness was too much.

"Hey, Reggie," Jason shouted to half the restaurant. "Half sausage and peppers, half pepperoni, and get us some Cokes."

"You got it, chief," Reggie said, poking his head out to where we could see it.

Jason laughed to himself. "Hey, remember that time Mom caught you playing dress-up?" Jason asked Naomi. He turned to me. "She wanted to try on makeup or something. She was, like, seven or eight, put so much on her face she looked like a prostitute or something. Bright red lipstick, like, caked-on eyeliner."

"Oh, you're a makeup expert now?" Naomi asked, offended. I got why she was short with Jason, since he was short with her, too. Maybe he was worse. And he was being unrelentingly negative. "You don't even want to talk embarrassing childhood stories, because you've got way more of them than I do."

Jason's eyes widened for a split second. "What have you got?" Jason asked, not backing down. This double date was building high-speed momentum in the wrong direction. I had to remember to stop having such good ideas.

"Two words: 'My Humps,'" Naomi said, apparently referring to the Black Eyed Peas song about Fergie's butt. "Jason actually pulled the family together for his one-man performance of freaking 'My Humps.' In front of Mom. Dad. Me. Alicia. I've got video—I could drop it on the Internet and kill your whole thing, Jason. No shame in your game, star child, like having Michael Jackson in our living room. 'My Humps,' top that."

Jessica leaned forward and burst out laughing. "That's a good song, baby," she said. Naomi leaned back and crossed her arms.

"Yeah, I know it is," Jason said to Jessica. "Walter, your girlfriend's getting a little out of control, wouldn't you say?"

"My boyfriend backs me up a hundred percent no matter what, Jason, but thanks for asking," Naomi said. Good to see they had this covered without me. I was good on the sidelines. I downed the rest of my root beer and signaled for another.

"You want to air out dirty laundry, Naomi, it doesn't get any dirtier than this," Jason said, nodding. "Fifth grade, school bus."

"Jason, *no!*" Naomi shouted.

"What's wrong?" Jason asked. "Sound familiar? Naomi poops her pants, like, a block from school. They had to drop off all the kids and turn around and bring her dirty ass back home. They're driving all the way to school with crap stink in the air, everyone trying not to throw up. Fifth grade—she was practically an adult! Mom and Dad were all freaked out, thinking we'd have to put her in adult diapers or homeschool her or give her up for adoption or something. Walter, you really don't know what you're getting into here."

Jason tilted his head, looking at Naomi.

"I was *sick*, Jason," Naomi said as Jason laughed like it was the funniest thing he'd ever heard. "And Mom and Dad were fine with it. I was sick! For, like, a week, jerk!" And to me, "He made up half that story!"

Jason laughed and laughed, while Naomi and I waited for it to stop and Jessica chuckled along halfheartedly. Crossing the lines of comfort. Naomi looked furious as I patted her back. "It's okay," I said. "That was then. You were sick."

"Jason used to make superhero outfits for his teddy bears!" Naomi shouted. "Chopping up his own expensive shirts. Mom was so pissed. He was making masks for his ragged old bears. He had, like, twenty of them, too, probably still does. Mr. Cool Rapper, playing with his stuffed bears."

"So?" Jason shrugged. "So what? That's cool. Superheroes are cool, teddy bears are dope, Mr. Foo Foo was the bomb. I'm a creative person, Naomi. You crapped your pants in front of a bus full of your peers. These are not the same thing. I got the worst one yet, even, and all you have is teddy bears and lady bumps, both cool. How's this? I come home from school, our older sister is teaching Naomi how to kiss. How gross is that? Right? My baby sister and my older sister fake-kissing their arms and stuff in the living room."

"Teddy bears are cute," Jessica said, in a desperate Hail Mary pass to turn a positive tide on this conversation. She held on to Jason's arm like a koala bear.

"You done?" Naomi asked Jason, her voice cold and flat. He shouldn't have brought up Alicia. Jason was going for the jugular. If he was trying to turn me off to Naomi, it wasn't working. She felt more real to me than ever. I took her hand in mine under the table.

"Yeah, I'm done." Jason chuckled to himself while his date smiled. Then he dropped the smiles and laughing and put on a serious face, locked in on Naomi for a second, and then on me. "Hey, I didn't start this."

Our pizza arrived and Jason's date and I dove in. I threw two slices on my plate and scooped up one. Food never tasted so good. Delicious diversion.

"We didn't start anything, either, Jason," Naomi said. "We wanted to do something fun, hang out and show you it's not the end of the world if Walter and I date. We're still the same people. We can still hang out, not that we did before." Naomi lazily took a small bite from her slice.

"Let's just put it all on the table," Jason said, picking up a large slice. "I don't think you two should be dating. At all. That's not going to change." Jason chewed on his pizza, waiting for a reaction. He didn't have to wait long.

"Good thing it's not up to you, then," Naomi said. She put down her slice and cut it with a knife and fork. She was relaxed enough to calmly cut up her pizza. She must deal with this stuff every day. It was too late for me, my face and hands were probably a mess already.

"Forget the fact that you're dating someone I used to be friends with," Jason said. I rolled my eyes. "But why can't you at least date someone black? I don't agree with it."

"Jason, you dated a white girl," Naomi said, a rising anger in her voice. She wasn't going to tolerate him much longer, and he was persistent in digging his own hole. "You dated several of them, in fact. You dated Jenna Cranby for, like, three months."

"Yeah, and I learned from it," Jason said, and put his arm around Jessica. Her eyes were fixed on the table. "I'm passing my knowledge on to you, grasshopper. You're supposed to learn from me. Besides, Jenna was bad news. All Taylor Swift and Starbucks. Walter isn't a real man, anyway. I know more than anyone." His gaze rolled over to me, like, *What are you gonna do about it?*

"Dude, come on," I said. Stray shrapnel was flying everywhere and I got hit. "We're still friends, all right? I'm not looking for a fight here."

"So you date my sister behind my back, but you're not looking for a fight, is that right?" Jason asked. "You don't get to pick and choose your fights, buddy. Not always. Besides, you're never looking for a fight—that's why you aren't a real man."

Naomi might have been used to this, but I wasn't. If he was like this with everyone, he should really get his ass kicked.

"What's a real man, then?" Naomi asked. "What does a real man do? Get a new girlfriend every week?" And to Jessica, "No offense."

Jessica smiled weakly and looked down. Probably not the date with Jason she'd been expecting. If anyone was an innocent bystander in all this, it was she.

"Walter's way more of a man than you'll *ever* be," Naomi said. "I didn't even want to do this! Walter's the one who wanted to salvage your friendship. He's the stand-up guy here. I just thought it would get you off our case if you saw how not-an-issue our relationship is."

"You guys care to take it down a notch? Put the weapons away," Jason said with a casual smile. He could change moods and tones and facial expressions to fit whatever he was trying to get at the moment. Now it was a smugness, that we were getting too worked up as if he'd been calm all along. "All I'm saying is this gets the thumbs-down from me," Jason said. "I'm entitled to my opinion."

"Well, tough titties to your opinion, Jason, because *this* is happening," Naomi said, pushing her body into mine and cupping my face with her right hand. "Mom okayed it."

"I don't care what Mom says," Jason grumbled, and ate his pizza while his undeterred date put her hand on his shoulder. He always got his way. With his parents, with his dates, and he thought he'd get his way with me and Naomi, too.

"How about a movie?" I asked. "Something where we don't have to talk."

∙   ∙   ∙

We lost Jason and his date after the pizza, and that was for the best. Tension was released as soon as we got out of there, and by the time we got to the theater down the street, we were both in a decent mood again. Jason might be toxic for a while, but I had faith it would pass. We were friends. That had to mean something to him somewhere.

We got our tickets for the new Thor movie and stood in line for popcorn. "I could just kill him," Naomi said, gritting her teeth. "Honest, I could. Is that bad? Is it wrong if I kill him?"

"I don't think so," I said. "I don't see why that would be an issue. He's your brother—it's almost expected."

"Right? If someone's going to kill him, it may as well be me," Naomi said. Hopefully no one in line with us was paying too much attention. "I'm just kidding," she said. "I'm not serious. I wouldn't do that, but I want to, strongly."

We were up next in line. "Popcorn?" I asked. "Do you want to get one and share?" Naomi nodded.

I looked around to see if anyone I knew was in the theater with us. I was actually there with a pretty girl and not my parents or sister for once, which felt pretty good. Naomi was looking around also, but she had other things on her mind.

"It's hard not to look at all these people and think of what they say on Facebook pages or on websites," Naomi said. "Do you think that or is it just me? Nobody ever says I deserve to be pulled over. Nobody tells me I look like a criminal. But they must be thinking it, because *someone* posts all that stuff."

"Everyone has something to say online. It's the Internet," I said. The theater was full, and everyone was lost in their own groups. "There's no consequence, so they say whatever stupid thing enters their heads. The rest of the time they're all too busy with their own lives to pay attention to anyone else."

"Well, stop right there. Racism exists," Naomi said. "It's not like it only happens when people are online and bored and anonymous. But you picture it in, like, really rural areas, and backwater places. Not . . . here. Why would you even live in the city if you thought like that? Those comments are on local news sites. They're about our neighborhoods."

"I didn't mean it like that. Really," I said. "I just meant I wouldn't take it personally. People are big shots online. Everyone wants to be the funniest, or the most controversial. Because nobody cares what you say online. You can get away with anything. So they just say whatever."

"So you don't think anyone's looking at us?" Naomi pushed. "They're all too wrapped up in their own lives?"

"No one's looking at us," I said. "If it's not their lives they're wrapped up in, it's their cell phones. Taking selfies. The lights will go off soon anyway. Everyone will forget everything as soon as the movie starts."

"So no one is paying attention and they'll forget us anyway?" Naomi asked, and pulled me in for a long, slow, very public kiss. She grabbed some popcorn out of my bucket and flashed a mischievous grin before popping one into her mouth.

"Wild child," I said, impressed.

•　•　•

Dad was on his laptop when I got home. He was always on there now. He had the large coffee mug out, a bag from the bakery down the street. His brow was furrowed. He didn't even seem to notice me come in. He was muttering to himself.

"Stop it, already," he said. "Leave it alone, just leave it alone."

"Hey," I said, walking over to the table, peeking at the laptop screen. "What's going on?"

"I was a hero just weeks ago," Dad said. "Everyone was celebrating the good deeds of James Wilcox."

"And now?" I asked. "What's going on?"

"The gorilla thing," Dad said. He pushed his laptop away. "Nobody cares about the gun stuff, the threat. It's the gorilla. Everyone's flipping out over some gorilla comment I made a year ago and nobody cared about then. It isn't even racial, you know? How is that a black thing? If a guy looks like a gorilla, I'm gonna call him a gorilla. I don't care what color he is."

I could see a comment thread on his screen that must have twenty back-and-forth replies on it. "Is that you?" I asked.

"This guy FThePolice95 won't drop it. He just keeps arguing. Every time I reply, there he is ten seconds later," Dad said. He was rubbing his temples, he could have been sitting there all day. "He's the goddamn King Arthur of the Internet. I'll write him all night if I have to. I'm keeping my name clean."

"Ninety-five is probably his birth year. It's some kid in his early twenties," I said. "Look at all those other responses. You've gotta get off of there."

"I'll get to them," Dad said. "I don't have a job to go to. I've got the time. I'm not letting Sharp win this one, Walter. You want to make yourself useful, there's a pot of coffee in the kitchen. Fill this up for me."

Dad pushed the mug over and pulled his laptop back in front of him. Barry already won. You can't beat FThePolice95. You can't beat them all.

Chapter Eleven

The Monday morning sky was a pale light blue with pink highlights. I stepped off the bus, which was mostly full of freshmen and sophomores this year, my head still trying to make sense of how that date had gone so wrong, so fast. As far as I knew, Jason and Naomi were laughing about it over green tea later that night. That was the way their family functioned. My goal for the day was to find Jason and see if we were cool, but somehow Lester found me first again. He was getting out of his dull-red nineties Mazda as I passed him, and he walked with me to the building.

"Wally Wilcox!" he said. "Do you want a ride to school, man? The bus is not cool. I've got a fresh new window and everything."

"Thanks, I'm good," I said. "It's just a few more months."

"Yeah, but you're dating now. You're going to parties, making friends," Lester said. "You don't want to be on that thing. Hey, we need to catch up. Your dad, man, what do you think? Officer Wilcox. I can't even believe the stuff I'm reading."

"That's about what I think," I said. "I don't believe it."

Lester got the door and kept walking with me inside as I headed to my locker.

"Well, I'm biased," Lester said. It was football season and he had his varsity jacket on. "It's kinda hard for me to side with the police on any issue. Did you know they can arrest you for just standing somewhere?"

"Like, loitering?" I asked.

"Yeah, *loitering*," Lester said. "You know Calvin? He's cool, and personally, I don't think he'd lie. But that's just me. Like I said, I'm biased."

"There's more to it, though," I said. But really I knew as much as anyone about what had happened. "Nothing I want to get into. I don't really want to talk about it, anyway. I want to keep as separate from all that as I can."

The school was filling up, as we had about ten minutes until first period. Lester kept walking with me, saying hi to people in the halls until we got to my locker.

"Hey, so Jason," Lester said to me, a little more quiet than his normal talking voice. I opened my locker, and he stood on the other side of the door. "I'm not supposed to say anything, but he's a little salty."

"Salty?" I asked. I'd say he was worse than salty, last I saw him.

"Yeah, angry," Lester said. "Did you really not tell him about the Naomi thing? That's bro code one-oh-one. If it were me, I wouldn't start a relationship dissing a girl's family, but that's just some free advice. That's a bad foundation, bad mojo, right?"

"I wasn't staking her out, going in for a move or something," I said, getting salty myself. I couldn't find my algebra book. My locker wasn't big enough to lose things in. "It just happened. When there was something to tell, we told."

"Hey, you like the CD I burned?" Lester asked, dropping the subject and ignoring my tone.

"Yeah, I did," I said. I wanted to stay friendly with Lester anyway.

"I knew it!" Lester said, and made a fist. He slapped me on the back. "Hey, take it easy, Wally."

Lester walked down the hall, light as air for a large guy and a spring in his step as usual. He joined up with some other kids not far down. I shut my locker and walked the other way.

•   •   •

We'd been getting rain and flurries the past few days, and the lunch-outside season was passing. Nate, Kate, and I had to eat inside the cafeteria for our break. The lunchroom scene was loud and smelly. Nate described it as a mix of bologna, tomato soup, and cleaning agents. Kids got their soda caffeine fix, saw the end of the day coming, and couldn't stay attached to their seats. Maybe we were old souls; our little group preferred to talk about TV and movies than to participate in the lunchtime noise factory. The rowdier tables sat any number of undesirables, Beardsley and Frankie included.

"Wilcox," I heard in a weaselly voice. He didn't even have to fight—his speaking voice was a punch in the face. Beardsley pulled his chair over to our table. He had a buttoned-up shirt over his skinny frame, shaggy hair falling into his eyes. "Wilcox, how's it going, man?"

"Fine," I mumbled, and bit into the grilled cheese I'd gotten from the café. There was no good way to get rid of someone like Beardsley.

"It's like a whole new Wilcox in the halls now," Beardsley said. Even his smile you wanted to smack off. "What's going on with your girlfriend, man? You hitting it?"

"Knock it off," I said, and put down my food. "I'm not doing this with you." I didn't want Naomi to even enter his warped brain.

"Leave him alone," Kate said. She didn't have an ounce of fear in her, and she barked her command full of disdain. "Go find someone else to pick on."

"Why does everyone always think I'm picking on them?" Beardsley asked. "I'm helping my buddy out, and no one asked you anyway, *Kate*."

"Don't talk to her, Beardsley," Nate said, more authority in his voice than Kate's, even. "Get out of here."

"Or what?" Beardsley asked. This could get ugly fast. Nate didn't back down from anything, and neither did Beardsley. I disappeared from the confrontation. I wasn't proud of it, but that was my instinct. To find a shadow and hide in it.

"That's up to you," Nate said. He was good. He seemed legitimately tough with essentially the same build as me.

Beardsley laughed. He put his arm on my shoulder, gripped tight, and made my skin crawl. "See? You see that? Nate *gets* it." He slapped his hand down on the table with a loud smack, drawing attention from other tables. "You've got a pretty girl like Naomi Mills and you can't do a thing to stick up for her. You can't even stick up for yourself. You're like a damn mouse."

"Beardsley," Nate said, "turn around and go back to your table before I slam your face into it."

"Nate, shut up," Beardsley said, showing no visible sign of fear. "Nobody cares about you."

"Just get lost," I said. Mumbled. Whatever. I was busy twirling my spoon in my yogurt.

"You know why I can't get lost?" Beardsley asked. He got in closer, talked quieter. "Because I'm *like* you. I like dark meat, too. I'd probably mess my pants with Naomi. That's why I have to ask you: is this whole thing some kind of cover-up? Did your dad make you do it? Everyone knows your family's racist. I mean, your dad should be fired, like yesterday."

"No, he shouldn't," I said, too flustered and angry for wit. "He's not racist."

"It's a fact, kid. Don't even argue it. You look dumb," Beardsley said. "My dad says every cop in his department is racist. Just be real about it. If I polled everyone in the cafeteria, one hundred percent of them would agree your dad should be fired. Come on, let's make a bet."

"You want to skip next period, Beardsley?" Nate said. He was as fed up as I was. "We'll go for a walk."

"You're so tough," Beardsley said. Frankie was laughing at the other table like this was a stand-up act. Big, dumb Frankie. "I've got a test after this, so I'll take a rain check."

Beardsley turned to a girl at his own table who had been listening to his performance. "Do you follow the news?" Beardsley asked her. "Do you know Officer Wilcox? The 'racist cop'?"

"Get the hell out of here," I said, and got out of my chair. "Leave me alone." Nate got out of his chair, too. Then Beardsley got out of his. Kate buried her head in her hands.

The standoff was over before it started; Mrs. Opton, with her absurdly large glasses, made her way over and asked us what was going on. By the time we all got our *nothing*s out, the bell rang anyway and that was the end of lunch. A second later, Beardsley pushed in his chair and grabbed a half-eaten slice of pizza from a plate at his table that wasn't his.

"Nice talking, Wilcox," he said as he took a bite, and headed off. Frankie was right behind him, laughing and shaking his head. I shrugged an apology to Nate and Kate, grabbed my stuff, and walked around Mrs. Opton to head out myself.

I was going to have to avoid the cafeteria, apparently. Everyone had bolted for the doors at the same time, and I couldn't breathe. I waddled one baby step at a time, someone's backward Yankees cap nearly touching my face. "Are you Walter Wilcox?" a tall blond freckled girl asked me on the other side of the cafeteria doors. "Your dad's . . ."

I gave a noncommittal nod. I kept walking, and she rushed ahead to keep pace. I had a math class to get to.

I'd felt a little more "fishbowl" since this whole thing started. People didn't go up introducing themselves to me, but I'd become something of a curiosity. Didn't mean I enjoyed it or wanted to answer anyone's questions, though. Or hear their opinions.

"That must be crazy," she said, and walked with me, out of the crowd. "Don't listen to Beardsley. He's a sad little boy. Your dad is a hero."

"Really?" I asked. I'd been consumed with the idea of being a target, worried about backlash or embarrassment. He wasn't "town hero" anymore, after all. He was "racist cop." I was taken aback to hear someone say something nice and actually acknowledge he wasn't trying to do anything bad. It just turned out that way.

"Truth is, we live in a crappy city," she said. "I know I don't feel safe at night. There's a lot of crime and bad things happening to people here. Like, I get the whole profiling issue, I get why it's controversial, and I don't think all blacks are crazy, violent people or anything like that. But," she said, and I could tell we were taking a detour here I wasn't on board with, "if you're a good citizen, then you have nothing to hide, right? And if you're not a good citizen, then I don't care what you think. If it'll make everyone else in the city feel safe to walk around at night, I don't think anyone should have an issue with getting pulled over or checked out. It's exactly what this city needs."

I didn't think that was what my dad was saying at all, but I really didn't know for sure. Maybe he thought like this girl did . . .

"But you or I wouldn't get pulled over and checked out, right?" I asked.

"If we looked threatening or suspicious, then absolutely we would," she said. "But my mom works in the court system, and she says it's a statistical fact that more crimes are committed by black people."

Why was she telling me this? Why did she even think it was okay to say this stuff out loud? I had to look around to be sure no one else was listening, or thought I was somehow contributing to this diatribe. She was talking to me like people talked online. Right after I'd told Naomi people didn't actually talk like that, that they were just looking for attention. You rolled your eyes reading it online. Hearing it out loud made me feel sick.

"It's part of living in a city," she went on. "Think about it, think of every building on every street and how many people are packed together in each one. You end up with people who have stuff living a short walk from people who don't. It's them and us, and we rely on people like your father to keep us safe. He's a hero."

If *stuff* was what separated us from *them*, then I was *them*, and so was Dad.

• • •

I was cutting in the kitchen: steak, potatoes, rosemary, lettuce, and tomatoes. We only had a few meals that we cooked, and this was one of them. I dropped the chunks of steak into the frying pan, and the olive oil popped and splashed. Dad had me cornered.

"So were you ever going to tell me?" Dad asked me, cleaning up some of the dishes we'd used in the sink.

"Tell you what?" I asked, although I could guess from his tone what he meant. There was only one thing I'd been keeping from him.

Dad turned off the faucet and dried his hands. "I have to see on Facebook that my son has a girlfriend?" Dad asked. "That's why you were hiding it every time I asked? 'Cause she's a black girl?" He tossed the dishrag to the corner of the sink and crossed his arms.

"No," I said. "I wasn't hiding anything. There's nothing to hide." What did he see on Facebook? I wondered if Naomi had changed her Facebook status, if it changed something on my profile. I wasn't even Facebook friends with my dad. I didn't even know he had an account until all this mess started.

"How long has this been going on?" Dad asked. How long officially, how long since I've been talking to her, or how long since I first saw her?

"Not too long," I said, putting the salad together. I couldn't read Dad, but he wasn't happy. "A week, maybe."

"No, this has been going on more than a week," Dad said. "You never thought to tell me? Walter, I asked you straight up if anything was going on. Repeatedly. I'm not blind. Coming home late, out all the time, that dippy smile on your face. I knew there was a girl. You lied to me."

"Whatever, it wasn't a lie," I said, which was kind of true. "I was figuring it out."

"And in all this figuring out, it didn't dawn on you to look at what's going on with us right now?" Dad asked. He got the spatula and passed me to the stove. "It's kinda bad timing, don't you think? Do I have to say why? All the girls at school and you picked the one that's gonna be news. Not smart, Walter, not smart."

"Timing?" I asked. I felt guilty a second ago, but now I was getting pissed off. "I met an incredible person, and it took me seventeen years to find her, Dad. The timing is fine. I wouldn't wait a day longer. I thought you'd be happy for me."

"It's different now. You know why," Dad said, tossing the potatoes into the pan with the steak. "Don't play dumb. If you wanted a nice father-son chat we could have had one weeks ago. Walter, you know I'm not going to ask you to stop seeing this girl, but try, just try, to think of what you're doing here, in terms of how it affects everyone and not just yourself."

"You mean how it affects you," I said. "And it doesn't affect you at all. Who I date has nothing to do with your lawsuit or job or some burglar at my school. It's not like I'm dating that kid's sister or anything. No one's going to care!"

"Oh no?" Dad asked. "Go check on your little Facebook picture, then. Welcome to the real world. It ain't pretty."

• • •

Dinner was quiet. When I got to my room afterward, I went right to Facebook. Naomi hadn't changed a thing on her profile and nothing had changed on mine, but I had become Facebook famous. On the Police and Community in East Bridge page, there was a picture of me and Naomi. From the movie theater the other night, kissing. It was captioned OFFICER WILCOX'S SON, WALTER, DATING A BLACK GIRL. DAMAGE CONTROL?

The same thing Beardsley had suggested at lunch. Naomi was always so stressed about people looking at us. How would she take someone snapping pictures of us and posting them on the Internet? She might never want to see me again. Let alone her parents were going to see this on Facebook.

There were already twenty-four comments on the picture. I got through a handful of them before I had to stop. I was convinced there was nothing good for me online.

Colin McNeil: I'm all for diversity, not racist, but we lose what makes us beautiful when we mix. Just being honest.

Crystal Hale: It's 2014, get over your outdated views.

Fred Mason: Gay is sick, color is fine.

Janet Perez: Gold digger? They're teenagers, that kid has no gold to dig.

John Hart: Well, she's in the news now.

Lauren Bailey: Sick of seeing strong black women lessen themselves. Really tired of it.

I tried calling Naomi right away, but it went to voice mail. A minute or two later she sent me an instant message.

11/24 7:58 NMillz: Hey

11/24 7:58 WalterW1014: Did you see it?

11/24 7:58 NMillz: Yeah . . . are you okay?

11/24 7:59 WalterW1014: I don't know, are you okay?

11/24 7:59 NMillz: It's messed up

11/24 7:59 NMillz: My parents are going to kill me.

11/24 7:59 WalterW1014: Who would do that? Whos taking pictures of us? Im freaking out.

11/24 8:00 WalterW1014: What if I'm being followed? What if my dad is? People on facebook have my address and everything.

11/24 8:00 WalterW1014: This is really sick. Do you think it's lester or beardsley?

11/24 8:00 NMillz: It's Jason

11/24 8:01 NMillz: Honestly I figured it out pretty much right away because that's the kind of scuzzy thing he'd do, but I checked his phone when he was in the shower, that pic was on there.

11/24 8:01 NMillz: And a lot of pictures of girls' butts at school but whatever

11/24 8:02 WalterW1014: Come on. I know he can be insecure but whats he even trying to do?

11/24 8:02 NMillz: And another thing, that photo was posted by the fb page, so either Jason runs it or he knows who does.

11/24 8:03 WalterW1014: So what do we do now?

11/24 8:03 NMillz: We fight.

Chapter Twelve

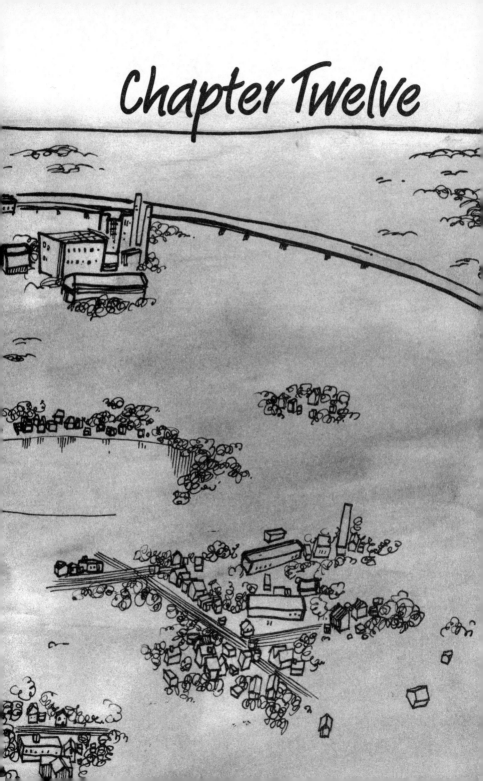

*O*n Thanksgiving morning Dad and I headed to his parents' house. We stopped for doughnuts so we at least had those to fill in the silence. Dad went over there some weekend nights to see his family, but I mostly was there on holidays.

Most of the city was known as East Bridge. Dad's family lived in the easternmost section, what we called King's Town. It was an especially white area, and more rural then anywhere else in East Bridge, with more yards, department stores, and strip malls.

My dad's side of the family was blue-collar. Hard work for little money, sharper language, and a lot more tattoos. Gran and Pop's house was the same little burnt-orange house they'd always lived in, up the hill from Foxon Avenue, home of defunct department stores from the early 2000s, tanning salons, and used-car dealerships. On a clear day they had a great view of the skyline across the city.

Dad and I were the last to get there around ten thirty. Smells of food and cigarette smoke filled the air. The decor had never changed, and the kitchen still looked like a seventies kitchen. My aunts and uncles were all there, and my cousins were there with their kids, who were busy running around and screaming. Gran Wilcox was hard of hearing, so she was the loudest, and we were met with a *"Here they are!"* when we stepped inside. She had a loud voice, but a frail body and dark poodle-like hair.

Pop Wilcox followed that up with *"Eat something!"* He was always telling me especially to eat something. He grabbed my arm and gave it a twist with his large hands to turn it red. It was his version of a hug. Pop had a sleeve of tattoos on his left arm, the centerpiece a large panther with yellow eyes. His own eyes were the trademark Wilcox light eyes, surrounded by harsh wrinkles. Dark tan from being outdoors so much. He had a motorcycle he used to ride until just a couple of years ago, when Gran had him sell it for extra money.

"You kids want some doughnuts?" Dad asked the kids in the room, putting the box on the already-full table. They said yes. "Don't you ever say no?" he asked. They shook their heads.

Dad pulled my cousin's kid, four-year-old Wendy, onto his lap, and she reached into the box to grab a doughnut.

"Powder?" he asked. "I put you on my lap and you pick a powdered doughnut? You spill any of that powder on me and you're under arrest. Don't give me that cute face."

My dad's brother, Uncle Joe, put me in a headlock. "Hey, kid," he said. He let go of me and picked up the half-empty box of doughnuts and said, "Glad you're keeping something off the streets!" to my dad. Joe was a tough guy, sleeves full of tattoos, too. A tangle of thorn-covered vines went down his right arm, a skull on the shoulder. His black hair was always slicked back. I thought he was the coolest growing up. I used to spend weekends at Gran's house when I was a kid with my cousins Danny and Samantha, and Uncle Joe would take us out bowling or to the arcade. He was a cop just like my dad, but for this district.

He married a much younger girl, my aunt June. The story I

always heard growing up was that my dad and Uncle Joe used to fight over her, even got into an actual fistfight, which my uncle won, and Dad relented. He ended up being the best man at their wedding still. The happy ending to the story was always how Dad met Mom just a few weeks after that fight.

"Hey, handsome," Aunt June said, which she'd called me for a long time. She never changed, either, always the big hair and makeup. "The girls noticing you yet? You're getting so big." She gave me a "precious" smile.

"Some, I guess," I said.

"Yeah? Some? One?" she pried. I really hadn't planned on talking about Naomi here. "Anyone special?" she asked, with that sly smile people get when they want details.

"Uh, maybe," I said, wondering how I could throw her off this track. "It's new."

"That's the best part, the new," Aunt June said. "I want to meet her! I want to see you with a little cutie, Walter. You're depriving us! How come you don't come around anymore? You used to be over here all the time. I miss it."

"Just busy," I said. "School, life stuff, new girl. I miss you, too." I did miss Aunt June, I did miss the family, but those had been simpler times. Things were changing—things had changed. I was a teenager now, and my parents had split up. I know I had changed, too.

"Bring her over sometime, will you?" Aunt June asked. "And don't be a stranger."

Aunt June patted me on the leg and went into the kitchen, and my cousin Samantha came into the living room. She had two kids now. The older boy, Jack, ran over to me and said "*Watch this!*" before clubbing his sister with a plastic sword. She started crying.

"Jack, give me that sword," Sam said. He shook his head. "*Now*," she said.

Sam sat down next to me on the couch in the living room, slouched into her seat, and relaxed her legs and the sword. She was only twenty-one, but I thought of her as a grownup. She caked on the makeup, too. Dark tan, blond hair, round face. Even when I was ten and she was fourteen, she was clearly the one with life experience. Sam had married at eighteen and already had one kid then. She and her husband, Dave, moved into a small house only a couple of streets away from Gran and Pop's.

"Just wait till you have kids, Walter," she said. "I'm gonna laugh so hard."

"You've got a long wait," I said. The idea of having a kid, let alone two within the next three years, was completely absurd. I felt closer to ten than I did to twenty. I'd only just now gotten a girlfriend for the first time in my life.

"It'll happen. It happens to everyone," she said. "Nobody plans on it, but we all end up with our litters." It was true for this area, especially. Or even in the suburbs with Mom and Dad. It felt like someone in the family was always announcing a pregnancy or wedding plans.

It was nice, Thanksgiving. The smells, the noise, the laughter. I felt too old to sit around with the kids, though, too young to have fun with the adults. I didn't know what to do with myself.

I wandered back into the kitchen and found some stuffed pepperoni bread to munch on. Dad was at the table talking to his parents about the case. The rooms had divided on their own with the kids all running around the living room now and the adults settled in the kitchen. With all the food in there, though, that wouldn't last too long.

"You'll be fine. You're one of the boys," Pop said. "I've never been a cop, but I know they take care of their own. Right, Joey?"

It was good to see Dad getting some support anyway.

"You want my advice?" Uncle Joe said, taking a cigarette out of the pack in his shirt pocket and lighting it. "Just keep quiet. You have a constitutional right to not talk. You've been there what, twenty years or something? It's not like you killed anyone. Guess what? It's a physical job sometimes. Just keep quiet and let it pass."

"You're missing the point, though," Dad said. He was finishing his first beer. "I didn't do anything wrong. This kid legitimately confessed. I don't need to be covered or looked out for. I just need my team to do the right thing by me."

"That's what I'm talking about," Uncle Joe said. "You're still fighting it. You keep talking, and eventually you're gonna say something they can use against you. And get the hell off that Internet, bro. If it wasn't for that thing, this would all be forgotten already. Every two days it's news all over again."

"No worries there," Dad said. "I've had my talking-to from the chief. Accounts deleted."

"Twenty-four-hour news cycle," Pop said. "Nobody's got anything important to talk about anymore. Imagine if your Grandpa was alive still." Pop coughed up a laugh. "He'd give you a reward for everyone you put behind bars."

It was embarrassing to listen to. Dad should have told them to shut up with that stuff, but he was laughing with them. God forbid he brought up Naomi. I'd wait in the car or walk to a bus.

My grandparents' generation thought those things, said them, and no one batted an eyelash at them. Our parents' generation was supposed to at least have some guilt over it. I'd grown up hearing this stuff, and I'd bring my iPod to drown it out with some

Eminem. I didn't pay it too much attention back then, but it all took on a new context now. I couldn't imagine bringing Naomi over. What would my great-grandfather say about her? About me and her? Would everyone laugh at that?

"Ain't that the truth," Gran said. "You don't see 'em around here."

"They didn't let any blacks in back in the sixties," Pop said. His mind seemed to wander. He looked a lot older since I'd seen him last. I'd thought of him as a big, intimidating figure, but he really wasn't anymore. He was just barely bigger than me. "Used to keep them out. I don't know if it was a law or an unspoken thing, but blacks knew you didn't come here. That all changed in the seventies. Now you got a few, but mostly they don't want to come here, still. Something in the air, I guess."

"Nah. It's changing," Uncle Joe said. "It's a slow process, but you see it happening, a little more each year."

"It's really strange," Dad said, hunched over in his chair. He grabbed one of the Boston cream doughnuts but didn't eat it. "Half of my team at work is black or Hispanic. My partner's Hispanic. They know me. I just don't get it."

Samantha's son Jack ran up to me and tugged on my pants leg. "Are you *gay*?" he shouted at me.

"Do you even know what that means?" I asked him.

"*No*," he shouted, before punching me in the balls and running back to the living room.

Thanksgiving left me feeling outside of everything, outside of my own body. Disconnected from my family, from Dad, from my school, and from the world. I sat in my room, on my bed, listening to the phone ring, hypnotized by the intermittent tones.

"Hello?" a voice on the other line answered.

"Hi, Mom," I said. I wasn't sure exactly why I'd called her, why I hadn't just called Naomi. I guess I wanted to save her from Melancholy Walter. So I reached out to Mom instead, since we were all about messy feelings and alienation. "Happy Thanksgiving," I said.

"Hi, Walter, that's a nice surprise," she said. "Happy Thanksgiving to you, too. What did you do today? Did you go see Dad's family?"

"Yeah," I said. "Did you go to Seth's family or somewhere else?" I didn't really have any idea what my mom did for Thanksgiving, or Christmas or any holiday. Maybe they were the hosts; maybe they did nothing. I'd been out of the loop for a long time.

"We did," Mom said. "Mel came with us, so that was nice. It gave me someone to talk to, anyway. It was a nice dinner."

"You needed Mel for company?" I asked. "Do you not get along with Seth's family or something?"

"I do, it's fine, and they're all very nice," Mom said, and then paused. "It's just a little weird. How do I even explain it? Let's see. We were both grown adults with marriages behind us, so it's not like bringing your high school prom date over."

"He's not sitting right there, is he?" I asked. "Don't incriminate yourself or anything."

"Oh no," Mom said. "He's downstairs painting. He paints these tiny little figures with a tiny brush. He has to use a magnifying glass to do it. It's a hobby."

Was Seth a nerd? This definitely called for some future investigating, but I had other things to figure out first. "So today was a little weird for me, too," I said. "I wanted to ask you something. Did you get along with Dad's family? It seemed like you did, right?"

"Sure I did," Mom said. "Aunt June and I used to go shopping together every weekend, and we'd laugh so much. We'd go get our hair done after. We had a ball."

"Oh," I said. Not exactly what I was looking for. "I'm not sure I fit in there."

"Well, you're pretty different from them, huh?" Mom asked. She sounded like she was settling in somewhere, getting more comfortable. I normally didn't like calling people, except for Naomi. I never knew what people were doing when I called, if they had time to talk or if I was being a bother. But this was going well. I hadn't been sure I'd ever talk to my mom again for a while. And now it wasn't even difficult. "You do take after me," Mom said. "We're sensitive types, masters of empathy. Not a lot of that on your dad's side."

"You think so?" I asked. It sounded like the opposite of what I was feeling. I didn't understand anyone and I hadn't empathized at dinner. I lay down in bed, getting comfortable.

"Sure," Mom said. "Remember when you stayed home from school and we saw the rabbit in the street? It got hit by that car and ran off into the woods. You were distraught all day over it. It's a good thing. It just means you can relate to others. You could have it like I do. Or did. I'd take on everyone's pain like it was my own. But that was different."

"Is that why you'd get depressed?" I asked.

"Well," Mom started, and paused. "Understanding someone's pain and actually being in pain are different things," Mom said. "And the lines got very blurry for me. Do you feel depressed?"

"No," I said.

"Well, good, then!" Mom said, uplifted. "Ta-da! Fixed!"

Maybe that fixed something. I felt less alone, anyway. "Just wanted to say Happy Thanksgiving," I said.

"Thank you, sweetie," Mom said. "Happy Thanksgiving to you."

●　　●　　●

I waited for Naomi on Friday morning outside the imaginatively named Café by the Park around nine. I sniffled. My cheeks felt like ice packs, but the sun was out and yesterday was a memory. I watched the traffic light turn green and red and back to green until Naomi arrived. And when she did, when I saw her walking fast with her winter hat on, I got up off the window ledge and nearly ran to her. I surprised myself by how much I missed her already. Only a month ago I barely knew her, and now she was a part of me, something I could feel when she was missing the way I'd know my arm was gone if I woke up in the morning without it. We gave each other a big hug that lasted somewhere in the vicinity of infinite time and space, and then we went into the café.

The café wasn't full, but there were a few people there. A group of five was sitting near the window; there was another couple there. A few people were there reading or on their laptops.

I ordered while Naomi got our seats. As I brought our heated-up pastries over, Naomi was looking at her phone.

"Friggin' Lester keeps texting me lately," Naomi said. "When have we *ever* hung out? And now he keeps asking me. It's getting really annoying, but I feel bad saying that."

"Really?" I asked, wanting to get a glimpse of whatever he was texting. I sat down across from Naomi. "That is kinda weird, though, right? I don't think you need to feel bad. It's a little disrespectful to us, too."

"How's that?" Naomi asked, and put her phone on the table. She took a sip of coffee.

"Well, he's been weird around me, too," I said. "I think he's jealous of us. He didn't say anything, but I definitely caught a vibe."

"No," Naomi said. "I don't know what it is, but it's not like that."

"I'm serious. I think it is," I said. "He's always asking me about you. It's not crazy to think he's jealous. He sees me with you, and he wishes it was him."

"Stop making it weird, okay?" Naomi said. "We do have some history. Maybe he's just going through something. I should probably see what's up."

I didn't say anything. It seemed naïve to completely discount it as a possibility, but I could see this wasn't going to be a productive conversation.

"Are *you* jealous?" Naomi asked, and then shook her head. "I'm sorry, forget I said that. I didn't mean it. That was mean."

"No, I'm sorry," I said. "I don't know Lester that well. I'm

jumping to conclusions. I just know I'd be jealous if I saw me kissing you. I'd kick my ass."

Naomi smiled. She picked her phone back up. "My parents are freaking out over the picture. It's one thing to have a bunch of nasty people talking about your daughter, and it's another to see a picture of her making out with her boyfriend. They think I'm going to pull an Alicia and go nuts, rebel child or whatever."

"Ugh," I said. My coffee cup was still really hot. I hadn't even sipped from it yet. Naomi was owning her coffee—she didn't care if it was hot or anything. That coffee was good to go. "I guess this wouldn't be a parent's ideal scenario for their daughter's first relationship."

"They're worried about your dad, too," Naomi said, sipping her coffee. "Worried about you. Worried about me. They're basically shedding years off their lives every day—it's out of control."

"Ugh," I repeated. I wondered what their worries were, if they lined up with my worries or Naomi's. There was getting to be a lot of worries to keep track of. Maybe we could meet up and swap worries and chart them out on a piece of paper.

"This is disgusting," Naomi said, eyes still on her phone screen. I wished she'd stop looking at the comments. "You see this? There's a hashtag on Twitter. My parents would kill me if I responded to any of this."

She tilted the phone to me, showing me the search results for "#racistcop."

So she responded in person, to me. "*Give him life or he keep on doin' it,*" she read. "*Hashtag racistcop. Ignorant.*

"*Leaving America over hashtap racistcop,*" another one read. "Boy, bye," Naomi said.

"Let's see." She scrolled for another one. "*Kid's got jungle fever, funny as hell.* What does that even mean? Who says that, '*Jungle fever*'? Give me a break.

"*That girl in the pics, tho,*" she read, referring to herself. "That girl's gonna beat your ass if she ever sees you. Hashtag pissed-off Naomi.

"*This hashtag racistcop ho, getting nasty in the theater,*" Naomi read. "'Ho'? I'm kissing my boyfriend—so what? Who the hell expects their picture to get posted on the Internet? I'm tired of these no-brain cretins online, can't think for themselves!"

"Don't look at that stuff," I said. "You're right, it's all idiots on there, and who cares what idiots say?"

"If it's about me," Naomi said, "then I care."

Even one comment like that can stick like a leech and worm its way into your brain. I felt now like Naomi did when she sat in the middle of a restaurant, like we were being watched or whispered about. Naomi was embracing the negativity with vigor. She actually insisted we sit in the middle of the room now.

I took a sip of the coffee. I grimaced.

"Is it bad?" Naomi asked. "Did you put any sugar in it?"

I shook my head. I had never ordered coffee before, so I didn't put anything in it. I took it to the counter to add some cream and sugar to it. "Mmm," I said, taking another sip. "Tolerable."

Naomi sipped her coffee and looked at her phone again. It had become addictive, for both of us. There was nothing good on there, just arguing and bile and hatred, but we were involved now. If there was ugliness around, we should at least know it was there.

"Who asked these idiots for their opinions, anyway?" she asked. "Why do they care who I date, or who you date? They don't know either of us."

"Bothers me, too," I said. "I wish they'd find something else to debate. I don't want the attention."

Naomi put her phone in her pocketbook. She took a deep breath and looked at me for a second. I raised my eyebrows. "Can we talk?" she asked.

"Yeah. We aren't talking now?" I asked. "That whole time you had the phone out, that was talking. Don't worry about it. I'll catch you up later."

"Do you like me? Like, really like me?" Naomi asked. Something must have popped in her head because her mannerisms were all different suddenly. "None of this was going on when you first kissed me and I don't want you to feel like you're stuck in it. With the websites and opinions everywhere. It feels different now."

"I like you. That's not different," I said. "I like you even more—you know I do. I like-like you."

Naomi laughed. "You're such a dork. You didn't have to say that."

"It is what it is," I said, looking around the room. No one paid any attention to us. We were just another dizzy couple getting coffee on Friday morning. "It'll pass."

"That's the problem. It doesn't just pass," Naomi said. She twisted her mouth with distaste. "I have it all right, I'll admit that, but I'm still a minority. I still get judgments, and I have fears that you don't really have to face. This sounds like an insult, and I promise I don't mean it as one, but you're *white*. All this stuff with your dad, that will pass. It may take a week or a month or however

264

long, but eventually it'll go away. But if you stay with me . . ." Naomi began to trail in her thoughts. "I'm just saying, it's a long road, and—"

"I'm staying with you," I said, touching her knee under the table. I wanted to take every fear and pain of hers entirely. "That's their world, okay? Our world is right here. It's a happy one."

"I like-like you, too," Naomi said, touching my hand on her knee. She nodded. "I really do. I like you a whole lot."

"I like you even more," I said. "I like you more than anything in the world. I want to be right here with you, right in the middle of this room, okay?"

Naomi nodded. "If that's true, we'll be okay," she said. I leaned over the table and she leaned in and we kissed. And with that kiss, I could tell her coffee was much sweeter than mine.

Chapter
Thirteen

School was becoming increasingly claustrophobic and one of my least favorite places to be. For a supposed empath, I didn't trust anyone there. As I walked between classes, the halls were flooded with faces I'd seen a million times but I'd never viewed them all as potential enemies like I did now.

"Walter!" I heard calling behind me. "Earth to Walter!" It was Kate's voice. Where had Kate been? I felt like I was on everyone's radar but couldn't remember the last time I'd seen Kate. She caught up to me.

"Where have you been?" I asked.

"Me?" Kate responded, and hoisted her bag over her shoulder. "Where have *you* been?"

We walked fast, navigating between oncoming people like a scene out of *Star Wars*. Kids were walking fast with a bounce in their step, everyone with direction and purpose, confident in where they were going. "I've been around, haven't I?" I asked.

"Not really," Kate said. "I'm guessing this Naomi is keeping you away?"

"Can I ask you something?" I asked.

"Can you stop asking things?" Kate asked. "What's up?"

We turned down the hall, still walking fast, although now we weren't walking to my next class. I hoped we were at least walking to hers. "Do you like Naomi?" I asked. "Like, do you think we're a good match? Or no? You can be honest. I mean, you haven't really hung out with her or us or anything—"

"Did I miss the invite?" Kate asked.

"Huh?" I asked, and then walked straight into a kid built like a brick wall and fell on my butt. The kid didn't even stop moving but muttered a "dude." Kate laughed and helped me up. I guess I hadn't invited her. I hadn't included any of my friends in my relationship. Maybe I was on another planet lately, one with just me and Naomi.

"You're such a nice guy, Walter," Kate said. "You're a goddamn sweetheart. Yes, I love Naomi even if I've never met her, and I can't wait to meet her, and she's incredibly lucky to have you."

I smiled. "Is your class this way?" I asked. She shook her head and laughed. "Mine, either. I'm back that way."

•   •   •

After school I sat in the library waiting for Naomi to finish her harp lesson. I'd been in the library a lot lately. The eternal refuge for thrill-avoiders. I could avoid everyone outside while I was there, but I was still drawn to the people I didn't know, online.

I parked myself at the computer and checked the Internet to see what hatred was being floated now. The news websites and comments sections were eye-opening, but there were other sites that reprinted the same articles on a more national level. The people leaving comments there weren't locals. They weren't people who knew anything about my family or our police department or what goes on in the city. These were people from wherever, *Anytown, USA*. Who were these people who felt so compelled to comment on everything?

The article was about Calvin Temple's lawsuit against the East Bridge PD, but the comments spiraled away immediately.

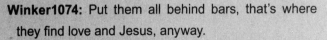

Winker1074: Put them all behind bars, that's where they find love and Jesus, anyway.

WakeUpPeople: Bunch o race hustlers!! Media turns everyone against each other and won't stop until there's war! Burn down the media, burn down every news station, only way we'll ever have peace!!!

CoolGuySammy: Blame the obamathugs, it's the ghetto people that cause all the violence and feel the most entitled to free everything, rent, food, gas.

It was addictive in the worst way, reading line to line, comment to comment. Every time you scrolled down, more popped up. You lost yourself in the noise of everyone else, and in this case you lost yourself to hate, you became one of the millions. Every time I sat at that computer I was leaving my body, joining some celestial primordial soup with every other thought and feeling floating out there, and when I got out of that soup, I needed a shower.

The soup and the world were blending. It felt like everyone in the school knew about Dad and knew who I was. I questioned every look I got. Everyone knew about me and Naomi, about my Mom and Dad, about every little thought I'd ever had.

I read those words online but they could have come from anyone at anytime. The kid sitting across from me. *"It just seems odd, is all. I mean, the timing is highly suspect. No one believes you're actually dating her."*

The librarian. *"People are going to look at you. Everyone's going to have an opinion. Get used to the whispers. Hashtag racist cop. Hashtag jungle fever."*

"We're all gonna look the same in another ten, fifteen years." The girl with her face buried in a book. As far as I was concerned,

every pair of eyes in a fifty-foot radius was set on me. *"If God wanted us all to be one race, then we'd all be one race."*

I looked back at the computer and opened Facebook. At least I didn't have to worry about Dad's online meltdown anymore. Not that he was doing much better without the Internet. When he was online trying to protect his image he'd been busy. Now he was just watching TV and eating, waiting for something to change. Jason was making all the commotion now, and the rhetoric had spun increasingly negative. The page was run over with trolls trying to out-funny each other. More comments on the infamous Walter and Naomi kiss picture.

> **Anonymous**: Hey I know that girl. Didn't realize she liked white guys. I've got something for that dark bitch, I'm gonna have fun with her.

Who the hell was Anonymous? He'd left a bunch of comments.

> **Anonymous**: I wonder if she's one of those ratchet ho's I hear about, guess I'll find out soon enough.

> **Anonymous**: I've been wanting to show one of these girls what a strong white man's capable of for a long time. I can't wait.

> **Dan P**: Real nice, sicko.

I clicked on Anonymous's page, but there was nothing there. The page was empty, no picture or anything. The page was fairly local, though. I mean the case had gotten some national attention, but the Facebook page was for people in East Bridge. It didn't even name the case or my dad or anything. Who was this person? Did he actually know Naomi? This was going too far, and I was ready to knock his teeth in and I didn't even know who he was. Who was talking about my girlfriend like that? Did people think this was funny?

Naomi dropped into the empty seat next to me, a dusting of snow on her shoulders and hat. A big smile, just for me. I shut the browser down fast before she saw what I was looking at. She didn't need to see it. Not this second, anyway. I wished I could get her away from the Internet or any of this stuff. I had a knight-in-shining-armor moment; I wanted to lift her up, put her on the back of my horse, find the dragon, and slay it. We'd trot off into the sunset, wherever that led. Some mythical warm place with no dragons, and no Facebook.

"I can't believe she didn't cancel my rehearsal!" Naomi said. She always seemed excited to see me when we hadn't talked, even for just a short while. "I know it's only, like, an inch of snow right now, but come on, snow is snow, right?"

"Yeah," I said. "They should just cancel, to be safe." Maybe Jason would step up and delete the comments. He obviously cares about her on some level or he wouldn't still be this mad. Maybe I could track down Anonymous and beat the crap out of him before she ever had to worry.

"I could be home right now, sitting in front of the fire in my fuzzy slippers," Naomi said.

"You don't have a fireplace," I said. And then I noticed Jason over Naomi's shoulders, looking through a shelf full of books.

"Well? You want to get going?" Naomi asked. Jason hadn't

looked over at us yet. I wasn't sure if he'd seen me or not during the hour or so I was there.

"Hang on," I said. "Jason's here. Should I check in? Like, just to say hi?"

"Could," Naomi said. "You want me to come with?"

"Better not," I said. "Didn't work out so well the last time we were all together."

Something about the library atmosphere, the familiarity of seeing Jason there, struck a nerve with me. Even in the summer when school was out, Jason and I kept our routine. But I had to see Naomi when I could, and there was homework to do still, and life in general had gotten a lot more chaotic in a short time. Comic stores and library chats were expendable. Not that it mattered now. Jason would take a bus to the next-nearest comic-book store before stepping in there with me. That was how it felt, anyway.

"How's the demo going?" I asked. Jason was standing by a wall of books with his eyes glued to a thick one he was holding.

"I don't rap anymore," Jason said, not looking up to acknowledge me. He turned a page in his book. "More important stuff to do."

"We need to talk," I said. "I know you're on there posting stuff about me. On that Facebook page. Is that your page? Are you running it? I get that you're mad, but this is serious stuff. And Naomi's getting hit there, too. It's messed up."

"It's just online," he said, and shook his head. "Don't worry about it." He shut his book and stuck it back on the shelf.

"This is our lives, not some game," I said. "You're riling people up and you're trying to turn people against my family. Have you seen some of the comments on there? What did I do to make you so mad?"

"I'm just being honest, and you guys are wrong," Jason said. He picked another book off the shelf, refusing eye contact, not making any effort to think of me as a human being. "If you disagree with anything I say, you can post there, too, like your dad does.

"I'm friends with Cal, so I have to take his side in this," Jason said. "That's that. I'm pro-black, I'm anti-cop, anti-profiling, and honestly I'm not really down with you dating my little sister, either. So none of this should be a big surprise to you."

Lester and Beardsley joined the circus, coming into the library out of the snow like a burst of unwanted cold air, and streamed right toward Naomi. Beardsley threw his bag on a table.

"Is that Beyoncé Knowles in our little library?" Lester asked Naomi at the computers. "Oh, no, that's Miss Naomi Mills, diva in her own right!" Always charming.

Jason went back to his book. "Listen to these facts," Jason said. "Traffic stops have grown seven times in the last decade. Young black men and Hispanics are five percent of the population, right? But we're over forty percent of the traffic stops. Only six percent of these stops lead to an actual arrest, and they give these cops quotas to meet, they tell them to go bring in as many people as they can, so where do you think they go? *Us.* It's not just that, either. I don't drive, so that doesn't happen to me, but I get followed around in stores. People walk extra far from me on the sidewalk, I see old ladies holding on tight to their purses. I'm not that guy. I'm friendly. Stuff you wouldn't understand. You aren't me, you aren't Calvin. You're Walter Wilcox, son of Officer James Wilcox."

"Nice," I said sarcastically, and shook my head. I was Walter Wilcox, period. And what was wrong with that? I wasn't going to apologize for being who I was. I didn't live in some blissed-out white paradise like Jason and Lester seemed to think I did, either. I was just a person, same as anyone. And I was sick of being compared to some kid I'd never met. He was as tangled as you could get into my life, but I couldn't verify his actual existence.

"It's nothing personal, okay?" Jason said, grabbing his book bag off the table. "May the right side win."

That was when Naomi got the attention of the library. "No one asked you to wait for anything, Lester," she said, standing up and drenched in attitude. Voice raised. "Walter was right about you. You're a jealous, insecure, egotistical clod! And not very truthful, either. I tried to defend you because I thought we were friends, but we are *not*. Bye."

Naomi was out of the door before the librarian was up to shush her.

"Oh shit," Jason said, looking at me.

Lester called after her. "Whatever, let's see what you say next week." He looked around at the library. He didn't see me, as far as I knew. "Let's see what she says then. I'll be here."

I had to pass Lester to get my stuff. I was the pissed-off one, he should be ducking me, but that wasn't Lester. He locked his sights on me, gave me a nod. "What's up, Wally," he said. I ignored it, got my stuff, and went outside.

People looked at us outside. They talked to each other still, but they saw me coming out, they were waiting for me, and they were watching Naomi.

She was pacing like an army lieutenant. "Can you believe that?" Naomi asked me. "He said you were my practice run and now I need to get with a real man. He said I'm making him look bad; he doesn't wait around for girls. I told him I'm with you. Then he said, 'Which one of us do you want on your arm? I'm bigger, better-looking, and my skin matches yours.' Who says that? Who even thinks it—this isn't 1960 or whatever. And Lester's supposed to be like family or something. What does Jason think of that? What's my dad gonna think about that?"

"Do you want me to go talk to him or something?" I asked, although I didn't intend to leave her alone. She was melting down.

"Here's another thing: I'm sick of anyone having something to say about me, or about us," she said. "Next time someone says something to me—I don't care if it's 'You're a cute couple'—I'm smacking them in the face! I'm taking my boots off and going at them!"

"Stop," I said, and put my hands on her shoulders, I tried to get her to stop pacing, get her energy down a notch before she went back in there and caused a bigger scene. "Stop, calm down. This isn't good. We need to cool down."

"Why?" Naomi asked. "I don't need to calm down. *You* need to get angry."

I brushed the dusting of snow off the brick wall rail that ran along the stairs, and sat down. "Take a deep breath," I said. She did, reluctantly. We sat there for a few seconds, but I didn't think she'd sit much longer without saying anything.

"What kind of stuff are you hearing?" I asked. "We can talk about it."

"Doesn't matter. Let them talk—let everyone talk," Naomi said. Her foot was bobbing up and down, her determined gaze settled on nothing. "I've got something for them."

"I thought everyone was preoccupied with themselves," I said. I laughed. She didn't. *Nope.* "Everyone's obsessed with everyone else. Look at those celebrity tracking sites, every sociopath murderer we know every detail about. Everyone wants to know everything. I mean, that's it—that's what we're stuck with. There's no way around it. No point in fighting it."

"So what are you saying? You want to break up?" Naomi said matter-of-factly.

"No," I said. It was hard to talk to her sometimes. "Stop it. I'm just talking. I'm just thinking aloud. There's a lot to process."

She crossed her arms and took a long breath.

"Sorry," Naomi mumbled. She reached over and touched my wrist. She took my hand, squeezed it. "I get it, this isn't easy. I'm sorry. I'm not going anywhere, 'kay? I didn't mean that."

"I wish I could skip school for the rest of the year," I said with a sigh. That would make things a whole lot easier. "Do you want to get out of here before Lester comes out and crushes my head?"

"I wouldn't let him," Naomi said. A smile crossed her face. "You know I'm tougher than Lester Dooley, right?"

I did know that. I knew it now, for sure.

Chapter Fourteen

I stood at my bedroom door after dinner, listening for footsteps or TV noise, or any indication that Dad was anywhere other than his own room. That was what it had come to; I stayed in my room mostly and Dad in his. It was down-pouring change, and neither of us dealt well with that. The Wilcox family plugged our ears and waited change out. Dad was on a mission, though. He was playing a character, the down-on-his-luck underdog detective, out to break the case and clear his good name, and I was in the audience, meant to sit back and idly observe.

I decided it was quiet enough that I could head to the kitchen, but once I stepped outside my door, I saw Dad was reading an article on the Internet. He shook his head.

"God, this is serious stuff," Dad said, eyes still glued to the monitor. Dad had been receiving threats in his e-mail, threats that apparently I was a part of. "Could be 'trolls,' as you put it, but I can't take that chance. I've seen this stuff too much."

"What stuff?" I asked.

"You name it. You think I haven't seen violence out there?" Dad asked, closing the browser and facing me. "I see kids with guns, knives. I respond to threats. I see what goes on in people's homes. I'm not kidding you when I say it's a slum. I'm not just being colorful. Bad stuff goes on out there. Daily. This is where we live now, and you can thank your mother for that."

"It's not that bad," I said. "At least not with the people I know and go to school with."

"You're not going to like this, but I need to do my job as a parent," Dad said. This was what I'd been hiding in my room to avoid. "I want you to come right home from school for the next few weeks. However long this goes on. And I want you to stay offline."

"I'm not going to stay offline," I said. He was trying to keep me from Naomi. He could use all the rationale in the book, but if the end result was that I couldn't see Naomi, then we both knew what he was doing. "I need to go online for homework and stuff."

"You know what I mean," Dad said. "There's a lot of sick stuff on there you don't need to be reading. A lot of lies, a lot of negativity, and, like I said, actual threats."

I'd read the threats and I'd had the same thoughts, wishing Naomi could stay offline, wanting to protect her. But we needed to know what was going on, and we needed each other.

"I'll do my best to stay safe. I'll spend more time at home, but I'm not going to stop seeing Naomi," I said. This wasn't the kind of change I was going to wait out.

"Naomi isn't my concern right now," he said. "Life is my concern. Paying the rent is my concern. Keeping you safe is my concern. And she's better off home with her parents, too, if you're really worried. Just give me some time, okay?"

"*If* I'm worried?" I asked. "You better believe I am." I wondered if he ever had a leg to stand on, if that kid did confess. I questioned it more and more each day.

"Stop with the drama," Dad said. "When did you get so dramatic?"

"This stupid case is ruining my life," I blurted out. It was as if some path to the darker cabinets of my brain had opened up. These thoughts were there already; I'd just never accessed them before this moment, and now they were wide open. "I'm trapped in this mess! I finally have a life, and it's ruined! Is any of this even true? Am I going to lose my girlfriend over some allegations you're too stubborn to admit to?"

"You don't know enough about anything to make those kinds of accusations. You're just a damn kid," Dad said. He was cornered, I had cornered my Dad and he was fighting his way out. Dad stood up from his chair. "And I'm ruining your life? You aren't exactly a ray of sunshine in mine lately."

"Sunshine? I don't even exist," I said. "You didn't even notice me at all until you lost your Internet privileges and stopped arguing with teenagers online. Is that how you acted with Mom?"

"What the hell's the matter with you?" Dad asked. "Don't you ever talk to me like that. I look bad right now, and part of that—a good part of that—is your fault." Dad was flustered and pissed off, and so was I. We never talked like this. He was close enough that he could get physical. "I got a kid dating a black girl, and I'm the racist cop. Those are the stereotypes. I don't need this extra baggage from my own family. I don't need to deal with this crap twenty-four-seven. You're throwing me under the bus, Walter. You think I'm ruining your little puppy love life. Well, you're throwing out my career, everything I worked my whole life for."

"Maybe you're throwing it out," I said. "I saw how you and Gran and Pop and Joe talk. Our whole family is racist, so yeah, maybe I do believe Calvin. I never met the kid in my life and I believe him over you. Just admit it and move on with your life."

"That's your family, too," Dad said. His voice was loud and

sharp enough to cut. "You're every bit the racist I am, if that's your thinking."

The lights in the room flickered briefly and then went out. It wasn't living room lights-off dark; it was dark-dark. I went to the window and there were no lights at all for blocks. The sky was a muggy dark brown.

"Maybe this can get me back to work," Dad muttered as he got out his cell. He dialed work and waited. "Don't go anywhere." Blackouts had happened before in the city, but usually during the summer, and during the day, so when the power went out this time, it was actually dark.

I went back into my room to get my own cell phone. I texted Naomi to see if the power was out there, too. *You okay? Power went out down here*, I texted her. I had to get out of the house.

Dad was on the phone with work. He sounded friendlier already, but it was a ruse. "Hey, Celebrity Cop, that's right," he said to whomever he reached. "Let me out there. We'll bring the cameras, get it on a network."

My phone buzzed a few seconds later. The light of the phone screen lit up the room. *Parents are out. Jason on a date. Babysitting. Power's out here, too.* She was alone with Kelly. I told her I'd be right there, and that was a promise I wasn't breaking.

"Come on," Dad said into the phone, sounding like he was responding to bad news. He turned to face the corner and ran his hand over his head. "You need me out there. I got this."

"I'm going to Naomi's," I told Dad, having grabbed my hoodie and phone and keys already. I was checking the closet for a flashlight. This was as good an opening as I was getting.

"Hang on a second," Dad said into his phone, and held it to his chest. "The hell you are. Get back to your room. You're not leaving the house, and she'd better not leave hers, either. You're safer indoors."

"She's alone with her baby sister. She'll be safer with me there," I said, clicking the flashlight on and off to test it.

"That's if you even get there," Dad said. "Bad types come out when stuff like this happens. You don't know who's out there doing what. Stay put, Walter."

"What bad types are those?" I asked.

"Don't do that with me," Dad said. "Crooks, that's who. I'm on the phone, Walter. Go back to your room."

Dad turned his attention back to his phone, and the door was shut behind me before he could say another word. I rushed down the stairs without a look back and stepped out into the dark.

"Walter!" I heard Dad yell out, but that was behind me now.

• • •

I got to Naomi's place pretty quickly. I walked fast with my head down, my mind racing with angry thoughts. Blind to both time and my surroundings, not deep in thought but with more of a white-noise-grumbling frustration. I didn't pass any looters or maniacs. Most of the few blocks I walked were quiet. I passed a few cars, a few people walking, and that was it. Another check in the "Dad's a crazy paranoid" column. I called Naomi, and she invited me up. She was doing better under the circumstances than I would have. Candles lit the living room, and Naomi was calm as could be, especially considering Kelly's wailing cries. I gave Naomi a big hug when I came in. It was therapeutic and I needed it. I felt the tension leave my body almost immediately.

Between the two of us, we managed to settle down Kelly. In fact, she had a blast. We played number games, counting from one to five, and five to one, getting sillier and more ridiculous each time. We read her short books by candlelight. Naomi insisted I at least try to hold Kelly, and the first thing she did was grab the glasses off my face. Naomi put them on.

"I love these things," she said. "Wow, these are strong!" Naomi had glasses, too, but only needed them for reading. I loved it when she had them on, though. She looked cute in glasses.

Naomi put them briefly on Kelly's face and snapped a picture before taking them right back off. "These things would ruin her eyes."

"My vision isn't that bad," I said. "Is it?"

Kelly got sleepy soon after that, and Naomi put her to bed. She was a natural with kids. Kelly was something out of a TV show, all cute squeals and smiles, not like my cousin's sticky-punchy, potentially homophobic kids.

We made our way to the couch in the living room and got

under a blanket for warmth. We kissed by the candlelight. Her face was a sliver of dark, soft orange. Her lips sparked and brought my whole face to life. It felt a world away from everything else. Even the blackout felt like an afterthought. I took a deep, cleansing breath.

"I want to look at you forever," I told her, and meant it. I wished it could just be like that all the time. I kissed Naomi between the cheek and nose, to the farthest jawbone, to the left of her chin. The bottom lip, and upper lip. I pulled her in as close as I could. Then I pulled her in a little closer.

We kissed a little longer. "What time is it?" Naomi asked. I rested my arm on the couch as she squirmed, looking for her phone. It was around nine, but it felt like it could be any time, or like time wasn't a thing at all. It was our own special time, apart from everyone else's. "We still have a while before my parents get home."

"Did you text them about the blackout?" I asked, but she wasn't worried about the blackout. She was just babysitting in the dark, and now parked on the couch with her boyfriend. Maybe I shouldn't have said anything.

"They never go out. Are you kidding?" she said. "Let them have fun."

"My dad's convinced war is going to break out in the streets," I said. I wished he could have fun, that a blackout could just be a blackout. "All the rioters and looters and crazies see the lights go out and grab their weapons. Start smashing windows and shaking down the innocents."

"That's true. It's happening right now," Naomi said. "Can't you hear all the car alarms? The whole city's burning down."

"I thought that was the glow of the candles," I said. "But you're right, the fire's reaching for the sky. I can hear the helicopters whirring by. It must be crazy out there." I tightened my arms around Naomi. "We're safe in here, anyway," I said. "Under this blanket, just you and me."

Naomi burrowed her head between my cheek and shoulder. "Of course, we'll need to go back out there eventually," she said.

"We've got everything we need," I said. "Let the police take care of it. It's apocalyptic out there."

Naomi was quiet for a moment. I heard Kelly stirring in the next room. I closed my eyes, content, a little sleepy myself even. Then Naomi spoke. "Okay, I'm going to say something again, because I'm thinking it."

"That's such a bad rule you have," I said. "You can really get into trouble with that."

"Please, can I say this?" she asked, and I nodded. "I'm worried about you."

"Why?" I asked. "I'm okay. Especially right now."

"But I am worried," Naomi said. She sat up and turned my chin toward her face, her eyes were searching for mine in the dark. "Look at me. I'm worried you're going to shut down because you don't like the attention. There's going to be attention, long after this stuff with your dad passes. Maybe you don't see it—I don't know. But if it's not your dad's case, it'll be some other news story or just your everyday racists. Or just curious people. I worry you'll shut down every time we're challenged and hide in your shell."

"Hide in my shell? Is that what you think I do?" I asked.

Her brow furrowed. "It *is* what you do," Naomi said. "I'm happy with you and you're happy with me, but there's a lot we haven't talked about that maybe we should at some point."

"Naomi, I want to be with you. That's all that matters. No, I don't like attention. I don't want to defend myself for liking someone. I don't want to fight people, especially strangers, and why should I have to? I don't even think fighting should be in the vocabulary of a relationship. I'm happy with you."

"Me too, but sometimes relationships are work," Naomi said. She turned my head back toward her, a little softer this time. "You have to work for happiness, and you have to fight for love."

"Fine, I'll fight," I said, and moved her hand from my face. Annoyed that she'd use that word for the first time in this context. "I'll fight—I'll fight dirty, okay? I'll gouge eyes and use a rock. Who do you want me to fight?"

"That's not what I mean," Naomi said. She was sitting up and leaning forward, away from me now, the blanket bunched up between us. "You're avoiding the issue again. This is exactly what I mean. I'm saying talk to our parents, talk to your dad, talk to *me*. I want to know what's going on in your head."

"No, that's talking," I said. "You said fighting, I'm gonna fight. I know a few wrestling moves. I've played some Tekken. I can turn anything into a weapon."

"Stop," Naomi said, annoyed. She was raising her eyebrows to accentuate her points. "You know that's not what I'm talking about. I'm glad you don't fight at school or pick on kids smaller than you, like some of those other guys, but you should want to fight on some level. That's the problem. I'm not talking fists and feet; I'm talking about facing the world."

"It's the same thing!" I said. They both led to people getting hurt. "I don't like it; it's not me. I don't like fighting, I don't like arguing, I don't like *this*!"

My parents had fought all the time—that's what she made me think of. Lying in bed, listening to Dad yell and Mom scream, and as a kid I couldn't think of why they were together aside from the fact that they were my parents so they were just kinda stuck there. And I fought with Mellie and sometimes I'd yell things I heard our parents say even though I had no clue what they meant.

"You don't like this?" Naomi said. She was mad at me now. If she wasn't before, she was definitely mad now. I'd seen her mad and did not want it directed at me. "You don't like talking to me?"

"Of course I do. Naomi, look at everything going on around us," I said. "No offense, but for all your talk about fighting, you can be a little unhinged. Frankly, it scares me."

"If you can't deal with me *as I am*—" Naomi pointed at me, her voice raised enough that I worried we'd wake up Kelly.

"Look at the comments online," I interrupted, trying to keep my voice low. "Look at the bile people are posting there!"

"And you *listen* to that?" Naomi asked as if I were disturbed. She had an immediate retort to everything I said. I wasn't even sure if she was listening to any of it. She was an argument robot, like one of those baseball pitching machines set to auto.

"I'm just saying the world is not a safe place," I said. She slowly turned her head away from me. "It's not some soft cushion you can go diving off of buildings and land on safely. You're mouthing off to Lester freaking Dooley, for crying out loud. That kid thinks I'm talking about him now. Who do you think he's going to come after? Me. And Jason? Your parents?" I asked. I got off the couch and started to pace. "You ever think all this fighting is just pushing everyone we know who should be in our corner really far away?"

"Lester's harmless," Naomi said, brushing aside everything else I'd said.

"Maybe you should be with Lester, then," I said, and instantly wanted to take it back. I needed to get out of there, fast.

"You are ridiculous," Naomi said, standing up herself now. "Relationships are hard. Sometimes there're bad things, hard times. You *really* need to learn to deal with them."

"How do you know what relationships are?" I asked. She didn't have any more experience than I did.

"Well, how do you know?" she retorted. It was a good retort. I chuckled. "Don't laugh. This isn't funny. God, it's only been, like, what, a month? Two months? And already we're—"

"I should leave," I said. I was in Naomi's hyperconfrontational world, and I didn't know which way was up here, or what wrong word was going to break us up.

"Walter, do *not* leave," Naomi said, shaking her head and moving toward the door.

"I have to," I said. "I have to because this is heading somewhere bad. I don't know where, but it's bad, and I want to go before we get there. I'm not ready for that." I got my coat and faced the door, with Naomi in front of it, and waited.

"Fine," Naomi said, as distant as I'd ever seen her. She turned away from me. "I'll lock the door."

Possibly a million different options at that second presented themselves: go, stay, talk, touch. But I felt I should follow through. I said I'd leave for a reason. I grabbed my stuff and fumbled my way down the mostly dark staircase and threw open the door as hard as I could. I still had that anxious, awful, angry energy tensed up in my body. The fast walk to Naomi's seemed like miles heading back. I could see the occasional headlights, the dull round areas my flashlight pointed to, and some twinkling lights that were mostly behind me, all in the distance.

I didn't want to go home. I wasn't ready to face Dad, and without home and Naomi's, the most I could do was wander and walk off some of the tension. Right through the war zone. Dad would flip. Truthfully, it was dead quiet out there save for a stray cat that I could barely make out.

My blood was pumping, head racing. Maybe that was how everyone else always felt, and why they fought so much. Admittedly, there was some life to it. It was natural, after all. The world was antagonistic by nature. Everything you did was a fight, every breath was a fight against death, every choice you made, every decision you made was a fight against another decision. We fought instincts, our better judgments—we fought nature. They say every story is broken down to a fight, man against man, man against nature, man against society. Everyone was against everyone, and it was tiring. Why couldn't we just be for someone, or for something? Why couldn't there be ideas we didn't fight, because they were good ones? Why couldn't we close our eyes and let nature guide us and pray everything turned out all right? But it was never that easy, and I was guided through the streets like I was drawn to a magnet; I realized I was chasing noise. There were other people out there.

The lights popped back on like a good idea well before I'd gotten home. Ahead of me in an apartment complex parking lot was a group of kids, Lester, Frankie, others I didn't know, five or six in all. Beardsley was there. They were standing there smoking, first in the dark, then in the light, posed like they belonged there, and me walking alone like I belonged there, and we looked at each other like this was expected and unavoidable. I was as ready for my ass-kicking as I'd ever been. Honestly, as I got closer and saw that face, I didn't care at all anymore.

"Wally Wilcox," Lester said with his usual grin. "Alone, walking down Lincoln Street. Must be coming home from Naomi Mills. How is the princess?"

I didn't answer. He was probably just testing to see if he could go pay her a visit.

"She isn't still mad at me, is she?" Lester asked, and took a drag from his cigarette and exhaled. "I was out of line that time—I know I was. I blew it."

"You didn't blow it with Naomi," I said. "You never had a chance with her to blow it."

Lester laughed—the whole crew laughed. "All right, you got me. I had a big crush on her, man," Lester said, walking closer to me. "I used to come over to the house, hang with Jason. She'd come out of the bathroom, hair all wet from her shower. Smelling like . . . What's that stuff girls use?"

"Lilac?" Frankie said. Lester laughed and shook his head.

"Yeah, we'll use that, lilac," Lester said, then turned back to

me. "Sucks to like a girl and know you're never gonna see her naked."

"Don't talk about her like that," I said. Lester laughed. He might have been a charmer or whatever, and he was your classic alpha male, but he was still a big, dumb, brainless, violent—

"I see how you look at me," Lester said. "Like I'm some kind of animal—you can say it. You think I don't get that all the time? But

here's the thing. I'm smarter than you. Surprised? Look at you, fists all clenched up, breathing heavy. Tell me, what do you think of this? You may be dating a black girl, but I still think you're racist."

That wasn't fair. He can't play the role of an animal and then accuse me of noticing it. I wasn't racist for thinking he was a bully when he was being a bully. I might have thought he was an animal, but he backed it up with his actions. He was planting the images in my head.

"You're picturing me heading up to Naomi's right now, checking in on her, big, strong black man on a scary night. That just pisses you off, doesn't it?" Lester taunted. His friends were laughing. "You dogged your friend Jason. He doesn't respect you, and neither do I. Your dad belongs here more than you. You don't belong here. You don't know poor. You definitely don't know black. Get it? You don't get to be with a black girl, and especially Naomi Mills. She's too good for you."

It was inevitable. I was weak. I wasn't good enough for Naomi; she should end up with Lester.

He turned to his friends. "Let's get out of here," he said, and put out his cigarette. He thought he was done with me, that the conversation was over, that the final line involved me crawling back into my hole and losing everything.

"Don't turn around on me," I said—I think I said. I wasn't weak. No, I wasn't going to roll over.

I've never fought anyone, not physically, but I ran right into Lester. He couldn't have seen it coming, because it felt like moving a truck with surprising ease, and we hit a parked car behind him. I got two or three fists and forearm punches into Lester's face before he tossed me back maybe five feet with one big shove. I ran back into him.

Rage and adrenaline really worked wonders because I had knocked Lester off his feet. Lester's arm swung. I thought he hit me with his muscle. I grabbed a rock while I was on the ground, but before I could do anything stupid with it, the rest of them were on me again. I was yanked into the air like I weighed nothing. The things I remembered after that were like snapshots, brief little snippets or ideas, images mostly. I remembered Lester laughing and touching his face, an uneasiness that broke when I was hit by someone in the stomach. I remembered my ribs hurting. I remembered my knee hitting the ground and trying my best to stay on my feet so they'd only be using fists.

"Knock it off," I remembered an older person yelling from a window somewhere. "Leave that boy alone!"

I also remembered someone on a doorstep talking on her phone.

I remembered swinging my arm, but I didn't know if I was trying to hit someone, or who if I was. Eventually I did get hit in the face. My glasses fell off. I got put in a headlock and saw blood on the ground. I wondered if it was mine.

I didn't remember the fight stopping, but I did remember the police car and the headlights streaming on me. Ricky asking me who did this and telling him "just some kids." Ricky held up some fingers, but I couldn't tell what he wanted me to do with them. Two fingers. Three. What did it matter now?

It would be a great story for Dad. Seventeen-year-old kid gets beat down on the night of a blackout, four on one, and get this: *he started it.* Maybe he had it coming. The kids all got away.

That energy still hadn't burned off.

Chapter Fifteen

"**N**o ambulance," I said as Ricky moved my head around, taking a look at my injuries. "It's my first fight. I'll take it like a man."

"Yeah, take it like a man, then," Ricky said sarcastically. "Great idea, wake up with a real manly concussion you can brag to all your friends about."

"I'm fine," I said. I didn't know if I was fine or not. Nothing actually hurt, I felt a little numb, but I had adrenaline rushing through me, too. People were out watching us. I saw my breath glow in the flashing lights of the police cruiser. Ricky reported something into his walkie-talkie.

"I'll take you home, but I'm calling your dad first," Ricky said. I groaned. There was nothing warm and inviting waiting for me back home. "I'm not letting him wake up tomorrow to find you like this, Walter. You know that. And if he wants you to go to the hospital tonight, that's his call, okay?"

Dad was up waiting for me when I got home. Ricky came in for a minute to drop off the goods. Everything was somber. I put a cold press on my face and settled in for the lecture. At least we had power now. Sort of, anyway. There was one dim lamp on, and

Dad was in his pajamas with a cup of coffee, waiting. It was shortly after midnight.

"You didn't listen," he said. I hadn't seen my face yet, but it was sore enough that I imagined it might get me some empathy. That was not the case. Mom would have empathized. "I'm a cop, you think I don't know what goes on in this city? You think I don't know what I'm talking about? I'm your father, which is reason enough for you to shut up and take notice when I talk, but I'm also an officer of the law. And you were very stupid disobeying me."

"Listen to yourself, you don't know anything that happened, but you act like you know everything," I said. I wasn't in the mood for this again. That same angry blood was coursing through me.

"You're damn right I do. Compared to you, I do know everything," Dad said, pointing at himself. He'd probably been rehearsing this since I left. "I've been a father nineteen years, a cop for more than that. I know every damn hoodlum and thief in this city. I know every crooked cop. I know girls, all right; I know how they get in your head. I know right from wrong. I know what's important, and that's your family, so you listen to me when I talk. You want to know what I know?" Dad nodded, confident. "I'll tell you exactly what this is: it was *black kids*. This was *revenge*. This was a message for *me*." He pointed at himself again, a smug smile. He hadn't even asked me what had happened. Not only was this a lecture when my cheek felt like it had it's own heartbeat, but it was a lecture filled with flat-out unhidden hate and unchecked ego.

"It wasn't black kids," I said. "It had nothing to do with you. They beat *me* up. This is *my* life, one you don't know anything about. Some detective." For an officer of the law, he didn't put any faces to it, he didn't apply any reasoning, and he didn't

304

acknowledge that these things happened all the time here. He took it all as an affront to him alone—that I was the method of delivery for this personal message. *Hey, racist cop, leave our kind alone.*

"I'm not a detective; I'm a cop, smart-ass," Dad said. "I uphold the law, and there's gonna be some laws this house. For one, you are done with that girl. She's bad news. How many times did I tell you? This isn't about high school crushes—"

"I get it, I know. We've gone over this already," I interrupted. We were spinning our wheels and going nowhere. "It's not about me; it's about you—I get it. I could do this whole lecture myself now: 'I have friends of every color. I'm the best cop, Walter, best there is. Everyone'll figure it out eventually.' News flash, you're not some ace detective; you're not even a good cop. They don't use you for anything. You're a slob and paranoid, and that stuff is in me now. That's your voice. I've heard it so much I have that paranoid voice running through my head. I'm scared of everyone and everything all the time. Why do I even listen to you? You lost your job, you lost Mom. I have to make an effort to think like a normal person. I'm embarrassed for you. I'm embarrassed for us both. I honestly don't believe a word you say anymore."

"That's some performance, kid," Dad said, clapping loudly and sarcastically. He was starting to sweat. "That how it's gonna be? You get a piece of tail and suddenly you're a big man?"

"Screw you," I said.

"Go to bed," Dad said, and pointed to my room.

"Go to hell," I said, and went to my room anyway and slammed the door.

"I'll put a lock on that door if I have to," I heard Dad yell from the other room. Then I heard his door slam, too.

My face was swollen and cut up. I didn't like to look at it. It hadn't really hurt until right then when nothing else was going on, and then it hurt like hell. I felt like the ending scene of a Rocky movie. I looked at my phone. No message from Naomi since our fight. She didn't check in with me. She was probably still mad. I checked Facebook in my room, and she did post something there. *If you can't fight me when I'm dating you, don't fight me when I break up with you.* Why would she post that there after all the trouble we've had on that site? I took a picture of my face with my cell phone and posted it to the East Bridge page Jason ran. Then I went to bed, lying on my back.

● ● ●

Sometime in the morning, I heard a loud thud. "Dad?" I got up and ran into the living room. Nothing there. "Dad?" I called again.

I looked in the kitchen, which was empty, but I saw Dad's arm in the doorway to his room. I wasn't ready for this. You didn't die from eating hamburgers or having an argument. A hundred horrible thoughts filled my head at once. Would he kill himself? Was he suicidal—was this way worse than I even knew? Was he on drugs? Was he right all along—did someone come after him? I hadn't heard any fight, though, or gunshot. I found him on his back on the floor of his room. His shirt was drenched with sweat, to the point where it puddled on the ground around him. His eyes were closed like he was asleep. He looked white as a ghost.

I didn't rush to ask if he was okay or try to do anything except grab the landline phone and dial 9-1-1 for an ambulance. That was something we'd gone over in school, and I'd paid attention to it, never knowing I'd need it, let alone so soon. But when your dad acts like mine does, it's something to know.

They let me ride in the ambulance since I didn't have a car or anything. It was supposed to be me being taken to the hospital, probably sitting in the passenger seat of Dad's cruiser, head against the window, quiet tension in the air. But my anger was swept away by a very real fear. My last conversation with my dad could have ended with "Go to hell."

In the hospital, everyone ran off to help Dad, who was stretchered in, and I was left alone to sit and wait. There was a lot of waiting. I'd always been somewhat prepared for this. Whether it was his diabetes and his fear of doctors, or his job, which could put him here on any given day. It felt different sitting in that waiting area, though, to see if this was the time. And I didn't have any answers as to what happened next.

My godfather was my uncle Joe, and I'd already decided I had no interest in living there. Maybe I was old enough to be on my own, but I had no money. College was right around the corner, in theory. I wished I had more of a plan. I'd make it on my own, I guessed. I was old enough now. I could get by. I was going to have to at some point. Dad was up to his neck in his own problems. Mom had her own life now. And Naomi . . .

I took my phone back out and dug around to see what I'd missed. Even a string of angry texts from Naomi would be something to make me feel less alone. She had texted, but I couldn't read the tone. She asked where I was, asked if I wanted to talk. That was it, really. She didn't send any follow-ups, no worried texts, no angry ones. No one else had tried to contact me.

I debated who should know about Dad. I called Mom, but I only got her voice mail. This didn't seem right for voice mail. I tried calling Mellie and got the same. I could send a text message to her, at least. *Dad's in the hospital . . . Stop by?* She had probably expected it like I did, but she didn't live with Dad. She hadn't even seen him in years now. But she deserved to know.

I checked Facebook. The East Bridge page had been taken down, or was removed. I didn't know if anyone commented on my picture, or even saw it.

There wasn't a ton of activity online without it. Maybe everyone had moved on. There wasn't much going on in the hospital, either. There was a receptionist fielding a few calls. Every now and again a doctor or a nurse walked by. They must have really hid the high drama, the buses full of injured bloody people, sobbing and screaming. That must all take place in the back somewhere. The X Games were on a TV, image after image of bicycles crashing, skateboarders dragged along concrete. I wondered if that was a dark joke by the hospital people and applauded them if it was.

I continued my game of Worst-Case Scenario. Worst-case scenario, my dad died that day. I'd go live with Mom and Seth and try to stay out of the house as much as I could. I'd still go to the same school, and I'd spend a lot of time there. I'd spend a lot of time with Naomi. Worst-case scenario, Naomi wouldn't talk to me anymore. She had to be mad at me. I wouldn't even listen to her when she tried talking to me. Worst-case scenario, she started dating someone else. Someone confident and cool, someone in control of his life, someone strong. Worst-case scenario, she was done with me forever. And Jason was done with me forever. Worst-case scenario, I went back to school, and everyone laughed at my red swollen face and held a parade for Lester and his friends.

This was a bad game.

A nurse in a white lab coat walked by, a short Indian woman with large, expressive eyes, and just as she was about to pass me, she turned to look at me, and from the look on her face, she saw mine. I must have looked like a beaten-down homeless ragamuffin who snuck in for shelter, nestled into some corner with my head down avoiding human interaction. At the very least, it was an easy assumption that I came here for me and not my dad.

"Oh my goodness," she said.

"You should see my dad," I said, only just after realizing the implication of domestic violence.

"Is someone helping you?" she asked. "Come here." I got off the couch, and we walked down the hall to a small office. The nurse told me to hold an ice pack to my cheek for a few minutes.

"I figured it'd heal on its own," I said. "Never got a black eye before."

"Well, that's some black eye. It covers half your face," she said, opening a cabinet and reaching for something. "It'll heal, but a little help and guidance won't hurt it, either. So, was it a fight or a trip down the stairs?"

"Fight, I guess," I said. She wet a towel with warm water and gently rubbed it over the wounded area. It felt nice.

"I wish I could convince you the drama passes," she said. "There's nothing worth breaking bones over. You take any Advil?" I shook my head. "You want an eye patch?" she asked. She dropped three Advils into my hand and filled a small paper cup with water. "Pirate look might scare off the other kids."

"No, thanks," I said. "But thanks for the Advil, and checking it out."

I walked back to the visitor area and sat on the couch. Mellie had texted that she was on her way. Mel's college was about an hour away from the hospital. At least I wouldn't be alone for too much longer.

"Walter?" I heard. It was a doctor, making his way over. He looked young, like a TV doctor. Made me think of Dad getting annoyed with all the young guys who'd been hired on the police force. He'd probably hate this kid taking care of him. The doctor didn't have the biggest smile, so I imagined his news would be less than great. "I just wanted to fill you in, if you've got a minute."

I nodded. He stayed standing, I remained sitting.

"So your dad is in a diabetic coma," the doctor said. "With diabetes, when the blood sugar gets to a low-enough point, the body and mind can lose consciousness. It could be set off by dehydra-

310

tion, exhaustion, shock. Stress." He counted those off on his fingers. My dad was a prime candidate, in other words.

"Is he going to be okay?" I asked. It had to be on the top three questions doctors received. His face wasn't promising.

"I can't say," the doctor said. "I can tell you that, personally, I think it looks good. We have him on IVs, he's getting the nutrients he needs, and you got him here early. But unfortunately I can't tell you for sure how long he'll be out, or in what kind of shape he'll be in when he wakes. The sooner he wakes, the better."

He must have seen the tear roll out of my eye because he quickly added, "But again, personally, I think it looks good."

After a couple episodes of the TV show *Jackass* in the lobby, the glass entrance doors slid open and Mellie walked in with a nervous strut. She eyed me and made a beeline over, and dove into me with a hug.

"Ow!" I said. Her shoulder rammed into my bruises like a bulldozer.

"Oh Jesus!" she said, seeing the browns and blues on my face. "I just glomped your face! I'm so sorry! What on earth happened to you?"

"I got hit," I said. I guess I had to figure out an explanation for that, because I'd be getting it a lot at school. Or at least a funny line. *Walked into an oncoming truck. She came in like a wrecking ball.* I told Mellie about the blackout and the argument with Naomi, and the walk home. I told her about the past few days. I told her about Dad and how he'd passed out on the floor and all the sweat. We had time now, so I told her everything.

"I'm sure he'll be fine," she said. "Everyone has diabetes now. This is probably routine for them here. They probably get, like, four of these a day." Mel and I were slouched on opposite ends of the couch, taking up the whole thing. Mel's legs on top and mine sliding to the floor.

"Ha-ha," I said. "It's not, like, a head cold."

"I know," Mel said. "Just trying to lighten the mood. Stay positive. They'll fix him."

"Yeah," I said. "Thanks for coming anyway. I wasn't sure if I should bother you."

"He is still my dad," Mel said, looking at me from her end of the couch. "I'm still your sister and you're still my brother, even if we're in different states. We're still a family, no matter what happens. So none of us are ever alone."

"It doesn't feel that way," I said. "Sometimes."

"Well, I'm glad you told me. I'd have been pissed if you hadn't." Mel held my hand. "He's my dad, too."

• • •

Dinner did nothing to combat the stereotypes of hospital food. Mel had a meat product served with a gelatinous vegetable serving, and, not trusting that combination, I went with the Styrofoam-textured grilled cheese, which I could only take a few bites from.

The TV was still on in the waiting room. Made sense—it was

a hospital, it was not like they shut the doors for the night at 10 p.m. or anything. The TV was showing a marathon of the game show *Wipeout*, more scenes full of bodily injuries. Well-played, hospital. We watched some of that, and then Mel fell asleep. My swollen face hurt twice as bad when I was lying there doing nothing. Advil was no help. Trying to sleep in a waiting room was even worse. And, of course, not far away there was my dad, lying in a coma. That was a surreal thought. I decided to walk around the hospital aimlessly.

Nothing seemed to be off-limits, so I kept walking, and thinking.

I thought about Dad. Like, how could you be told you had a disease and willfully do nothing to fight it? Maybe you didn't like doctors, but when you were ill, you went anyway. You went to your doctor, you took your medication, you changed your diet, you exercised. You might hate all those things, but were they really worse than dying? The idea that he just sat there and let his body rot away, and was so passive about it all . . . And what was I doing?

You're sticking your head in the sand like an ostrich, Naomi would say. Maybe we'd play the question game again. *Why are you so mad at your dad?*

Because, he's being stupid, I'd say. *He thinks he can shut his eyes and somehow he'll wake up and the diabetes will be gone, and he'll be back to working full-time. Maybe he's back with your mom—I don't know—and everything will be great again. But what if he shuts his eyes and they don't open at all?*

Naomi would put her head on my shoulder, her arm around my waist. *Things don't fix themselves when they're broken.*

No, they don't, I'd say. *They just stay broken. He's being so stupid.*

Are you being stupid? Naomi would ask me, stepping away. *Are you going to let us stay broken?*

There was a large window at the end of the hallway, next to a staircase. The ground below was orange from the streetlight, the buildings and trees across the street were black, and the sky was a dark blue with a tiny piercing of moon. I followed the exit signs, one in the hall, one down the stairs, and out a set of doors until I was under the moon.

There were no exit signs to follow outside, so I kept walking forward until the hospital was long behind me.

Chapter Sixteen

The hospital was just blocks from the High Hill section of the city, heavily populated but empty at this time of night. Or morning.

I felt like the ghost of Sam Spade, or any of the detectives Dad and I had watched. Haunting the city, shadows twisting around each building, darkness battling artificial light. I hadn't slept in a long time.

I was somewhere between person and animal. Between the detectives and the crooks they chased. I wanted to find this criminal. If I could just catch this kid doing what Dad said he'd done, it would make everything right again. Everything I believed would be confirmed, and the world would be right and I could trust and feel safe again.

Naomi hovered in the front of my mind, taking up most of the real estate there. Maybe that chapter of my life was already over. Maybe a relationship with someone like Naomi wasn't something I was capable of handling, or was ready for. She wanted someone to fight for her, not get nearly killed over her.

I knew that Naomi had nothing to do with what had happened, but at the same time she was so connected to it all. To me, at midnight out in the streets, looking for dangerous people, love equaled a bruised and split-open face. Love was a concussion with a promise for more.

Down the hill, the storefronts on Main Street were all lit up for Christmas, even when the lights inside the buildings were off. I wondered if I'd be alone at Christmastime.

I heard a noise on the other side of the building I was passing. I heard voices. I stopped moving, tiptoed along the wall, and listened. I heard someone laughing. A dog bark. The last time I followed voices on a dark night things had ended poorly, but that didn't stop me. I followed the wall and peeked around the corner, but there was nothing but streetlights and the hill off in the distance. I followed that wall, along the street front, still hearing the voices, and peered around that corner. But it was just an alley. I could still hear the voices, but I looked up, I looked down the street, I ran down the alley. Nothing. Not even a bedroom light was on.

I wasn't a ghost haunting the city; I was a damaged human being haunted by ghosts. Was Calvin Temple even real?

I knew at some point the thief would strike again, and I wanted to see it with my own eyes. I wanted proof. I wanted to know what all this was for. I knew the Basement pretty well, and that was where the majority of the crime had happened. I stood a chance of seeing it, if it happened while I was out there. If anything happened at all.

I was my dad, out on the street, looking for that kid to be doing that thing. I wanted Calvin Temple to be the criminal and I wanted Dad to be the supercop, the ace detective. I was walking in my dad's shoes and thinking how he would think and hoping he was right, but I was chasing a phantom. There was nothing there. I didn't like the feeling. I didn't like being Dad.

That Halloween party I went to with Naomi, watching Lester talking to her, convinced he was bothering her, that he was up to no good. I was being my dad, the same person I kept saying was wrong. I had him pegged, flagged. He was hitting on my girl. And what did I focus on? The laughing. She was laughing so hard with him.

I turned around to walk back to the hospital. I took out my phone, and I listened to the voice mail Mom had left me.

"I'm just thinking about you, how much you've changed. All in good ways, better than I could have hoped for." I had felt different, but the feeling had been short-lived. *"I'm so glad you came over, and I hope we can do it again. And I'm glad you brought your friend over. She's really a sweetie."* She was . . . *"I feel like a huge weight is off my shoulders.*

Do you feel that? I was really sick and really worried for a long time, and I want you to know how much better you made me feel. Anyway, I should get to bed." So should I. *"I love you. Talk to you later."*

• • •

I opened the Internet on my phone when I got back to the hospital, sitting at an empty table near the windowed wall. The Facebook page was still down. I couldn't find the phantom burglar. All evidence of this whole ordeal went down with the Facebook page, face bruises aside, and everything seemed to be back to normal. Everything was okay, except for my messed-up face and my anger.

Everything else in the world had disappeared, but my rage was alive.

Chapter Seventeen

When Mel woke up, we got breakfast, just the two of us. The food was much more tolerable than our dinner food had been. At least they were clearly pancakes, and eggs, and I devoured them both.

"I miss you like swearwords I shouldn't say in a hospital," Mel said. "How's Naomi?"

I twisted my mouth a little and looked to the side.

"Oh," Mel said. "Have you talked to Mom?"

"Just a little," I said.

"Dammit, Walter, don't be that person," Mel said. "You've got everything in the world going for you. You piss me off because you're so much like me. I started seeing a therapist." Mellie was quiet for a minute and let that thought hang in the air. "It's been really good. You may want to sometime, too."

"Therapist?" I asked. She had tattoos. I'd thought that was her therapy. "Why?"

"What do you mean *why*?" Mel asked. "Because I needed someone to talk to. Because I wasn't thinking normal."

"So what? No one's normal," I said. "Normal is stupid anyway."

"That's exactly what my therapist said, that there is no normal.

But—and this is why I think you could benefit as much as I have—the way we were raised was definitely *not* normal. We think it was, because it's all we knew, and all we had to compare it to was TV shows, and everyone knows that's all crap."

"It was normal before Mom cheat—before Mom and Dad split up," I said. I tried to finish my eggs before they got any colder. "I don't need therapy."

"Someday you're going to figure out that our logic is a little faulty, and I'm just suggesting you be a little proactive about it," Mel said. "Ever ask yourself this: Who raised us? I mean, who taught you confidence? Who told you how handsome you were when you were growing up, who taught you how to talk to girls, or stand up for yourself, or fix a car or even how to drive? No one. Dad was a workaholic. Mom was depressed. Who told you you're worthwhile, that you're special? No one told you these things growing up. No one told me, either. So that's the voice in our heads—it's saying, *I'm not special. I'm not worthwhile. I'm not handsome. I don't know how to do this. I'm not a part of this.* But that's what you learn in therapy. Walter, you *are* special. You are worthwhile. You're handsome, and you're sweet, and the world is yours if you want it. And that's the truth. That's what we should have learned a long time ago. That's what I'm trying to learn now."

I smiled uncomfortably. I didn't take compliments well. Maybe therapy fixes that, too.

"You think I'm just talking out of my ass—therapy nonsense," Mel said. "But Naomi saw it. I could tell. She knows how special you are."

"I don't think you're talking out of your ass," I said. We did raise ourselves, and we did a pretty poor job of it, too. In a way, I'd been thinking similar thoughts myself, just not that precise.

Hearing Mel voice them was like jumping to the back of a book and seeing how it ends.

Dad was still out. The doctor had said the sooner he's up, the better, and now it had been twenty-four hours. Was that considered soon, or no? That was too vague. Was it already too late? Sitting around the hospital made time drag; the importance of time made it all hurt. I needed to get out for a bit.

•   •   •

Nate skipped school. Something, he told me, he can now do as a single bro. With nothing much going on besides old episodes of *Celebrity Boxing* (where did they even find that?), I left the hospital and met Nate at the court. Not for a fight, but for some actual basketball. We were trying to sink the ball from half-court, both shocked to see the hoop didn't fall right off the second it got hit.

"This is fun," Nate said, chasing after the ball. "Can I toss this to you? I'm worried I'm going to make your face look worse."

"Not possible," I said. "Toss it."

It felt good to be out of the hospital, out in the sun, away from the drama, even just for the morning. I dribbled the ball to about halfway down the court and hurled it. Nowhere near the net. I followed the ball and passed it back to Nate.

"There's no win to my situation," Nate said. "I like Kate, obviously, but I don't want to be tied to her, either. We're graduating. We've got our last summer here, then college. It's a good time to be free."

"Have you ever actually explained to me why you broke up?" I asked. "I'm still confused, months later."

Nate threw the ball again—nothing. He chased the ball this time. "All right. It's kind of my fault," Nate said. "I may have had a crush on someone and mentioned it to Kate, not something I recommend. I just had one of those moments, like, *Am I with this one person forever, or do I play the field a little?* I tested the waters, and, Walter, the waters were turbulent. So Kate cuts me free, says go be wild, only I don't actually want to go be wild. So we've been in limbo ever since."

"So it's a 'grass is always greener' thing," I said.

Nate took the ball back to half-court. "If I make this shot, I find a million dollars today," Nate said. "No, let's keep it realistic. A hundred dollars."

He missed. I walked after the ball. "Should have made it fifty," I said, squinting in the late-morning sun.

"So what happened with Naomi?" Nate asked. "You made it sound like it was over."

I took the ball to half-court. "It's confusing," I said, and threw the ball. I hit the board, which was closer than Nate had reached, and it bounced back toward us. "There was some conflict, drama, arguing. It was like flat-out war for a brief moment, and it's been quiet since then. I think we just got exhausted or something. And my dad flipped out after the fight, and now he doesn't want me anywhere near her."

Nate walked to the ball. "All right, take out the dad part, 'cause that's a stupid reason to do anything, and forget the warfare, because that just happens. Take all the extraneous debris out of the way. How do you feel about her?"

"She's amazing," I said. "Best thing to ever happen to me. Easily."

"So what's with the silence? Why are you talking like it's over?" Nate asked. "Don't be an idiot."

"I told you it was confusing," I said. Nate bounced the ball to

me. "Okay, if I get this shot, my dad gets cleared of all charges and the state issues a public apology. And I find fifty bucks."

Miss.

"We should keep talking about you, though," I said. "Your situation isn't even complex. There's no nuance at all. Just go back to being Nate and Kate. Everyone's happy."

"If I make this shot," Nate said.

He missed. Half-court really was a long distance, and I should mention the wind was a factor as well. I couldn't even feel my fingers.

"All right, Mr. Complex," Nate said. "You want to go back to Naomi. So do it."

"I need to talk to her," I said. "I know. It's a two-person decision, whatever we do. If I make this shot . . . whether I make this shot or not, I'm gonna talk to Naomi." My shots were getting worse. I hit the cage fence behind the hoop.

"You're right. It is a two-person decision," Nate said, and tossed an easy layup. "I'm gonna talk to Kate, too. We gotta talk to our girls."

"Actually, I have to do something else first," I said. "Before I talk to Naomi. I'd feel better, I think. I want to talk to Lester."

"Dude, Lester almost took your face off," Nate said. "You fought the beast and lived to tell the tale—let it go. But if you're serious, I'm gonna go with you. I don't have any plans today."

"Okay. Thanks. It really wasn't like that, though," I said. "I was more of a beast. He's not bad." I took the ball back from Nate to the middle of the court. "Whatever happens. Here we go. If I make this shot, we're going to track down Lester Dooley."

I threw the ball, and it sank right through the hoop.

• • •

Nate took the basketball with us as we walked southeast through the city. A steady dribble formed a beat along the sidewalks.

"Are you planning on using that thing as a weapon?" I asked.

"You could do that cool move if we get in trouble, where you throw the ball and Lester catches it, and—*wham!*—deck him right in the face."

"Like in *Good Will Hunting?*" Nate asked, and tossed me the ball. "Every damn movie, this guy's seen."

We crossed Main Street into the Basement. The city was like a mood ring. When I'd been falling for Naomi, it'd felt impossibly large, like something out of a fairy tale, friendly characters everywhere out to greet me on my way. In my dad's world, it was a corrupt urban crime town and everyone had an ulterior motive. Somewhere in there was reality. On our way to the Jungle, the buildings felt cold and stiff. Like nothing dared move. Today I was in a western and the townsfolk were frozen till the first gun was drawn.

The Lester confrontation had to happen. If I was going to apologize to Naomi, if I was going to fix things, I needed to show that I wasn't going to make the same mistakes. I didn't want to hide from my problem. And where things stood with Lester, it was a problem. I had to show I could fight, or at least stand up for myself. Or at least work through an issue. At worst, get my ass kicked again.

"Is this really stupid?" I asked. "Is this a kamikaze mission or something?"

"It's absolutely stupid," Nate said. "That's how I know it needs to be done. Congratulations, Walter, on your entry into adulthood."

Somehow this was comforting.

"He was out of school yesterday," Nate said. "Someone said he's suspended through the end of the week. Maybe he was ratted out for the fight."

"Ratted out?" I asked. "Honestly, he barely hit me, and I was the one who started it."

"Walter Wilcox, you *are* a beast!" Nate said. "Remind me to stay on your good side."

"What about Beardsley?" I asked. "Or Frankie? Are they in school still?" Nate nodded. Lester probably took the fall for the whole thing to protect them.

When we got to the rows of similar-looking buildings, I hoped I caught the right one Lester pointed to when we got off the bus all those weeks ago.

We walked up the front steps and rang the doorbell. There were a few seconds before we got a response, from a very irritated lady. Her face was mostly obscured by door as the chain only let it open a fraction. "Who are you?" the lady I assumed was Lester's mom answered.

Nate spoke. "Hi, is this Lester's house? We're classmates of his."

"It's my house. But Lester lives here." The door slammed closed and then opened fully. Lester's mom was short and frail-looking, the opposite of Lester's hulking frame. I wondered what his dad must look like.

"Are you the kid?" his mom asked, looking at Nate and then at me. "Oh, look at you, of course you are, come in. You want to see Lester?"

She called out for Lester and shut off the TV. The house smelled like dust, or wood or something. The floors were hardwood. There was an olive-green couch that really drew all the attention of the room, with a bright orange-and-yellow knitted blanket on it. There was a bicycle inside the house near the door. Nate and I stood there awkwardly, Nate still holding his ball. Lester bounced up some stairs to the living room area, saw me, and ducked his eyes away.

"Oof," he said. "Hey, Walter, come on downstairs. We're hanging out."

Downstairs was a mostly empty basement-man-cave kind of deal. I was surprised to see Jason over playing a football game on the Xbox. He looked up at us. I guess no one was in school today. "Oh, damn," he said, seeing my face. "Hey, Walter."

"You want some pizza?" Lester asked, and grabbed a slice himself. I shook my head, and he got a closer look at the bruising. "That's messed up. You get that looked at?"

I nodded. "Did I do anything?" I said, looking at his face. I knew I hit him at least once. He had a tiny bruise on his cheek. "Is that it?"

"Yeah, it's a little shiner," he said, and smiled. "Hey, it's more than anyone else ever got on me. Nothing to sneeze at."

We laughed at that, if it was something to laugh at. It seemed funny at the time. Nate grabbed the other controller and sat with Jason on the couch, I grabbed a chair off to the side of the room.

"I crossed a lot of lines, like, personal lines I don't like to cross,"

I said to Lester, who was still standing near the pizza box, which was on a table with a computer setup. "I don't even know what I'm doing here, but I felt like I should say something. I dunno." I really could have used some more time to rehearse this. "I threw the first punch. I had my guard up around you. I had some preconceived notions. I mean . . ." This was difficult. "Whatever happened, I had a role in it. So. Sorry."

"I said some dumb stuff, too," Lester said. "That's how fights happen, usually."

"Yeah, but," I said.

"Yeah," Lester agreed.

"It's not a bad suspension situation anyway," I said, looking around. "Games, pizza. Are you stuck in the house?"

"No, I do what I want. She doesn't care," Lester said, rolling his eyes up, referring to his mom. "It's not the first time, probably not the last."

"Damn, who taught you to play?" Jason said to Nate, who was apparently upping Lester's team's score in the game.

"All I need is a controller," Nate said.

"Even up the score," Lester said with a smile, closing the pizza box and throwing away a napkin. "Someone's gotta humble Jason. The kid beats me every time."

Lester stood by me, then squatted down a bit. He looked at Jason, playing the game, then at me.

"Do me a favor," Lester said in a hushed tone. "Forget that other stuff I said out there. I feel like crap over it. It makes my stomach hurt. We don't need to repeat it here, but I didn't mean it, all right? You know what I'm talking about. Really, any of it."

I nodded again. It wouldn't be easy to forget anything he'd said, particularly about Naomi, whom I assumed he was talking about. But if we wanted to move past this, we both had to forgive. He wasn't going to be the only other guy to have a crush on her. That was something I'd have to learn to deal with.

"Walter, you got a minute?" Jason asked me with his eyes still on the game. "Can we step outside?"

Lester took over Jason's controller. "You lift?" was all I heard Nate say before I went upstairs and outside with Jason. We didn't stray too far from Lester's house, walking slowly to the trees lining the road. A large sheet of old cardboard leaned against the building, and I guessed Dad hadn't done anything about Lester's problem with the homeless man.

"How's the face feel?" Jason asked. I pulled my coat back on. Jason was wearing just a long-sleeve shirt. "No offense, man, but it's ugly as sin."

"Honestly?" I asked. "It feels how it looks. You skipping or did you get suspended, too?"

"Skipping," Jason said. Shrugged his shoulders. "Probably get in trouble. Oh well."

We watched as a cop car passed. Had a split-second thought that it was my dad before remembering he was in the hospital still. "Something you wanted to talk about?" I asked.

"Yeah, I'm kinda pissed off a little," Jason said, something that could wrap up the past month or two of my Jason interactions. "It's cool that you came over here to talk to Lester after everything, but why couldn't you talk to me like that?" Jason leaped up and grabbed a tree branch. His feet scurried along the trunk, and he hoisted himself up into the tree. "Like, no offense, but anytime anyone tries to talk real, you slip into some clever retort or you ignore it altogether. It's no way to live, Kemosabe."

"I'm changing," I said. I leaned against the tree.

"Get up here," Jason said from the tree branch. He threw an acorn at me.

"I don't know how," I said, looking up. I jumped, but it was too high. I tried kicking off the tree for a boost. It took a few tries, but once I reached the branch, I was able to climb the tree. The weight of both of us dragged the branch down pretty low.

"All right, well, if you'd do it different now, do it different," Jason said. "Talk to me."

"I like your sister," I said. "I like Naomi, a lot."

"Too bad. Stay away from her or I'll beat your ass," Jason said. "I'll throw you right off this tree." We laughed at that. I could jump off the branch and he'd probably get hurt more. "She likes you, too," Jason said. "Talk to her. She's a mess right now."

"She is?" I asked. I'd thought about Naomi, but I hadn't pictured her a mess. Last I saw her, she'd been pissed off and rightfully so, and that was the image I'd been carrying with me.

"I want her to be happy," Jason said. "She won't talk to me, won't say my name. She won't even look at me. That's my sister, my blood. She's a pain in the ass, and she really did poop her pants in the fifth grade—not sure how you're okay with that—but she's still my sis and I don't want her mad at me anymore."

"So you want us back together?" I asked.

"Forget about me," Jason said. "Just call her, dude."

• • •

Nate and I left Lester's with our lives intact, but now it was time to find Naomi. I felt aware of time suddenly, like with every passing second she might be forgetting me a little more. Naomi felt immediate and urgent, and my heart started racing. The school was a few blocks west, and Nate and I walked fast, the adrenaline kicking in. It was twelve fifty when we got inside and plotted what was next in the main hall. Nate dribbled his ball once, and it might have echoed through the entire school.

"All right, so Naomi should be in biology right now," I said. "I'm going to wait outside that room, maybe down the hall a bit. Then, when she gets out, she'll see me. Maybe I can get her to cut class or something so we have more than two minutes to talk. That's the plan."

A classroom door opened, and Mrs. Medley stood in front of us. I turned my head away and looked at a poster on the wall. "Nate?" she asked. "Are you going to join class or stand in the hall all day?"

"Oh, was that today?" Nate asked.

"It's every day," Mrs. Medley responded.

Nate handed me his basketball. "I gotta go," Nate said. "Good luck and Godspeed."

With that, I was on my own. I went ahead with my plan to wait for Naomi. Just outside of sight from the door. Ten minutes went fast when you were crossing the city with your friend and a basketball, but it could be painfully slow when you were standing still in the quiet, completely alone, waiting to find out if your girlfriend was going to run into you arms or deck you. Especially when you knew you deserved the latter. Finally, the bell rang. And a possibly more excruciating thirty seconds passed before Naomi came out of the room.

"Hi," I said when she saw me. I slowly raised my hand into a wave, or possibly as a sign of truce. I could swear her pupils dilated, like she saw a ghost. I should have worn a mask, maybe something fancy you held with a stick like they did at parties in old movies. Anything to cover the bruising. It was way too real.

"Hi," Naomi said. And then the last thing I'd expected her to say: "I have to go to the bathroom."

Naomi ran to the bathroom, and within the next minute the hallways emptied. And I waited. And I waited some more. And then I took Nate's basketball and I left.

●　　　●　　　●

I took the bus back to the hospital. Mel had texted me already that Dad was up, so I had a cocktail of emotions bubbling by the time I got there. I needed some good news. I needed something positive to grab on to. The first thing I heard walking in was from one of the nurses: "Your dad is so funny!"

I took the elevator to the third floor. The elevator was huge—it had to be to fit beds and stretchers in there. When the door opened, Rosie was in the hall like my own welcoming committee. "Walter, we've been waiting for you. Hurry up and get in there!"

"Hey, Rosie," I said, surprised to see her. "How'd you find out about Dad?"

"Are you kidding?" Rosie asked. "I know when my routine is off, and if your father doesn't answer the phone, something is wrong. They don't call me Nosey Rosie for nothing, you know." She gave a wink. *Nosey Rosie*, it was perfect. How had I never thought of that? I saw Ricky there, too. Rosie must have gotten the word out, quick.

It was a small room with a big window and plenty of sun. Dad was sitting up in his hospital bed, laughing with Mel, but he still had all the tubes going into him. I'd seen that kind of thing on TV, but not in real life and not on someone I knew. I thought the first thing you did after waking up was tear out all those tubes and patches.

Mellie gave Dad a hug and then gave me one, and left us alone.

Dad was looking at his phone. "They're gonna settle the case," Dad said. His voice was rough, like he'd been up for days and then crashed for days. I guess that was exactly what had happened. He put his phone on the little table beside him. "Settle it behind closed doors, probably exchange some money. Well, I won't be involved, in any case."

"What about your job?" I asked.

"I dunno. We'll see," Dad said. "I haven't been fired yet, so that's a good sign, right?"

It wasn't the happy ending "Dad's Alive" party I'd hoped for. I sat down in a chair beside the bed, and Dad held my hand.

"Christ," Dad said, shaking his head and trying to drum up a chuckle of some sort. He let out a cough. "Father of the year."

It was quiet now, a different scene from what I'd walked into with the nurses laughing and Rosie and Mel in the room. Dad was at a loss for words. My throat was closed off, too. Friggin' hospitals, wringing every last emotion out.

"Hey," he said, and lifted his hand lifelessly for a second. And that was all he said for a while. He looked out the window, around the room. At me. He had the makings of a tear forming in his eye, and I prayed he didn't cry because then I probably would, too. "Gotta meet this girl," Dad said as he lay back into his pillow. He looked about as tired as anyone I'd ever seen.

"Naomi," I said, and nodded. "You'll like her."

He offered me a weak smile. Those smiles took a lot out of him, but he kept trying. I gave him one back.

Chapter
Eighteen

heard from Naomi after dinner, which I spent with Rosie and Mel at a restaurant down the street from the hospital. *Do you hate me?* Naomi had texted me.

Never. Do you hate me? I texted back.

Never.

Our building, and I suppose Alicia's, since she discovered it, was about halfway between the hospital and Naomi's home on the other side of the park, so I didn't have to wait too long before I saw her. I felt like a musician about to go onstage, all nerves and bracing until I saw Naomi coming up the hill. Then I was onstage. The nerves dropped off me and I was okay.

Naomi walked with purpose to the top of the hill. I walked as fast as I could up my side of the hill until I was nearly out of breath. Naomi stopped once she saw me. She picked up her pace and reached out to touch my cheek. "Walter—"

"It's fine," I said. Naomi walked into my arms. The palm of her soft glove slid along my cheek as she looked into my eyes. "It doesn't hurt." The lights above us shimmered in her pupils. She blinked. I brushed a tear away with my thumb. Neon signs painted her face pinks and purples.

"And your dad," she said, looking worried now, maybe even anxious.

"He's fine," I said.

"I'm really . . ." Naomi didn't have the words, either. She nestled her head into my chest. "I'm really mad at you."

She pulled back and was smiling. I was, too. "I know. You should be," I said. "I'm mad at me, too. You can be mad. I'm sorry."

We kissed. It had been too long since we kissed, our hands on each other's faces and necks; it probably looked like we were strangling each other. Naomi pulled back.

"So mad," she said, looking into my eyes and touching my cheeks again. We laughed. It really didn't hurt anymore.

On top of our building, we sat on the roof and leaned on the edges, our arms touching, our heads aimed upward, looking at the sky and the stars with no city in sight. No people, no buildings, no cars or lights. Just the dark night sky.

"So I'm gonna say something, because I'm thinking it," I said. "You were right. I was an ostrich with my head in the sand."

"Huh?" Naomi asked.

"And I talked to Mel, and I am handsome and worthy of you," I continued. "I just get intimidated easily. I mean you're really intimidating because you're so amazing, but you push me in all the right ways. You're the best thing to happen to me, and I want to be that for you, so I really think we should stay together."

Naomi smiled and nuzzled into me.

"You sound like my brain," she said. "I was really worried. It's just what my parents always warned me about—my big mouth, always getting me into trouble." She shook her head. "You were so . . . Why couldn't I just chill and enjoy it? I thought you were done with me; I almost got you killed with my drama. I couldn't even call you, because I knew I'd just cause even more pain."

"Talking to you would have been a much better pain than being alone with a face half made of hamburger," I said. Naomi laughed. "I'm not done with you. Not by a long shot."

"It was too real, seeing you at school," Naomi said. Now she couldn't stop looking at me. "It's one thing to hear rumors, but something else to actually see it."

"Yeah," I said. "I wouldn't want to see it, either."

Naomi took off her glove and touched my face again. "So I can be your girlfriend still?" she asked very softly. She cupped my bruised cheek in her hand and looked into my eyes. I placed my hand over hers.

"Yeah, you can be my girlfriend still, if I can be your boyfriend still," I said. We were close enough that I moved my head near hers, ran my nose up her cheek. "I think that would be good."

It was as if a bomb had gone off, or a land mine. Debris went flying everywhere, but somehow it all came back down just right. We had ground again. I hoped it would always be that way, that things could scatter and chaos could strike, but we'd always land softly—we'd always get back to here. Everything worked when I had Naomi.

"I think I might love you," I said.

Naomi laughed, a happy laugh. "Oh, you think so? Yeah?"

"I do, I do love you," I said.

"I love you, too," Naomi said with no hesitation, a big, wide grin. "God, you're hot." She turned her head away and slammed her eyes shut. "Oh my god. I'm such a dork. Don't break up with me." She opened her eyes. "I say the stupidest things."

I leaned back into her. She put her arms around my waist. "You're right to be mad at me, you know," I said. "I was scared and I was holding back."

"Why would you be scared?" Naomi asked. And she didn't scare me. I felt more comfortable with her than I did in my own skin. It wasn't her I was scared of.

"I'm not good with change," I said. "But I'm ready and I know it now more than ever. And if you're mad and you can't give me a hundred percent, then I'll give you more, okay? I'll give a hundred-twenty or a hundred-thirty percent. It'll add up. I did the math."

And Naomi gave me a hundred percent kiss. That was how I fought: by being with Naomi, by being together and being happy. That was the fighting. Because no one can fight the world we live in. You can't punch the concrete walls, you can't pull a gun on the city and tell it to change its ways, because you're not gonna win. But you can change it by existing inside it, by being a part of it. You can replace all the broken bulbs and relight the darkest alleys, one at a time, until the whole thing glows bright like Main Street.

Author's Note

BRIGHT LIGHTS, DARK NIGHTS wasn't the book I set out to write three years ago. It was a much simpler story originally. Some things remained; in fact most of the characters in the book now were there from the start. Naomi was there, Jason was there, Walter had a different name but he was the same kid. Their relationship was central to the story but the fact that one was white and one was black wasn't ever supposed to be an issue.

My projects tend to be very personal. I write about what I've gone through, how I think and feel. And while I certainly kept to that, this story was bigger. An image I kept coming to while working on this was of a couple looking deeply into each other's eyes, while we slowly pull back and see the rest of the world around them. This was my first outward-looking project.

The inclusion of the world at large opened a lot of doors for the story. Once I made the decision to bring up an awareness of color in the book, things fell into place almost immediately. The tone of the book made sense, the characters' motivations suddenly popped. The universe seemed to be frequently commenting to me that I was on the right path.

There were times I thought it was silly to even write about it. There are TV shows with interracial couples with lead characters, there are celebrities that date outside their race and people are all for it, right? But that's not really accurate, not everywhere at least. If you spend any time online, you've seen your share of racism. The Internet has given racists a voice and peers.

This was one of the things I wanted to tackle with this book— where is racism today? What does modern racism look like? It's changed, it's a little mysterious, and it's a little faceless. Sometimes it's not even intended or expected, but views and ideas are ingrained and come out even in friendly well-intentioned places. And other times, it's just rude and in your face.

Like everyone, I have my thoughts and opinions, but I'm a fairly non-confrontational person. I don't like to argue, I don't like to force my views on anyone, and I don't ever intend to persuade anyone to think any way. Books work best as a conversation, not a monologue. Once the topic is presented, I want to converse through the characters, I want to talk about it from each point of view.

In this story, Walter comes to terms with his own racism, and that's as someone who is dating a black girl and listens to hip hop and considers himself young, cultured and open-minded. And yet he still struggles with his heart and his head and some deeper rooted fears he's barely aware of.

I really enjoyed my time in this city of East Bridge. I can't say for sure if I accomplished every goal I had. I've never written anything like this before, but I gave it my best and it's time to pop the bubble I've worked in and let it out into the world. Hopefully, you love Walter and Naomi as much as I do.

Acknowledgments

Pretty much any acknowledgment I attempt to write has to start with my editor, Connie Hsu. This is our third book together, and she read this story over and over, watched it evolve, she knows this world as well as I do if not better. She saw what this book  was before I did and she helped me see it, too, as long as it took. It sounds weird that someone could read your work and say "Do you see what you're actually writing here?" but that's what happened. She looked through the cracks, saw the real story that was bursting to get out, and it took a long time, breaking down a lot of walls piece by piece and doing a lot of cleanup after, but we got there. I don't think this book would exist with anyone else on board. She astounds me with the things she picks up and kept me on track like a mouse in a maze. She sounds like an evil overlord when I say it that way, but that's not how I intend it. I'll leave it in regardless.

I want to thank my agent Kirby Kim, who had a lot of patience  as I pestered and pestered and pestered him. It's been a long road but I am glad we're still on it together.

There's a whole ton of people in the book industry I want to thank, a massive team of people that have their fingerprints on this novel, from test readers to designers to sales people and copy editors and foreign market teams. Every time I visit Connie, she's introducing me to people that have done crucial things with my book. Full disclosure: I have very little business sense, that's why I write and draw all by my lonesome, and without these people this story would be a stack of papers in a storage bin somewhere instead of a physical book sitting on shelves in stores.

I would like to thank those who championed my book through acquisitions (Alvina Ling, Victoria Stapleton, and Simon Boughton), the early readers who helped make the book what it is today (Allison Moore, Leslie Shumate, and Zoey Peresman), and the team who turned the final manuscript into a book (Christine Ma, Jill Freshney, and my designer Beth Clarke).

I want to thank my family, of course. Without them there's no me, everything I think or feel or believe in stems from my

upbringing, who I am comes from who I was. So thanks to my parents, brother, grandparents, cousins, aunts, uncles, dogs, cats, bunnies, and babies. A special hi to my buddy Aria.

Cori gets a big thank-you for being the friend who read the whole book in an early stage and offered her advice. She's heard me talk about this book more than anyone not on my book team, and always listened and offered her thoughts and excitement and encouragement. If anyone was sure this book was going to get finished and be great from the get-go, it was her.

More thanks:

Takarra, some things you said to me and probably don't remember helped lead to this book, and I'm sure bits of silly conversations we've had have slipped in some-where in these pages. Carly, you were a sign that I was on the right path with what I was working on and I had you in my thoughts as I worked through it. Thanks to Sara Rhine for listening to me talk about this book, thanks to Elaine, Briana, Ben Kowalsky, The Bob, CD for inspiring, and, last but never least, thanks to the wider book-reading world, anyone who's sent me an encouraging e-mail, bought or read one of my books, librarians, booksellers, book lovers, fellow industry people and authors who have reached out or replied to me when I've reached out or inspired me with their own works.

I'm very glad and thankful to be a part of this awesome world.

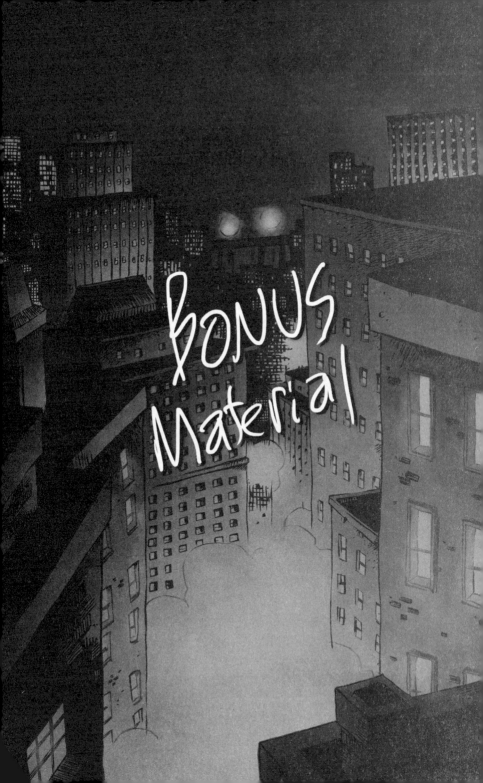

Playlist

1. Act 1, Part 1, Eternal Sunshine of the Spotless Mind—Jay Electronica
2. Electric Relaxation—A Tribe Called Quest
3. Find Your Love—Drake
4. Love Unconditionally—SWV
5. Cinnamon Tree—Esperanza Spalding
6. Neon Valley Street—Janelle Monáe
7. When Can I See You—Babyface
8. Everlong (Acoustic)—Foo Fighters
9. The Prettiest Girl in the Whole Wide World—Weezer
10. Like a Lovesong (Back to Back)—The Pillows

11. That Girl—Justin Timberlake

12. Ask Myself—Robin Thicke

13. XO—Beyoncé

14. We Found Love—Rihanna ft. Calvin Harris

15. Run to the Sun—N.E.R.D.

16. Enemy Gene—of Montreal

17. It Ain't Over 'Til It's Over—Lenny Kravitz

18. They Don't Know—Jon B

19. My Love Is Your Love—Whitney Houston

20. Ordinary People—John Legend

Alternate
Cover

This book went through more iterations than anything I'd previously worked on, so there's a wealth of material to share. I've got a few pages, so I'll show some of the unused art here.

Noir, while still being an aspect of the book now, was a much bigger part of it in earlier drafts. In fact, for a while each chapter had its own noirish theme and narration. The chapters were going to have these '40's-style movie posters, I did a handful of them before moving in a different direction.

Another idea I had was to have Walter narrate his story like a film, and these watercolor images would be framed like movie stills, sometimes showing sequences of action alongside the text.

As always, thanks for reading another of my books. Find me online at stephenemond.com, or write me at emoboyrocks@yahoo.com.